A Deadly Truth

Rachel Goldenberg

A Deadly Truth
Copyright © 2021 by Rachel Goldenberg

All rights reserved. No part of this publication may be reproduced, distributed, or transmitted in any form or by any means, including photocopying, recording, or other electronic or mechanical methods, without the prior written permission of the author, except in the case of brief quotations embodied in critical reviews and certain other non-commercial uses permitted by copyright law.

Tellwell Talent
www.tellwell.ca

ISBN
978-0-2288-6444-8 (Paperback)
978-0-2288-6445-5 (eBook)

DEDICATION

This book is dedicated to my incredible family: Harris, Paige and Chase. And to the languishing we all experienced during the COVID-19 global pandemic, which drove me to write a book (after I had mastered the art of baking banana bread and watched all of Netflix).

PROLOGUE 1

There is blood everywhere. Is it mine? I don't feel any pain. I do a quick scan of my body, checking my feet, legs, stomach, arms, neck, face. I don't think I'm injured. So where is this blood from?

I look around me. All I see is red. Red blood. Red flowers. Red rose petals, to be specific.

The blood is warm. I don't think I ever realized how warm blood is. I've had a cut before, but I've never been so covered in it that I could really feel the temperature, you know? It's sticky. Red, warm, sticky blood.

I look over at the bed and there he is. I think he's dead. Did I do that? I don't remember doing it. The last thing I remember is talking to him. And now he's dead. And there is red, warm, sticky blood everywhere.

Huh. I killed him.

I should go shower. Yes, a shower. That's what I need. And maybe a latte, that would be great. From that good coffee shop nearby, The Bean. I love the coffee there. You know, it was rated the number one coffee shop in all of Toronto, by *Toronto Life* magazine. I will shower, get rid of this blood, then grab a coffee. I wonder if The Bean will have any more of those delicious pies they make. All this blood is making me crave cherry pie.

PROLOGUE 2

2015

The alarm went off at 7:00 a.m., but it didn't have to. Rose Davis was awake. She was too excited to sleep. Today was going to be one of the best days of her life. Everything was about to change. If only she had known how much would change, maybe she would not have jumped out of bed so quickly.

But she did not know.

What did she know? Today was June 6, 2015. Today she was officially graduating from law school. All of her hard work is paying off. The brutally long lectures from professors who love to hear themselves speak, the endless hours of tedious studying, and the five-hour exams that almost gave her carpal tunnel syndrome. Not to mention the summer internship she suffered through last year, where she worked late into the night, every night. She was lucky to land an internship at a prestigious corporate law firm, where she spent her days poring over financial statements, preparing minute books (although she still has no idea what a minute book *really* is), and doing other menial tasks assigned to the summer students. There was one brutal day where she stood at a photocopier all day copying a company's employment records because that was part of the "due diligence" for a large transaction.

Ugh, she hated that job so much. She hated corporate law, period. Her passion was criminal law. She firmly believed that every person deserves a good defense, no matter what they were accused of. Innocent until proven guilty, right? She had grandiose dreams of being the next big shot criminal defense lawyer. She could picture it already: the high-powered suits, the beautiful office, close to the courthouse, of course, so she would not have to travel too far for her days in court. She had her life all laid out ahead of her, and it was starting today, June 6, 2015.

Again, if only she had known how drastically her life would change that day.

Rose rolled over in bed and gave Will a final look before forcing herself to get out of their warm bed. God, he was gorgeous, even while he was sleeping. Tall and athletic, with short dark brown hair, and brown eyes so dark they were almost black.

Will Sutton. She and Will had been dating since high school. He was the popular jock, the guy that every boy in school wanted to be and every girl wanted to be with. And he was hers. She still couldn't believe it. Ten years later and she still loved him more than ever. She felt butterflies every time he walked into a room. Every time he looked at her, with those dark, sexy eyes, her stomach did a little flip.

He wanted to marry her. Her! Rose Davis. She could not believe her luck. And she was pretty sure that he was going to propose today, after her law school graduation. This was the real reason why she did not sleep all night. She was too busy planning her wedding and her life with this wonderful, handsome man.

Will must have sensed she was staring at him and he opened his eyes.

"You like what you see?" Will teased.

"It's okay, I guess," Rose replied with a smile. Will reached out and grabbed her arms, pulling her close to him. He pressed his body against hers and touched his forehead to hers, their noses touching, their lips just an inch apart.

"Just okay?" Will asked.

"I've seen better," Rose teased back.

Will looked up at her with a cheeky grin. He then started kissing her neck, down the left side, to her shoulder. He made his way down her upper body, his lips softly brushing her breasts on his way down. He kissed her stomach and continued to work his way lower. Rose was arching her body in response to his touch, to his lips. All of a sudden, Will stopped.

"Okay then. I'll go." He started to move to get out of bed.

Rose, filled with desire, grabbed Will by the arm and pulled him back down on top of her.

"You are not going anywhere, buddy." She then kissed him with a desire so intense, it felt like the world disappeared. This is what it was like with Will. He made her feel like there was no one else in the room when she walked in. He made her feel safe, special, and loved. He was everything to her. He was home.

Without separating their lips, Will whispered, "Never. I will never leave you."

"Good to know," Rose said as she nipped at his lower lip. "Because I have to go!" With that, Rose jumped out of bed. "I have to get ready for my big day! Save some of that for me later, tiger."

Don't trip, Rose, she thought to herself. She was nervous. She had always been a little clumsy. Her mom said that she was like that as a little girl, running around and exploring the world, too fast for her own good, and bumping into walls, doors, tables, pretty much anything sturdy. She had so many cuts and bruises as a girl that her kindergarten teacher actually thought about calling child services to make sure she was not being abused at home. But she was just excited and liked to run.

If there was ever a person to trip while walking across the giant stage to receive her law school diploma, it would be Rose. It didn't help that she had to wear that long, silly robe that lawyers wear when they get called to the bar in Ontario, the same robe they wear when they appear in court. The robe looked like a giant blanket wrapped over Rose's slender shoulders. Underneath the robe she wore the requisite black pencil skirt, white blouse, black waistcoat, and white-collar tabs. She wore a pair of black high-end pumps that she had bought as a graduation gift to herself upon completing law school. She had brushed her straight blonde hair and pushed it off her face with a black headband.

She was lined up at the side of the stage with her fellow students, waiting for their names to be called. She was a few feet away from her best friend, Anne Jacobson. Anne was dressed in an identical outfit for her call to the bar. Her long, brown hair was styled in a perfect blow out (as always!) and she paired her robe with nude pumps. Anne was always fashionably put together, down to perfectly manicured nails. Rose could always tell when Anne was stressed because her normally polished nails would be chipped and peeling.

Rose and Anne had been best friends since they were five years old, along with Stella Taylor. They met at the beginning of kindergarten and were inseparable ever since. In high school, their threesome quickly became a foursome when they met Lauren Williams. The four women jokingly referred to themselves as "LARS," an acronym for their four names. Rose knew how lucky she was to have such supportive friends, and even luckier to be celebrating this momentous moment, graduating from law school, with Anne.

From the angle near the stage, Rose was able to look out into the crowd and find her family. There were her parents, her brother (whose wife and baby were home for naptime), and ... an empty seat. Will was not there.

Rose felt a flash of worry which then quickly turned to anger. *I know he's busy planning the proposal, but this is important to me,* she thought. *The least he could do was take a break and show up for this big moment in my life.*

She looked over at Anne and signaled to the empty seat.

"Where is he?" whispered Anne.

"I don't know," Rose whispered back. "But as soon as I find him, I'll kill him for missing this!"

"Rose Davis." She heard her name called. She walked out, head held high, with a new determined purpose: she was ready to wring out Will's neck for not being here. *After the proposal, of course*, she thought.

All the anger she felt disappeared the second she opened the door to their house. She looked around and all she saw was red. Red flowers. Red rose petals, to be specific. And candles. The candles were not lit, which Rose admitted was a little weird, but she did not care. *Probably a fire hazard, anyway*, she thought.

The house was set up beautifully. Rose decided that she would forgive his absence at her graduation, as disappointing as it was, if this was what he had been busy with. It was exactly as she had pictured it, how she had dreamed of it as a little girl. It was finally happening.

She called out his name, but he didn't answer. *Where is he?* she thought. She walked through the main floor of the house, but she did not see Will.

"Will!" she called again. Still, her call was followed by silence.

That was when Rose noticed that the rose petals lined the stairs heading toward the bedroom. She followed the path of red, as she realized that he wanted her to come to the bedroom.

She slowly crept up the stairs, careful not to disturb the beauty of the red rose petals everywhere. Her bedroom door was slightly open, and she saw rose petals on the floor. She took a deep breath as she reached for the door handle. This was it, the moment she had been waiting ten years for.

She opened the door. There was Will, on the bed, with red rose petals all around him. So many rose petals. *How did he display them like that?* she thought. *And why is he not sitting up?*

She looked closer and realized that the red was not petals, but his blood. There was blood everywhere. Rose screamed. That was the last thing she remembered before she passed out.

CHAPTER 1

PRESENT DAY

There is blood everywhere. Why is there so much blood? she thought. *Is it mine? I don't feel any pain.* Then she sees blood is dripping from her fingers, from her arms, from her neck. She spreads her hands over her neck, trying to stop the blood. But there is too much of it. She can't stop the blood. She tries to scream, to call for someone to help her, but no sound comes out. She is desperate and crying, covered in blood, but unable to do anything. *HELP!* She tries to scream, but all she hears is silence. She starts gasping for air, but she is unable to inhale the sweet taste of oxygen.

Rose wakes up, panting, gulping for air. She is wet, covered in sweat, not blood.

It is a nightmare. One that is all too familiar for Rose. She has had nightmares at least a few times a week for the past six years. Since the day Will was brutally murdered.

The nightmares vary, but they usually end up with her covered in blood. Sometimes she is the one dying, other times she is watching Will die. Sometimes she dreams of getting there on time, calling an ambulance, and saving Will's life. Those are the worst nightmares, because every time she wakes up, she is forced to face the reality that it was just her imagination. In fact, it is her life right now that is the real nightmare.

Rose looks over at the clock. It is early, but she gets out of bed anyway. She knows she will not be able to fall back asleep now.

She puts on running clothes as she brews a pot of coffee. As she listens to the low hum of the coffee percolating and starts to hear the wonderful *drip, drip* as the smooth liquid falls into the pot, she turns on her tablet and checks her email. From there, while she sips her coffee, she peruses the newspaper, specifically looking for stories of homicides. This is how she starts every day. Coffee, crime check, run, repeat. Then it's off to work until the late-night hours.

It's funny how she never drank coffee before becoming a lawyer. She was proud of herself—she didn't need caffeine; she was full of natural energy! She laughs at the thought of that naïve girl. Her first month as a young prosecutor pushed her deep into the addictive world of java.

Yes, that's right. A prosecutor. Gone were the days where she thought she was destined to save people from confinement behind bars. Now it is her life's mission to *put* those criminals behind bars.

After Will died, Rose could not bear the thought of going back to the home they shared. In fact, she never stepped foot in that house again. Her parents gathered some of her belongings and she moved into her parents' house that day. A few weeks later, they packed up the house and sold it for her. Rose moved to Vancouver, British Columbia within a week after that. She studied for and passed the British Columbia bar and shortly thereafter secured her job as Crown counsel for the Ministry of the Attorney General.

She moved into an apartment in the downtown east side of the city, on Cordova Street. It may not be the fanciest part of town (in fact, the area is known for its indigent population, including marginalized communities, homeless people, mentally ill people, and sex workers), but Rose is happy here. She has always felt safe, and it is a close walk to work. It looks a lot worse than it really is.

Rose is very good at her job and has become a well-respected criminal prosecutor, even at such a young age. Yes, she is innately smart and is quick to piece together bits of information that seemingly appear as if they have nothing to do with one another. But it is the deep, empty hole of grief and the desire for revenge that push her.

She works long hours and has very little time for anything else. She still talks to Anne, Stella, and Lauren on a regular basis, but since moving to Vancouver, she doesn't see them very often anymore. The same with her family. She sees them whenever they visit, but that's about it. She has no personal life. Work is her life.

That's not to say she has no friends in Vancouver. She does. Her closest friend in Vancouver, Paige Maxwell, lives in the same apartment building, just a few floors above Rose. They met on the day that Rose moved into the building, when some creep tried to hit on Rose in the elevator. Paige grabbed Rose and pretended she was her girlfriend. They become fast friends. To this date, they giggle every time they see that guy in the elevator.

Paige is always encouraging Rose to go out more, pushing her outside of her comfort zone. Rose pushes back and usually wins the battle, convincing Paige to stay in with her, opting for comfortable pajamas, a bottle of wine and a movie instead of high heels and a fancy restaurant. Paige has tried many times to set Rose up on dates, but Rose has very little interest in dating. She firmly believes that she had her one chance at love with Will. Will was her soul mate, the person she was meant to be with. He is gone now. She has resigned herself to live without love. And she is okay with that.

At least she tells herself she's okay with that.

CHAPTER 2

Rose has always felt a deep connection to music. She connects songs to times in her life, to people or to moments. Sometimes the songs lift her up and embolden her, like "Stronger" by Britney Spears, which she listened to on repeat after a breakup. Other songs remind her of her childhood and innocence, like head banging to Queen's "Bohemian Rhapsody" while dancing with her dad in the living room after dinner. Then there are the songs that she listens to when she is consumed by her sadness, which allow her to wallow in it and just *feel*.

Today, as she steps out of the shower after her run and gets ready for her day, she puts on one of her melancholic playlists. She listens to Dave Matthews crooning "Grey Street", identifying with the subject girl in the song, who feels like the red blood bleeding from her is actually cold blue ice flowing from her heart. Rose's heart is made of ice. She remembers what life used to be like, six years ago. She vividly remembers waking up to see the sleeping form of the love of her life. All she had to do was reach out a hand to touch his body. This memory quickly shatters into pieces as Rose looks over at her empty bed. And just like the subject of the song she is listening to, all the vibrant colours of her memories muddle together and turn into a muddy grey. Rose feels the empty loss in her life on a daily basis. Everyone tells her it's time to move on, that she'll be okay. But she's not okay, not really.

It doesn't help that Rose has immersed herself in the world of criminal activity since Will's death. Rose tells herself that she chose to be a criminal prosecutor to make the world a better place. But she suspects that it goes deeper than that. Rose is committed to a life of revenge. She wants someone to pay for what happened to Will. The fact that no one has been charged or convicted for his gruesome murder is appalling to her.

She focuses on homicides. While she is still too junior to choose which cases she is assigned to, her boss Charles Mitchell always assigns the most horrible murder cases to her.

Charles has been with the prosecution's office for over 30 years, and he has taken Rose under his wing since she joined 6 years earlier. Despite being a busy senior prosecutor, he still makes time to help Rose, to discuss her files with her, and to problem solve any issues that arise. He is infamous at the office for being blunt and straightforward, often to a fault. Sometimes, he can just be an ass. Before Rose began working with him, he rarely spoke to his fellow prosecutors and did not make time for playfulness. But after she joined, he began to soften a little. She made him … well, fun!

Charles has been a dedicated mentor to Rose. He taught her to believe in herself and her work and not to let people push her around. He encouraged her to challenge assumptions and instructions given to her, to not blindly follow what she is told. At the start of her career, Rose would ask him to review her trial strategies and her opening and closing statements. She remembers receiving copies of her work marked up in red pen, so much ink that you could hardly see the original text. At first this horrified Rose, she was embarrassed that her work was of such poor quality. But she slowly realized that Charles was just trying to make her a better lawyer and she appreciated all the feedback he gave her.

Rose knows he is very proud of the lawyer she has become under his guidance.

Charles assigns her the gruesome homicides because he knows she wants to prosecute them. He also knows that she will work harder than anyone else at their office to secure a conviction.

What he does not realize is that in every case that Rose takes on, she is secretly hoping to find evidence that can lead her to Will's killer. Every criminal that Rose puts behind bars is an attempt to lock up the animal that destroyed her life.

Rose pores through the details of each case, looking for a pattern similar to Will's death.

It is not easy. Will's murder was particularly horrifying. Rose's mind frequently goes back to that night. The blood. It was everywhere. Will had been stabbed over twenty times, at different angles and in different places in his body. Each time the killer plunged the knife into his body and flung it out, they sprayed Will's blood everywhere around him.

And it wasn't just the stabbings, as awful as they were. The medical examiner reported that there was evidence of anal trauma. A bloody tennis racquet was found beside his body. She could barely think about this without feeling sick to her stomach. Whoever this animal was, they made sure that Will felt pain. They made sure that Will felt violated. They wanted Will to suffer.

Will's ultimate cause of death was bleeding out. Rose couldn't bear the thought of him, lying there, with his lively blood draining from his body, knowing there was nothing he could do to stop it. Did he feel the pain every time the knife pierced his skin? Every time the knife slid out of him, cutting his skin like it was butter? Did he pass out from the pain right away or was he aware of every moment, of every last breath he took?

Rose catches herself thinking these thoughts on a daily basis. She jogs her memory back to that afternoon, almost as if she wants to torture herself. She doesn't actually remember seeing all of Will's wounds in person. The only thing she remembers from that day is blood. The next thing she remembers is flashing lights and ambulances. She was sitting outside the house. She doesn't know how the ambulance even got there that day. Did she call 911? Did a neighbour hear screaming? She doesn't know.

She shakes her head, as if trying to shake out these disturbing thoughts. On that day that Will died, she vowed to avenge his death. She has dedicated her life to doing just that. Her parents and her brother tell her to stop. Her therapist tells her to stop. But how can she stop? While this monster is out there? She believes, deep down in her core, that she will find them and bring them to justice.

CHAPTER 3

Rose was always an anxious person. She comes by it naturally. Through undiagnosed and untreated, she knows that her mother shares a similar sense of anxiety. So she comes by it naturally.

Growing up, she did not exude obvious signs of anxiety. She was not particularly fearful, worried, or restless. She slept well and had no difficulties concentrating on her studies. All in all, Rose had a pretty normal childhood.

Her anxiety manifested itself as a desire to achieve, to succeed. Which wasn't a problem for her; it served her quite well. She always earned top grades in school, had many friends, and was beloved by all her teachers. She took piano lessons and ballet lessons until she entered high school, at which time she chose to focus all her attention on her studies. She had tried to participate in sports, but ultimately she was not very good at them and she gave up. In fact, Rose barely made it through one skiing lesson before picking up her skies and marching right off that hill. She never skied again after that. She also tried basketball, swimming, tennis, and skating, with similar results, and her parents did not push her to continue. If she was not good at it, she did not have to do it.

Through therapy and self-reflection, Rose now understands that this was not helpful. She knows her parents believed they were doing what was best for her. They were supporting her interests and saving her from feeling like a failure. The problem with this approach was that Rose never really faced adversity—she was either great at something, or she didn't do it. And the problem with being good at everything is that Rose never learned how *not* to be good at something. So whenever something challenging comes up, Rose is not equipped to handle it.

Her anxiety therefore turned into this intense need for perfection. She had to be the *best* in order to do something. She needed external validation, someone telling her she did a good job. It was not enough that she felt proud of herself or that she felt that she did a good job. She did not even know how to feel that type of inner validation. She looked to others for approval. Rose developed an inner critic that told her she wasn't good enough if she was not the best. And every time she faced some version of a challenge, whether it was not getting the top grade in her class or making a mistake in court, Rose's inner critic came out loud and strong to remind her of her various failures. Her sense of self-worth came from succeeding, so any time she did not succeed, she was worthless.

This drive to succeed and be good at everything continued throughout university and law school and has helped Rose secure the prestigious job as Crown counsel. But, as Rose's therapist constantly reminds her, at what cost?

Perhaps if Rose had sought therapy earlier on, she would have been able to overcome this inner critic by now and undo years of feeling unworthy. Perhaps the anxiety would have always been there, underneath the surface, instead of creeping up on her and affecting her personal and professional life.

But that is not the case. Her anxiety slowly bubbled under the surface, ready to explode, until one day, it was met by a dear friend: depression.

Following Will's death, Rose fell into a deep pit of depression that, if she were being honest with herself, she has never really climbed out of. The depression mixed with the anxiety have become a dynamic duo of sorts, meddling with Rose's confidence, self-worth, and happiness.

It's not always bad. Many days are good. She is still outgoing, personably, likeable. Most people wouldn't even know she suffers from any form of mental illness. But with the ebb and flow of depression come days of sheer hopelessness and helplessness. On these days, Rose lives in a daze. It's as if this thick fog of malaise follows her around. She cannot put into words exactly what the problem is, she just feels this general despair, that nothing is okay, and things will never be okay. The sun is still shining on those days, but the sky is not bright and clear. The grass and trees are not a vibrant green, but rather some murky shade of khaki. The food is a little more bland, the coffee a little more bitter.

Some days she cannot get out of bed and she opts to work remotely from home. Other days, she forces herself to get up. As her mother always says, "put on some lipstick and a smile and get over it." Don't bother people with your "dirty laundry," people do not want to hear about your sadness. People have no tolerance for sadness. So Rose pretends that everything is fine. Perfect, in fact. Even her closest friends do not know the true inner demons she faces every day. Rose figures, if you keep pretending to be happy, eventually that happiness will manifest itself, right?

Six years later, Rose is still waiting for the false happy persona to become her reality.

Can she blame Will's death for her state of depression? That would not be fair, she has always had an underlying imbalance of chemicals and hormones. But it definitely didn't help. Rose might have always faced inner demons of depression along with the anxiety. But with the tragic death of the love of her life, she feels that she has been stripped away of the right to be happy.

Her therapist disagrees, of course.

Rose has been seeing Dr. Charlotte Hill for three years now. She has been helping her learn self-acceptance, self-love and gratitude. After last night's nightmare, Rose is glad she is seeing Dr. Hill this morning before work—she could use a lot of those things right now.

Rose walks into her therapist's office and takes a seat on the small grey sofa, covered with fluffy pillows in soft, muted tones. The office is located in the financial district, close to the Vancouver Art Gallery, just west of Rose's apartment and the courthouse. Found on the third floor of a tall, modern building, the office is painted a soothing cream colour and the walls are adorned with simple watercolour paintings in light blues and purples. Next to the sofa is a white and gold end table with a box of tissues, ready to be used to wipe tears expelled during self-discovery. On the other side of the sofa is the therapist's desk and computer. There are no framed pictures of family members or pieces of imaginative artwork created by a child, like you would find in many offices. In fact, there are no personal details in the entire office. At first Rose was put off by the coldness of the room, but over time she has come to learn that it was purposeful, and that the clean canvass allows the patient to take over the room and make it their own. The office can become a safe haven for any patient, whatever their malady. For Rose, it reminded her of a coffee shop, hanging out with a good friend. It was a place where she could let her guard down and say the things that she truly feels, not the things she thinks she *should* feel.

Directly across from the grey sofa on which Rose sits, Dr. Hill is sitting in a comfortable chair. She starts their session the way she always does: "How was your week?"

"It was good thanks! I was able to enjoy a lot of free time, watched a bunch of movies, exercised, and baked a cake. And I didn't cry at all." Rose's tone is uniquelt both genuine and sarcastic.

Dr. Hill smiles at her. She knows that Rose uses humour to cope with her issues. Humour is a perfectly useful and productive tool, so long as it is not used to deflect the real feelings.

"So, the usual?"

"Exactly," Rose says with a smile. "Oh, and I went on a bunch of dates with men who fawned all over me. I can't decide which one of them I shall marry, I will have to ask my father about the size of my dowry. My suitors may not want me for less than three cows and a donkey."

"You know, if you actually went on a date once in a while, men might actually fawn all over you and want to marry you."

"I'm not getting married."

"You can't say never, Rose. You're young, you're only thirty years old."

"We've been over this. I don't expect to feel love again. I had my love, then I lost him. You don't get that kind of love more than once in a lifetime."

"Do you actually believe that?" Dr. Hill challenges her. They have had this conversation more than a few times before, and Rose always insists that she will not love again. But Dr. Hill does not think she truly believes this. Dr. Hill knows that, like all people, she wants to love and be loved. She just needs to learn to love herself and allow herself to feel this love.

"There is no time for love or relationships. Not if I'm going to stay on track with my career."

"You don't think you can have love and a family at the same time as your career?"

"Definitely not. There's just no time for everything. I remember a conversation with my boss, Charles. He was helping me prepare an examination outline when all of a sudden he looked at the clock and jumped up. It was 5:02 p.m. and he had to leave to go home to his family. I told him I was impressed that he was able to be such a great lawyer and such a great dad. That he makes it seem like we can have it all.

And you know what he said to me? You can't have it all. Simple, blunt. You can't do it. He explained there are three main categories in most people's life: work, family, and health. One of those three things will always have to give. For him, it is his mental and physical health. He jokes on a daily basis that he is so stressed he thinks he is having a heart attack. And yet there he goes, running off to watch his daughter compete in a swim meet."

"You don't think you could balance family and work?"

"Not if I want to maintain my mental and physical health. And that is important to me. Coming to therapy, working out, being active. So there it is. Charles gave up health. I gave up family. And that's okay. I don't have time for it. I'm busy. I have a wonderful, fulfilling life. And when I die, in my fuzzy bathrobe and slippers, all alone, my cats will keep me company until someone eventually notices the decrepit odour emanating from my apartment, at which time eventually the police will discover my body. It's all good. I have it all planned out."

Dr. Hill just stares at her in response. If she is patient enough, she knows Rose will succumb and tell her how she is honestly feeling.

"I'm not joking. It's my reality. I will die alone," Rose says.

"That is a bold statement. How did we go from dating to death?" Dr. Hill questions.

"It always ends in death."

"Yes, it does. We all die. But hopefully not for a very long time. Hopefully you will live until well past one hundred. Which means you have many more years to develop relationships, to live your life to its fullest."

"I am living my life. This is how I choose to live my life."

"You're hiding from life."

"I am not hiding."

"You're hiding because you're scared. Scared to put yourself out there, scared to feel again, and scared to be hurt again."

"Wouldn't you be scared? I put myself out there, I let myself be vulnerable, and look where that got me. The man I love is dead."

"He is. And that is awful. Tragic. But Rose, you cannot live your life in solitude, worried that the next person you fall in love with will die the way Will did. In a sense, you are letting Will's killer win. You are letting this horrible event define you, define your career, your relationships. You can choose to try again. You can choose how to define your life."

"Easy for you to say. I am consumed by death. At work and at home. I relive his death almost nightly. Either he dies, or I die, or someone else I love dies. I can't keep going through this."

"You had another nightmare last night?" Dr. Hill gently asks. Rose nods. "Who died this time?"

"Me," Rose sighs.

"Rose, it was a dream. A horrible dream, but a dream, nonetheless. You are alive, you are healthy, you have your whole life ahead of you. Do not live in your dreams, awaiting death. Live in the daytime world with the rest of us."

"You're right. I'll try."

"No, you won't," Dr. Hill challenges. "You're just saying that to appease me. Rose, you do not need to tell me what you think I want to hear. I am here to listen to you, to listen to your truth, whatever that truth may be."

"Okay," Rose says, nodding. "Thanks."

But Rose knows deep down that that isn't really true. People do not want to hear her truth. They do not want to hear the silent, violent screams wracking her body. They do not want to see her darkness. No one wants to see darkness. So Rose continues to live in that darkness in her mind, alone.

CHAPTER 4

"You ready to kick some butt, Rose?"

Rose looks up from the mountain of books and folders on her desk and smiles. Her assistant is standing in the doorway to her office. Mia's wild purple hair is as frizzy as it always is. Mia does not even pretend to control it anymore, she just lets the natural curls do their thing. While some people in the legal profession might find this unprofessional, Rose sees it as one more thing that makes Mia special.

Matching Mia's bright, unruly hair is a sleeve of tattoos, wildflowers and vines climbing their way from her wrist to her shoulder. Rose suspects that there are many more tattoos underneath Mia's clothes, but she would not dare to ask what and where.

Mia's unique exterior deceptively hides the true treasure she is. She is quick and sharp, a fast learner, and helps run Rose's life. Without her, Rose knows that she would be lost. More than all of that, she is a true friend to her.

"You know it. Is my bag ready?"

Mia has packed Rose's case, which contains everything she will need for court that day: document briefs, case law briefs, copies of evidence, her notes, her examination outlines, paper, pencils, pens, highlighters, and of course a copy of the Criminal Code.

"You know it," smiles Mia.

Rose is an exceptional lawyer. Her perfectionism propels her to learn the details of every case she prosecutes inside and out. She is prepared with arguments to dispute any defense along with case law to support her arguments. Her written arguments are concise and persuasive. She spends hours working on these, often to the point where Charles forces her to stop, telling her that "done is better than perfect". Rose still strives for perfect. She knows exactly what evidence she will be eliciting today and what questions she will be asking the accused, who testified all day yesterday and will be subject to her cross-examination today.

The key to being a good lawyer is to never ask a question you do not know the answer to. So to prepare, Rose makes sure she knows every single answer that will be given during the examination today. She is just sitting doing some last-minute preparations.

Like most of her cases, Rose is prosecuting a homicide today. It is a particularly brutal and barbaric murder, and Rose is steadfastly determined to secure a conviction. Elizabeth Diaz was found in an alleyway just off Granville Street, propped up against a large garbage bin. The original entertainment district in Vancouver, Granville Street has the high energy and neon lights of the Las Vegas strip. Bars, pubs, and dance clubs line the street and people can be found drinking and partying there until the early morning hours.

Elizabeth Diaz was found around 4:00 a.m. on the morning of August 19, 2019. The call came from a couple of hipsters who were sneaking off for a place to hook up. Elizabeth's body was propped up against the garbage bin, swollen, bruised and cut, and her wrists had indentations from ligature, likely some type of rope or fabric, indicating that her hands had been bound together before she was killed. Her hands were purple, as if all blood circulation had been cut off. She had sustained multiple injuries, which indicates that either the murderer was hurting her in the course of an interrogation, looking for information, or that the murderer was just a perverse human being who took pleasure in causing pain in others. The police who had investigated this crime firmly believe that it is the latter, and Rose is inclined to agree. Based on everything she has seen in her preparations for this case, the murderer is a sick psychopath.

But it was not the tortured beating that Elizabeth sustained that led to her death. Cause of death, as confirmed by the medical examination, was a single gunshot to the head. The murderer had had his fun, then he was done. The green garbage bin was painted in red blood and grey brain matter, which led to the medical examination's conclusion that the fatal shot took place at that location.

A year and a half later, Rose is now prosecuting this case. This is the third week of trial, and Rose feels she has done a good job so far at presenting the prosecution's case. She is looking forward to examining the horrible man accused of this murder. His name is Arthur Lewis. It is quite unusual for Rose to have the opportunity to question him today, since most accused people do not testify. This just supports Rose's theory that this man is twisted and takes pleasure in hurting others and drawing out the process.

Rose looks down to the folder on her desk, where photographs of Elizabeth are splayed out. Rose has seen some pretty horrible things in her tenure as Crown counsel, but these pictures make her feel sick to her stomach. She can't wait to destroy this monster in court.

She closes the folder of pictures and drops it into her bag. She stands up from her desk, straightens out her black skirt and jacket, and prepares for battle. Right before leaving her office, she quickly looks in her pocket mirror and puts on a dab of lipstick.

Mia wishes her good luck, and with that, Rose stands up straight, pulls back her shoulders, and marches off to court.

"Mr. Lewis, you testified yesterday that you met the victim, Elizabeth Diaz, that night, on August 18, 2019, at around 11:00 p.m. Correct?"

Rose is face-to-face with the murderer. Staring into his cold, hooded eyes, Rose sees a darkness. His eyes are black, as if he has no soul. Framing his eyes are pale skin, a pointy nose, and dark black hair. He is wiry thin. He was thin before, but jail has made him even more gaunt, making him appear almost fragile. Almost. His dark, deep-set eyes reveal a different story.

Lewis is sitting in the witness seat, directly to the left of the judge. The judge's dais is deep, rich mahogany with elaborate detailing. Above the judge, the B.C. Supreme Court coat of arms is on display: a shield in the middle, with the Union Jack on it; the blue waves; the setting sun; the two supporters on either side of the shield, a stag and a sheep; and the motto "Splendor sine occasu," which is Latin for "Splendour without diminishment." Rose remembers the first time she appeared in court. The judge had not come out yet, and lawyers, witnesses, and spectators were sitting quietly in the courtroom. She stood and stared at the coat of arms, in awe, vowing to honour it and fight for justice.

Rose is standing behind the Crown counsel table. Lewis's lawyer is sitting at the table to her right, feverishly jotting down notes, no doubt to try to rehabilitate Lewis in reply after Rose is done her cross-examination. She is looking expectantly at Lewis, waiting for his response.

"Yes."

"You had never met her before that night, had you?"

"No."

"You had never seen her before?"

"No."

"You first noticed Ms. Diaz at the bar at The Belmont, correct?"

"Yes."

"You talked, then …"

"Yes. We talked, I offered to buy her a drink. She accepted, but then she ditched me to go dance with some other jerk."

"So you bought her a drink, then she walked away. And you say that that was the last time you saw her."

"Yes, that was the last time I saw Elizabeth. And she was—what's that saying, again? Alive and kicking."

The way he says her name, it is as if he is taunting her. Lewis killed her. Rose knows it, and he knows that she knows it. He is daring her to prove it. Rose is disgusted by the way Arthur Lewis says Elizabeth Diaz' name—as if it is just a name. Not a person. Not a living, healthy person, with hopes and dreams, with friends, with a family. Is this how Will's killer speaks of Will? Just one more notch on the bedframe, so to speak? How dare these animals speak the names of their victims. They have no right to utter their names, as if they have no significance.

"Ms. Davis?" Rose realizes that she has been staring and distracted, pondering the victim's name. The judge's voice brings her back and she tries to focus on Lewis again.

"Sorry, Your Honour. I'll continue.

"You testified earlier that you went home from The Belmont around 1:00 a.m.?"

"Yes. Would you like me to go through my whole testimony again?"

"That won't be necessary, Mr. Lewis. You went home around 1:00 a.m. You were alone?"

"Yes."

"And you, um, you went straight home?" Rose begins stammering involuntarily. She can't seem to clear her head, to shake the fog away.

"Yes, I went home. It was 1:00 a.m., where else would I go?"

Rose pauses, looking at her notes. She tries to find her place in her outline. After a few minutes of silence, while Rose awkwardly flips through her notes, the judge suggests that the court take a short recess. Rose insists that she is able to continue.

"And … um … you, um …" she stammers. Which confuses her, since she has never stammered in court before. She is always extremely confident and articulate, that is how she won her law school moot trial.

"You …" Rose realizes that she's sweating, and she can't seem to put her thoughts together to speak. The room begins to spin as she feels a wave of dizziness take over her. She is not sure what is going on, but she continues to power through, like she always does.

"You …, um … went straight home?"

"Objection. Asked and answered," Lewis's lawyer interjects.

"Sustained. Ms. Davis, do you need a minute?"

"No, Your Honour, I am fine. I just … um … I'm just a little tired, I didn't sleep well. I'm fine."

"Then do continue, please, and try to stay focused."

"Yes, Your Honour."

The pen in Rose's fingers that she has been fidgeting with slips from her sweaty fingertips. She stumbles as she picks it up, reeling, trembling. As Rose lifts her head from picking up the pencil, her vision goes blurry. Rose's heart is pounding fast, as if it is trying to explode from her chest. She can't breathe properly, she is gasping to take in a gulp of air. If only she could get a good gulp of air, her mind will clear and she'll be fine.

But she can't seem to get that oxygen. She just keeps getting dizzier, and her heart is palpitating. She is mortified for breaking her icy smooth surface—no one has ever seen her falter like this. All she can hear is a voice in her head telling her: *you're pathetic, you're weak. You can't even get through one lousy examination without freaking out. Just give up and leave.*

Out of sheer panic, embarrassment, and desperation, Rose stands up and runs through the double doors out of the courtroom, leaving the judge, defense counsel, and the accused staring at her, mouths agape.

CHAPTER 5

Rose runs out of the courthouse and heads toward Oppenheimer Park, just a five-minute walk east of the courthouse. She sits down at a picnic table in the park, her favourite, where she often brings her lunch and laptop for a quiet bite to eat away from the office. Rose sits there, taking deep, calming breaths. She practices the techniques she has learned from Dr. Hill, counting her breaths (inhale count to four, exhale count to six) and focusing on grounding herself. She observes the details of the park, the buildings around her, and the people walking through the park. She listens to the sound of kids playing and inhales the smell of wet grass from last night's rainfall. After twenty minutes, Rose has calmed down and she heads back to her office.

Charles Mitchell appears at Rose's office doorway just as she sits down. Rose begins to apologize for what happened, but he stops her. In a paternal tone, he expresses concern for her well-being and insists she goes home to rest for the rest of the day. Rose agrees, with the stipulation that she will be continuing her cross-examination prep from home. Charles shakes his head and sighs as he leaves her office.

Rose feels almost like herself again as she curls up on the couch in her apartment with a blanket. She takes a sip of her coffee and sets the mug down. She smiles a little bit to herself as she hears her mother's voice in her head, *Coffee? Do you really think caffeine is a good idea, sweetheart?* Rose knows it is not a good idea, given that her heartbeat just returned to a normal rate within the past half-hour. But she couldn't help it. There was something soothing about coffee, it made her feel better. Also, she needed the extra energy and focus to prepare for court tomorrow.

I have a lot to make up for after that little performance today, she thinks to herself.

Rose knows she is being hard on herself right now. But she also knows that she can do better, be better. So she pushes herself past the point of anxiety, exhaustion, and fear. This is what makes her one of the best prosecutors at her office.

It is right as she gets settled reading transcripts from the pre-trial examination that Rose hears a knock on her door. She rises from the comfort of the couch and peeks through the peep hole on her door. She smiles as she opens the door.

"Did you come over to be a bad influence on me?"

"Who me? Never!" Paige Maxwell barges right into Rose's apartment, with the comfort of someone who has been here many times before.

"How did you know I was home?"

"I called your office and your assistant told me you left early. Seeing as how you have *never* left work early before, I figured something must have happened, so I came to check on you. I come bearing gifts." Paige holds up Rose's favourites: a pint of chocolate chip cookie dough ice cream and a bottle of rosé wine.

"You know me too well."

"I know," says Paige. "Which is why you're about to roll your eyes."

Paige is right. Rose knows what Paige is about to say, because it's not the first time she has suggested it. "I'm not taking a leave of absence, Paige," Rose says as she rolls her eyes and grabs spoons and glasses from the kitchen. She appreciates Paige's concern, but the last thing Rose needs right now is a leave of absence. No, she needs to get back to work, even harder. She needs to secure a conviction in this case.

But she knows Paige means well. Paige Maxwell was the first real friend Rose made when she moved to Vancouver. They both love watching cheesy romantic Christmas movies together and listening to serial killer podcasts with a bottle of wine. Paige is the only person in the city that could get Rose to take a break from working.

Sometimes.

Rose briefly fills Paige in on what happened in court today, describing how she felt an intense mixture of anxiety, shame, and fear.

"Rose, you need to slow down a bit. You have been working around the clock lately. Even more than usual. You deserve a break."

"I enjoy working. I don't need a break."

"You are so stubborn," Paige says, as she flops onto the couch, pushing Rose's files away.

"I know," Rose replies and sticks her tongue out at her friend.

"I'm serious, girl. You have been working way too much lately. You barely answer my calls, and we haven't hung out like this in a few weeks."

"That's not true—we hung out last week."

"You came over to borrow my laptop charger, that hardly counts as a hang," counters Paige.

"Potayto, potahto," Rose quips back.

"Have you spoken to your therapist about today?"

"Not yet. I'm going tomorrow after court. I called her for a last-minute appointment."

"You're going back to court tomorrow?" Paige cries.

"Of course I am. Why wouldn't I?"

"You know ... because you had an anxiety attack and almost passed out during court today? Because you are clearly overtired, overworked, and overwhelmed?"

Rose looks over at her friend. "Paige, I know you care about me, and I appreciate it. But I am fine. I promise. I am going to work tomorrow. I can do it." Rose refuses to admit that she is, in fact, overtired, overworked and overwhelmed. She will not ask for help. Asking for help is a sign of weakness. She can do this.

Paige looks back at her friend, reading her mind. "Just because you *can* do this, does not mean that you *should*."

"Thank you, Dr. Maxwell. Now, I really do have to get back to work. Thanks for the ice cream and wine." And with that, she ushers Paige out of her apartment. She turns around and looks at her apartment.

"I'm fine. I can do this. Right?" she says to her empty apartment. Not surprisingly, no one answers back.

CHAPTER 6

Rose is at her desk the next morning before 6:00 a.m. She knows she has a lot of work ahead of her in court, and she is now a full day behind on her examination outline. She is exhausted but fueling herself with caffeine and a deep sense of fear that she will not be able to finish her questioning today.

Sometime around 8:45 a.m., Rose senses Mia getting to her desk and settling down for the day. She barely looks up from her notes, she is so deep in concentration.

The loud knock at her office door startles her and she jumps up from her seat. She is on edge, more than she would care to admit. But she tries to shake off the fear and anxiety as she sees Charles in the doorway.

"Feeling any better today?"

"Yes, much better," Rose lies. He knows she is lying.

"Your appearance suggests otherwise." Rose looks down at herself. She barely looked in the mirror this morning as she got ready for work. She realizes now that she has put on a mismatched suit: dark navy pants and a black blazer. Her white buttoned shirt is tucked in but has a noticeable coffee stain over her right breast. She also realizes that she is extremely hot and sweaty, and she can sense the clammy texture of her hands and her face. She cannot see it right now, but she suspects that the glistening face staring at Charles right now is also quite ashen and pale.

"I'm just tired."

"Rose, you know how much I respect you. How much we all respect you here. You do an amazing job. But something has changed. There is something going on, and you do not seem able to address it or accept it."

"I'm fine, really," Rose counters. But before she could go further, Charles cuts her off. "You're not fine. And I know you want to push through whatever this is that is going on with you, but I'm telling you, you cannot. You are going to lose this case."

Rose just stares at him, mouth agape, caught off-guard. He has never spoken to her this way. She does not know what to say.

"I know that's harsh, but it's the truth. And you need to hear it. Someone else can take over this case for you. Go home. Go rest. Take a leave of absence."

Part of Rose knows that Charles is right. She had a panic attack yesterday. At first after Will's death, they happened a few times a week. Slowly, over time, they slowed down and then stopped. She hadn't had an anxiety attack in over two years.

But it was just a one-time thing. Rose tries to argue with Charles, to explain that she is fine. But he is unwilling to listen or to accept her point of view. Realizing that she was not going to win this argument, Rose packs up her things and stands up. She is furious. She feels like an all-star basketball player being benched in the finals of the NBA Championships. Feeling betrayed, glaring at Charles, she marches past him without saying a word.

"Thank you again for taking the time to talk with me today. I know I just saw you yesterday."

"Of course, Rose," Dr. Hill says. "You know I'm always here for you. It just so happened to have worked out, that I had a last-minute cancellation and had this time open for you. Tell me what's going on."

"I don't even know what to say. I was in court, feeling totally fine, and then out of nowhere, I felt like I was losing control. My vision was blurry, and I couldn't breathe. It felt like … it felt like I was in the middle of a tornado, in the eye of the storm, and this horrible storm was swirling around me, and I couldn't get out of it."

"It sounds like you had an anxiety attack," Dr. Hill says.

"Yes," Rose agrees. "But this one was worse than any attack I have had previously. I've never felt like that before."

"What did you do?"

"I ran. I left court and went to go calm down in a nearby park. I practiced my deep breathing and used the grounding techniques we've been working on. Eventually I calmed down enough to start to head back to the office. By the time I was at my desk, I was feeling much better again. But my boss insisted that I go home, so I did.

"Good. Did you get some rest?" Dr. Hill asks.

Rose shakes her head. "No, I didn't need to. What I needed to do was work to make up for that embarrassment. I prepped for court all day. I worked my butt off, getting into the office this morning at 6:00 a.m. Only to be told to leave."

"You were fired?" Dr. Hill asks.

"No, but it feels like it. My boss told me to go home. So, I left the office and went back to my apartment, where I stuffed my face and watched Netflix all day until my appointment time with you," Rose explains

"Go home," Dr. Hill says, as if wondering aloud. "That might be a good idea. Why don't you do that?"

"I did, I just told you," Rose says, with a hint of confusion, and maybe a little bit of annoyance. Was Dr. Hill not paying attention?

"I mean really go home. Go home to Toronto. Go home to see your family."

Rose is quiet for a moment. Finally, she states, "I haven't been home in six years. Since Will…"

"I know," Dr. Hill says kindly. "Maybe it's time."

"I can't."

"You can. You are strong. So much stronger than you know, than you give yourself credit for."

"I don't want to," Rose says. "Going home … I'll have to face it all. The life I lost. I can't imagine living in Toronto without Will."

"I'm not saying it's going to be easy. It will be very hard. But facing up to the negative feelings in our life is one of the best ways to try to get past them. Rose, we have spent the past three years working together, and you have come so far, working on yourself and showing yourself compassion. And that is great. But there is more to healing than just self-compassion. The constant repression of all negative emotions relating to the loss of Will is not helping you."

"What if I can't do it? What if I have another anxiety attack while I'm there?" Rose asks, fearfully.

"Then we'll deal with it. You can always call me. And if it is really bad, you can always come back home to Vancouver if you are really struggling. Your life will be here waiting for you."

"But don't run away from the struggle," Dr. Hill continues. "Notice it. Label it. Tell yourself, 'I'm having a really hard time.' Just that sentence will help you, by validating what you are feeling. Remind yourself that it's okay to not be okay. There is so much power in naming your emotions and validating them."

"But how will I remember to do that? Sometimes, when I'm really deep in one of my depression waves, I remember those words you always tell me: 'Label your feelings then validate them. Allow yourself to feel the feelings, whether good or bad. All feelings are valid.' But it's really hard to actually do that. I have this voice in my head that I can't fight, telling me that I'm not worth the validation, I don't deserve the compassion."

"Do you truly believe that?" Dr. Hill asks.

"Now? No. But when I'm deep in that zone, I fully believe it."

"I have an idea. When you get home later this evening, I want you to write a letter to yourself. In this letter, I want you to say all the things that you know you need to hear, like 'this is hard, but I am strong.' Pretend you are writing to a friend and say the things you would say to a friend who was struggling. Would you tell this friend that she is worthless because she is struggling? No. You would be kind and show her compassion. Write down all the things you're proud of, all the things you have accomplished.

"And then when you are home, if you are really struggling, if you feel yourself sinking into a depressive hole, read this letter. Give yourself the love, compassion, and validation that you would give to a friend."

Rose sits in silence for a moment. Dr. Hill can see that she has gotten through to her patient and that she is mentally preparing herself to go home.

"You can do this. I have full confidence in you," Dr. Hill encourages.

"At least someone does …" Rose sighs.

'You. Me. Shopping. Melrose Boutique. 6:00 p.m. Then dinner after. Note the periods here: this is not a question. We are doing this.' Rose looks down and sees this incoming text message from Paige.

'Can't. Need to pack.' she texts back.

Paige calls immediately. "Are you listening to my advice? Are you going on vacay?" she asks, excitedly.

"Yes, I'm following your advice, sort of. No, not a vacay. I'm going to visit my family in Toronto."

"Rose! I'm so proud of you!" Paige shrieks.

"Thanks, girl. I appreciate it."

"I'm serious. This is a huge step for you. Just promise me one thing," she says, her voice turning serious.

"What?"

"You'll go to Haddingtons for me and buy something pretty in my honour!"

Rose laughs. "You got it!"

CHAPTER 7

It's amazing how certain smells can take you back to a different time in your life. As Rose walks into her parents' house, the house she grew up in, she immediately smells home and feels like a child again.

The first smell to hit her is lavender. Her mother's favourite. She keeps beautiful handmade lavender soaps in every bathroom in the house. She also has lavender incense in the kitchen and a lavender-scented candle that she uses when she is cooking fish, or when she has burned something in the oven and doesn't want anyone to know that she did.

Cutting through the fresh, floral lavender scent is a spicy smell. Her father's aftershave. One whiff is all it takes and Rose is transported to when she is four years old, falling down while learning to ride her bike, and her father scooping her up and nuzzling her close into his neck. She remembers feeling so safe and protected, as her father wiped her tears and kissed her booboos. How many times has she breathed in that scent while being cuddled and soothed?

Rose smiles. She didn't realize how much she missed home. She hasn't lived here in ten years and hasn't been back in Toronto for six years. Ever since Will died.

Not died. Was murdered.

Rose calls out. "Hello?"

Her mother comes running towards the door and envelops her in a wonderfully tight hug. Rose jokes, "Okay, enough!" but she does not let go. Secretly, Rose loves it and doesn't want the hug to end.

Finally, her mother pulls back, holds out her arms and looks at her.

"Honey, you look terrible. Go shower, then put on some nicer clothes and some lipstick. Dad will be home soon, and Tyler, Emily and the kids are coming over for dinner."

Yup, it's good to be home, Rose thought, rolling her eyes but smiling despite herself.

For Isabelle Davis, it was a cardinal sin to leave the house without "some lipstick" on. Rose's mom is strikingly beautiful. Her rich chestnut coloured hair is smooth and always tied back neatly with a pin. Her dark brown eyes are framed by long lashes that are always perfectly coated in a thin layer of mascara. Her skin is smooth and glows (and no, she never had any work done, although most of her friends have). Isabelle always looks put together. Even her leisurewear matches, with her shirt neatly tucked into her pants, with a pair of expensive designer running shoes.

Isabelle always expects Rose to be dressed the same. Rose is naturally pretty, but she does not put in the effort that her mother does. Her blonde hair either has a natural, untamed air-dried look or is tied back in a messy bun. Her makeup regime is limited to mascara, blush, and a tinted lip gloss for a bit of colour. She is either dressed in a formal black suit for court or she is in unmatching workout clothes that she has picked up from various stores over the years.

Growing up, her mother always nagged Rose to brush her hair or put on some lipstick. While that used to bother Rose and make her feel insecure, Rose now knows that she means well. There is no malice behind her mother's comments. Rose knows that her mother thinks she is beautiful. That the focus on appearance is her mother's anxiety manifesting itself. She recognizes that while you can't control everything that happens to you, you can control how you look and how you're perceived. And according to her mother, the best way to look and be perceived is … well, perfect. Rose has spent the past three years fighting this conviction and trying to develop a tolerance for less than perfect. She's a work in progress.

Smiling to herself and thinking, *I hope I brought my brush and lipstick*, Rose climbs the stairs up to her room.

Her room looks the exact same as it did when she moved out before law school. It still has the small twin bed tucked into the left-hand corner of the room, with pink floral linen and an eyelet bed skirt. Her treasured stuffed monkey (named Mokey, because Rose could not pronounce "monkey" when she first got it) sits in front of her numerous pink throw pillows. Her wall is covered with hilarious cringe-worthy posters, like 'Nsync, Zac Efron, and Adrian Grenier from his *Entourage* days (even though Rose insists that she fell in love with Adrian after seeing him in *The Devil Wears Prada*, way before everyone else noticed him). Rose rolls her eyes at her younger self.

Her desk is in the far righthand corner, still lined with framed pictures of her with Anne, Lauren and Stella and with Will. There are also picture of Rose and her brother, Tyler. She and Tyler have always been extremely close. Best friends from birth, they grew up playing basketball on the driveway, fighting over who was better at video games, and going for long bike rides that always ended with them getting ice cream.

She misses her brother so much and can't wait to see Tyler, his wife Emily, and their two kids, Logan and Sloane. Tyler is a C-suite employee at a tech company. Rose can never remember what he actually does but she knows it's important. Emily is a veterinarian. *Leave it to Tyler to have the perfect million-dollar family*, she thinks to herself. A brilliant, gorgeous wife, and two adorable, well-behaved kids. Tyler is one of those truly great guys who deserves all the good he has in his life. He is smart, funny, and athletic. He plays pretty much every sport, although his most beloved game is hockey. Tyler is teaching both Logan and Sloane how to play hockey. Rose is a proud aunt who adores her nephew and niece, and she looks forward to playing with them.

People are always shocked to learn that Rose and Tyler are siblings. Rose is of average build, petite but curvy, with blonde hair, fair skin, and blue eyes. In contrast, Tyler is six-four, with a strong athletic build. He has dark hair and dark eyes. Simply put, they look nothing alike. They also have very different personalities. While both share a wry, sarcastic sense of humour, Rose's wit is punctuated with a determined seriousness, while Tyler has always been more playful and silly. Perhaps it is these contrasts that allow them to be so close; like they were choosing to be siblings, not just siblings by birth. In any event, Rose knows that her relationship with her brother is very special and she feels so lucky to have him in her life.

Rose reaches out to pick up her favourite picture of her and Tyler as children. They had been dressed in costumes for the superhero club they created for just the two of them. They would don their superhero costumes and run around pretending to save their toys. Both Rose and Tyler loved all superheroes, but their favourite was Superman. They were obsessed with the man of steel. When Rose was old enough, she started to babysit to earn some money. Shortly before her brother's sixteenth birthday, once she had saved up enough money, she went out and bought him a Superman keychain. She remembers how proud she felt, giving him something that she herself had earned. He smiled and promised her he would never take it off his keychain.

The two of them fought over who could be Superman in their superhero club, so they finally agreed that neither would be. Instead, her brother dressed up as The Flash, wearing the full costume with a lightning bolt on his chest and a face mask. Rose had decided to create her own superhero, she said she could come up with one that was better than Wonder Woman, Batgirl and Supergirl combined. She wore all pink, with pink cat ears, black marker whiskers, and a pink nose (which she drew on using her mother's fancy lipstick). She called herself Pink Pussy.

The first time Tyler and Rose presented their club to their parents, they snickered and insisted on taking numerous videos and pictures of her. Rose did not understand why. When she was twenty, Rose's parents showed her (and Will and most of her friends) one of these videos, and Rose could not stop laughing. She could not decide if it was hilarious, horrifying, or a combination of both. She remembers Will was quite proud of her and even asked if they could bring back the Pink Pussy superhero. Rose feigned indignance in front of her friends and family, but discretely winked at Will with a slight nod that she hoped no one saw.

Rose remembers these memories fondly. She picks up the picture of her and Tyler in their full superhero getups and smiles. She can't wait to see him.

CHAPTER 8

Rose is once again staring into the face of Arthur Lewis, his dark, black eyes fixed on hers. But his skin, normally waxy and pale, is bright red, covered in blood. She does not know whose blood it is. She never knows whose blood it is. But there is blood everywhere. She is screaming, but this just makes Lewis laugh. The more she screams, the more he laughs. She has fallen to the floor, lying in a puddle of blood. Lewis starts walking towards her with a gun, laughing.

"Look at you, alive and kicking. Scream all you want. No one is coming for you. You are all alone."

Rose begins screaming, a high-pitched wail. The type of scream that could crack a glass window. Then she hears glass cracking all around her, and she screams even louder.

Arthur Lewis laughs and continues to walk toward her. Finally, he is right on top of her. And the gun in his hand has turned into a knife. He arcs his arm back, ready to plunge the cold, sharp metal into her belly. Right as he knicks the surface of her torso...

Rose wakes up, covered in sweat. She had decided to take a quick power nap before Tyler, Emily, and the kids arrive for dinner. Panting, Rose looks around her room and tries to slow her breath. *It was a dream*, she reminds herself. Not wanting to be left alone with her thoughts right now, Rose puts on some calming music as she changes into clothes for dinner.

"First we have to say our favourite part of our day. Then we have to say something we didn't like or something we want to work on, then something we want to do tomorrow. I'll go first!" cries Sloane excitedly, sharing her favourite mealtime ritual. Sloane is five years old and is in kindergarten. Rose laughs to herself that everything is still fun and exciting for Sloane, and everything she says is in an extremely loud voice, as if vying for attention over her older brother.

"My favourite part of my day is seeing Auntie Rosie, duh." *Where did she learn to say duh like that?* thinks Rose. "Something I didn't like today is that Logan didn't let me play video games with him and his friends," she glares at her older brother as she says this, "and tomorrow I want to … hmm …. eat treats all day!"

Everyone around the dinner table laughs. "I don't think your mother will be too happy with that," Tyler says.

"A girl can try, can't she?" Sloane asks. "Now it's Logan's turn!"

Logan, who is eight years old and still at the stage where he is willing to play his little's sister's game without trying to "look cool," says, "My favourite part of my day is playing video games with my friends. Something I didn't like is that Sloane was annoying when I was playing and wouldn't go away," he glares right back at his sister, "and something I want to do tomorrow is play more video games."

"Okay, we have to get you outdoors tomorrow before you turn into a screen zombie." says Emily.

"Grandpa's turn now!" declares Sloane.

"Let's see, my favourite part of my day?" Cohen Davis put his hand on his chin as if he is pondering the very meaning of life. "I would say this dinner with all of you. And I don't have anything I didn't like—I had a great day. Something I want to do tomorrow is spend more time with all of you."

"Grandpaaaaaaa," cries Sloane. "You always say that!"

"And I always mean it," he says with his special smile that he reserves for grandkids. Cohen prides himself on being a confident and strong-willed man, and a hard-as-nails businessman, and yet ever since his first grandchild was born, he has become a total ball of mush. He smiles when Logan and Sloane smile; he cries when they cry; he spoils them with gifts and sweets, always sneaking things into their tiny hands or pockets, thinking that Tyler and Emily do not see. Of course, they do see it, but they pretend not to, allowing Cohen to share a special secret with the kids.

Rose and her father were very close when she was growing up. They are very similar—they share the same witty sense of humour, the same passion for art and books, the same guilty pleasure of watching *Looney Tunes* on weekend mornings, laughing every time Wile E. Coyote gets hurt while trying to catch the Road Runner. They share the same sky-blue eyes and fair skin, as well as a perfect cupid's bow in the middle of their upper lip. Unfortunately, they also share a stubbornness, a lack of patience, and a lack of tolerance for stupidity. This has led to some fights over the years, but they have always been able to overcome these disputes by bonding over their common interests. After one particularly epic fight when Rose was sixteen (she thinks it had something to do with leaving her blow dryer or flattening iron plugged in), they did not speak for two days. Eventually, Cohen came into Rose's room with a great new Stephen King novel, telling her she had to read it. And without a word, their fight was over, and they began discussing the latest King novel, which in Rose's opinion was not his best work.

"Can I go now?" asks Isabelle.

"Don't steal my answers, Izzy!" Cohen warns.

"I would never, dear. My favourite part of my day is Rosie coming home." She pauses amid a chorus of "aws" and reaches across the table to hold Rose's hand. "We have missed you so much, sweetheart. And my least favourite part of my day is that the children are just eating plain bread and cheese, the way they always do."

"Mom, give it a rest," Tyler interjects. "They're kids. They don't have to eat lamb if they don't want to."

"Maybe if you had told me that they don't like lamb, I wouldn't have made it, Tyler."

"Nobody asked you to make lamb today, Mom."

Cohen, sensing that the conversation was heading down a slippery slope, says, "I think the lamb is delicious."

"Auntie's Rosie's turn now!" exclaims Sloane with delight, oblivious to the tension between her father and her grandmother.

Rose was sitting quietly, enjoying listening to everyone chat and bicker. God, how she missed them all. Now, called upon to take her turn, Rose pretends to think long and hard. "Hmm … my favourite part of my day … was seeing my favourite niece and nephew in the whole wide world!"

"We're your *only* niece and nephew," Logan groans.

"And my favourite," Rose laughs.

"But I'm your *real* favourite, right?" Sloane lowers her voice into a whisper: "Like, more than Logan, right?" Rose winks at her and whispers "elephant shoe," which is their secret code. Rose once told Sloane when she was younger that if you mouth the words "elephant shoe" your mouth moves the exact same as if you had said "I love you." She and Sloane loved to whisper "elephant shoe" to each other to share their special secret.

"Daddy's getting jealous, guys!" Tyler cries. "Why does Rosie get all the love? What about your dear old dad?"

"You're okay, I guess," Sloane says, and everyone bursts out laughing at this young girl growing more precocious every day. "Can I have a treat now?" She asks, changing the subject abruptly.

"Why don't we work up an appetite first? Earn our dessert?" suggests Tyler.

"What did you have in mind?" asks Emily.

"I think I can guess," says Rose. Tyler gives her a huge grin. "Basketball."

"Two on two! Me and Sloane against Rose and Logan."

Rose grumbles and they head outside to the driveway to play. She is terrible at basketball and doesn't want to play. But she always wants to make her niece and nephew happy, and she can see their eyes light up at the thought of playing ball with her. She is torn.

Tyler can sense her hesitation and says, "I get it Rose, I do. You don't want to play because you know you suck," Tyler says.

"Tyler!" exclaims Rose, laughing. He is teasing her. He knows her struggles with perfectionism and the reason she quit basketball back in sixth grade. It is only because she knows that he doesn't mean it, that she doesn't smack him for that comment.

It really is an unfair challenge. Even with Logan by her side, who has become a pretty decent basketball player, Tyler and Sloane dominate them and win the game. Tyler is as limber and athletic as he was in high school. Rose thinks about how easy it has always been for him: always well liked, charming, and good at every sport. His senior year of high school, he was named the MVP of his hockey team, basketball team, and baseball team. Rose tries not to be resentful at his natural ease with everything. As easy as it would be to be jealous, Rose knows that Tyler deserves it. She also knows that he works very hard, despite his natural ability. In fact, that year that he won all three MVP titles, Rose remembers hearing her dad and brother wake up three mornings a week at 6:00 a.m., getting ready for practice. Sometimes he would have special training sessions with the school coach, Ed Hutchison. Tyler worked so hard, he would always quote Coach Hutchinson whenever Rose gave him a hard time, saying that earning the victory makes it taste that much sweeter when you get it. Tyler idolized his coach growing up. Rose wonders whatever happened to Coach Hutchison and if he and Tyler kept in touch.

"Can I have my treat now?" asks a sweaty Sloane, interrupting Rose's reverie.

Laughing, the adults all agree and everyone heads back into the house for dessert. Rose is so happy to be home, she didn't realize how much she needed this.

CHAPTER 9

I'm going to be sick. This guy's apartment is disgusting. Not surprising. He's not the definition of cleanliness himself. When he walked over to the bar stool, I was sort of hoping he wasn't the guy I was waiting for. But then as we started talking, I realized he was absolutely perfect.

The way this guy droned on at the bar about some fancy new computer game he was trying to create, it was torture to listen to. Well, to be fair, I barely listened to him talk. I just put on a charming smile and nodded here and there. At some point I began touching his arm gently. I could see that he was getting excited by the thought of me. I was excited too. Just in a different way.

After I could no longer stand listening to him rattle on for another minute, I took a final swig of my drink, looked him in the eye, and said, "Let's get out of here." Silently, he stood up and put on his thin windbreaker jacket. I can't believe how easy it had been.

I look down at him now, lying on his bed, his arms and legs hogtied behind his back, a pair of socks in his mouth as a gag. His eyes are wild, almost bulging out of their sockets, silently screaming for help. He is naked and shivering from the cold. I am sweating from the anticipation and excitement.

I have been planning this one for a while. Well, not this guy specifically. But I was itching for this. It's been a little while since I've allowed myself this indulgence.

It's not easy, you know. A lot of time and preparation goes into this. I'm not some monster that just tortures and kills people on a whim, you know. No, I spend hours planning my moves. Choosing my targets. Preparing myself, both physically and emotionally. You can never be too prepared, that's what my parents always said growing up. We were always prepared for everything. My mom always had an extra snack or set of clothes for us in case we spilled something. My dad always had a wrench and screwdriver in the car because you never know when you'll need it. They both ran a tight ship to make sure we were always good, obedient little soldiers.

Don't pity me or feel bad for me. I had a happy childhood growing up. We weren't rich, but we had enough money to get by. We were a typical family. My dad didn't hit me or abuse me, if that's what you're thinking. I wasn't bullied in school. I didn't skin the neighbour's cat or torture animals. I was a regular kid.

But I didn't want to be regular. I wanted to be special. To stand out. To feel strong, to feel powerful. When I was given the chance to learn how to be extraordinary, I took it. It took a lot of hard work, building myself up into what I am today. But it was worth it. Hard work pays off. You gotta earn your place in the world.

That first time, it was mostly an accident. It was this crazy, out-of-body experience. It was me, but it wasn't me, you know? We were just talking, and I got so frustrated. He didn't understand his place in all this. He didn't understand that we were special. I just wanted him to get it. Without even realizing what I was doing, my body went into autopilot mode and I just attacked him. I didn't mean to do it, I don't think. Although now, looking back on it, if I'm being perfectly honest with myself, I probably knew that something was going to happen. My intentions were not pure, that's for sure. But I didn't know I was going to kill the guy. And I did not plan for it. At least not the way I do now.

Now, as I was saying, the planning can take days, even weeks. I need to make sure I have all the things I'll need, all my equipment. That first time, I had to look around and find everything on the spot. The next time I did it, I made sure I was fully prepared. I got my gym bag and filled it with everything I could possible need: rope, duct tape, gloves, a knife, a flashlight. I'm honestly not sure why I thought I would need a flashlight, but hey, always be prepared, right?

I learned that time that I didn't need everything. All my gear just got in my way. Sometimes it was better to use what was around me, adapt to my surroundings. So now I make sure I have the essentials: rope and gloves. The rest, I've discovered, I can improvise once I start.

I know what I'm doing is dangerous. If I ever get caught, my entire life will be over. But hey, no risk, no reward, right? And it's not like I do it every day. I only allow myself to do it every so often. An intermittent indulgence. A guilty pleasure. But I must admit, it's become harder to ignore the urge.

The guy is whimpering and he disrupts my thoughts. He is staring up at me. I think he's trying to use his eyes to communicate with me, to plead with me to spare him. I can see the fear in his eyes. He is hoping to find some compassion, some form of humanity in me, to let him go. His attempts have the opposite effect on me. I am aroused..

This is my favourite part, the foreplay. Sure, killing is fun. Watching the light go out in a man's eyes is extraordinary—I make sure I watch every time. But the lead up, the anticipation? It's intoxicating, knowing how much power I have over another human being. I decide if this man lives or dies. Not God, not some other being. Me. I am extraordinary.

He will die, of course. But he doesn't need to know that yet.

I smile at this man. He tries screaming but the gag muffles any sound.

"Ssshhhhhh… it's going to be okay. I'm not going to hurt you," I say smiling. But we both know that is not true.

CHAPTER 10

The smell of coffee hits Rose as she enters The Bean, her favourite coffee shop. It is located in the heart of the Forest Hill Village. The Village, while rich in history, has become a hot spot for trendy restaurants, fancy gym studios, traditional barbershops and dry cleaners, and chic fashion boutiques. It is constantly buzzing with fitness aficionados going to and from their workouts, old men sitting on park benches sipping coffee and people watching, and "yummy mummy" mothers pushing expensive strollers while chatting with one another about their baby's latest milestone. Rose's parents live on Dewbourne Avenue, just a 10-minute walk from The Village, and she came here often when she lived at home, whether it was to grab a coffee, work out, or pick up some fresh produce from the market.

In the center of the stretch of shops along Spadina that makes up the heart of The Village stands The Bean. The walls of the cafe are all exposed brick and are adorned with rustic and eclectic lighting fixtures. One wall is a giant chalkboard, where the baristas write the daily specials and customers can write messages to the shop. Distressed white chairs and benches line the walls with long wooden tables sitting across them. The barista bar has a tall glass case displaying their daily delicacies. In addition to their amazing coffees, The Bean offers delicious daily varieties of pastries and pies. Rose orders a cappuccino with almond milk. When the barista hands her the drink, the wonderful, slightly bitter and slightly sweet combination wafts over her. The first sip hits her, dancing over her taste buds. Each sip brings up memories from her childhood days, and then her university and law school days, back when things were simpler. When she would come study here in the café before meeting up with Will or her girlfriends.

She takes her cappuccino and the tiny biscotti cookie that is served with every coffee and finds a booth toward the back of the shop. Just as she sits down, she hears her name.

"Rose!" shouts Stella as she runs into the coffee shop and throws her arms around Rose. Right behind Stella are Anne and Lauren, and the four girls are squealing and laughing and hugging. They had made plans to have a mid-afternoon coffee that day. It feels so good to see these women in person, not just over video chat like they do every Sunday evening.

"LARS, back in da house!" cries Anne. The women groan and laugh hysterically at this.

"Oh my god, you did not just say that," Rose cries.

"I sure did," replies Anne, "and I have zero regrets!"

Lauren offers to order the coffees for herself, Stella and Anne, so she goes to wait in line while Stella and Anne settle in the booth. Rose looks over and sees the tiny, round ball protruding from Lauren's tummy. Lauren is six months pregnant with her first child. Her normally short, blonde curly hair has grown longer with the pregnancy hormones, and her blue eyes are dancing over the display of pastries. She is truly glowing, and Rose could not be happier for her friend.

Lauren has always been super athletic and fit. She works out every day for two hours (although even Lauren admits she's not sure she will be able to keep that up once the baby is born). She looks incredible, like a maternity model. Rose looks down at her own belly. While not pregnant with a child, it is definitely not as tight and flat as it used to be. But instead of being hard on herself and seeing this as a failure, Rose approaches this feeling with compassion. She is learning to love her body just as she is.

"So tiny, right? I hate her," announces Stella while rolling her eyes.

"I know," chimes in Anne, "doesn't she look amazing?"

"Just like I did when I was pregnant with Penny," jokes Stella. Stella's daughter Penny is nine months old now. She is the sweetest girl, very smiley, with Stella's dark, thick curly hair and gorgeous bright green eyes. Stella is a wonderful mom, just like Rose knew she would be.

"Stop it, you looked amazing and you look perfect now!"

Stella sighs, "So true! I am amazing!" and they all laugh.

Lauren arrives just as their laughter subsides, and the four women settle into their conversation, filled with a lot more laughter. In fact, at one point, they laughed so loud the owner of The Bean had to come to their table and ask them to keep it down. This, of course, only fueled their laugher further, to the point where the owner asked them to leave if they could not quiet down.

Rose's belly aches from laughing so much. The sight of these three women, who have been her best friends for so many years, has brought her a calmness and a peace that she hasn't felt in months. Now that she thinks of it, she hasn't felt this good since the last LARS vacation they took, two years ago.

Forget Dr. Hill, this is the therapy Rose needs. She smiles contentedly, listening to Stella regale them with stories of midnight feedings and Penny's cute facial expressions.

Just then, out of the corner of her eye, Rose notices that the TV on the wall directly across from her has cut to a breaking news story. A normally bubbly news anchor is standing in front of an apartment building with police tape across the lawn, with the flashing lights of ambulances and police cars lighting up the view. Rose sees the news tickler at the bottom of the screen and her blood turns cold.

"Man found brutally stabbed to death in his bed."

CHAPTER 11

The apartment building is tall and decrepit, located in Cabbagetown, one of the seedier areas of Toronto. Some of the bricks on the outside structure have fallen off, while others look like they may crumble with one large gust of wind. There are police cars in front of the building, and one patrol officer is out front standing guard.

Rose steps up to the officer and signals that she needs to go inside, and the patrolman steps aside and allows her to enter. *Well, that was way too easy,* thought Rose. *Terrible security. I should tell the officer in charge to secure the building more carefully.*

Not knowing which floor to go to, or even which unit, Rose climbs the stairs slowly, hoping to get a glimpse of a stronger police presence to indicate where the crime scene is. The first five floors are clear and quiet, but by the time she reaches the top of the sixth stairway, she can hear the mumble of police two-way radios and of people talking quietly. Treading quietly, Rose starts walking towards the sounds. She hears, more than sees, the commotion at the end of the long hallway. Coming up to unit 624, Rose sees yellow police tape and three police officers huddled just inside the apartment. The officers are enrapt in conversation, allowing Rose to sneak past them toward the bedroom where the victim must be.

There, lying on the bed in a pool of blood, is Will.

The room is spinning now, then everything goes black.

Somewhere deep down, Rose knows that she fainted. She also knows that the dead body lying on the bed does not belong to Will. Her love died many years ago. This is someone else's love, not hers. That reality hits her hard, as she starts opening her eyes, like it does every morning when she wakes: he is gone.

Once her eyes are properly open, Rose sees that she is staring into another pair of eyes; these eyes belong to another man, someone she does not recognize. She does not know who he is. She would know if she had seen those eyes before. They were the most gorgeous eyes she had ever seen—a beautiful shade of teal blue, like the ocean, with a ring of emerald green around them. Such unique eyes. They are gentle, kind, and loving eyes. Right now, these eyes are worried. Are they worried about her?

"Hi," Rose says to the face attached to those eyes.

"Are you okay?" the eyes ask.

"Yes, thank you. Low blood pressure," Rose excuses.

"What the hell are you doing here?"

Rose sits up and can now properly take in her surroundings. The face attached to those spectacular eyes is similarly attractive and is framed by luscious brown wavy hair. It's the kind of hair you just want to run your hands through: tidy around the ears and through the sides, but longer on the top, allowing the thick waves to naturally frame his face. An unruly curl keeps falling on his face and threatens to block those blue eyes. Rose is staring at him and notices that now those eyes are not showing the same gentle concern as they were a minute earlier. They are angry.

"I ... um ... I saw on the news and wanted to see ..." Rose stammers. The man who had been leaning over her stands up and she follows suit. She can see that he is tall and has a trim, toned body. He is wearing jeans and a leather jacket, and she is wondering just who this man is and why he is here.

"This is a crime scene, so unless you have a badge showing you're a member of the Toronto Police, get out of my crime scene."

Ouch. Fully alert now, Rose snaps, "I may not have a badge, but I am fully competent and likely more equipped to handle this type of scene than you are, Mr. …" searching for his name.

"Detective Cooper," he fills in.

"Detective Cooper. My name is Rose Davis. I am an experienced Crown prosecutor with the Attorney General in Vancouver. I have seen hundreds of crime scenes, gang fights, domestic abuse, arson, murder, you name it. I can help you here. You should check for signs of a struggle. Sexual assault? Is there a tennis racquet nearby? You should also make sure you sweep for prints."

"Ms. Davis, I have been to a crime scene before. I am perfectly capable of inspecting a scene," Cooper says.

"I'm not telling you how to do your job or anything," she says, as she literally tells him how to do his job.

"Ma'am, I'm going to have to ask you to leave."

"Ma'am?" Rose stammers. Who does this guy think he is, speaking to her that way? "I am a respected criminal prosecutor. I can help you. I'm staying."

"No, you're not," Detective Cooper responds.

"Yes, I am."

"No, you're not." Motioning for another officer, Cooper continues, "Officer Mathison, please escort this woman off of our crime scene. Now."

With that, a short, doughy man in a too-tight uniform approaches Rose and reaches out to grab her arm.

"I can find my own way out," she says with a sneer. "But you will regret this."

"Doubtful," Cooper says smugly.

Asshole, Rose thinks as she storms out.

CHAPTER 12

Detective Ben Cooper tries to shake off his exasperation at the woman who is being escorted off the premises. He runs his fingers through his hair, trying to hold back the messy waves. Luckily, he thinks to himself, he had noticed her right as she entered the room and passed out. He happened to be at the doorway, still putting on his paper booties and latex gloves to be sure not to alter the crime scene or leave any of his own prints. If she had been conscious or had gone unnoticed, she could have tampered with the evidence or altered the crime scene. His captain at the TPS would not have looked too kindly at that, Cooper is sure.

Everyone thinks they're a cop, he thinks. *I will not let anyone interfere with this investigation.* He takes a few deep, calming breaths, and focuses on the scene ahead of him.

He takes a few steps closer to the victim to examine the body. The victim, who Cooper has now identified as Marco Ramirez, was found early this morning by his roommate. Lying in the middle of his bed, he appears to have been stabbed over twenty times. *What a barbaric way to go*, thinks Cooper. His wrists and feet had purple marks and abrasions, indicating that the victim had been tied up prior to death. There was blood splatter all over the bed, on the carpet around the bed, and on the walls. Detective Cooper assesses the patterns. The coroner's technicians will have to come in and analyze it properly, but based on his experience, he infers that Ramirez was stabbed while lying on the bed. Continuing this line of thought, Cooper concludes that the man died on the bed, and has not been moved post-mortem.

In addition to the stabbings, Cooper notes extensive anal trauma, with blood and bruising around Ramirez's anus. Lying nearby is a baseball bat. This must have been the weapon used to molest him. *Weird that that lady asked about signs of sexual assault or a tennis racquet*, he thought. *How did she know to ask about that?* He also notes that the knife used to kill the victim is missing. He wonders whether the murderer took the knife with them or whether they used one of the victim's knives, cleaning and replacing it in its drawer.

He also makes a mental note to ask the coroner's team about defensive wounds and any other evidence of a fight, like DNA under the victim's finger nails.

He feels a wave of sickness come over him as he looks around. He has been a detective with the Toronto Police Service for over ten years now, but these crime scenes still get to him every time. You just don't get used to seeing such horror. While he wishes he could become desensitized to these violent crimes, a small part of him is grateful that he feels it every time. It motivates him to do his job, to get justice for the victims. Once he becomes numb to these crimes, he knows that is when he should stop.

Cooper continues to look around the room. Ramirez was a slob. He had dirty clothes strewn across the floor, landing everywhere except for the laundry hamper. There were empty and half-empty boxes of takeout food, with plastic cutlery still hanging out the side. A large pile of empty beer bottles and Coke cans could be seen on a small table that held a TV and some various video gaming consoles. Directly across from the table was Ramirez's bed, and at the foot of the bed was a dark blue bean bag chair. In short, the room looked like a typical college dormitory being lived in by messy nineteen-year-old boys who just moved out of their parents' house.

Just as Detective Cooper started looking in the drawers, the forensic team arrives. He is quickly ushered out and told to let the team "do their magic." Cooper has worked with this team before and he trusts them implicitly. He leaves the victim's bedroom, turning his attention to the rest of the apartment.

It is a two-bedroom apartment in Cabbagetown. It is small; too small for two people, but it was probably the best they could do. Rent in Toronto is sky-rocketing these days, Cooper thought. He walks around the common kitchen and living room area. There is an eclectic mix of dishes, pots, and pans. The fridge is nearly empty, just some beer bottles, a bottle of ketchup, and a jar of pickles.

Turning his attention to the main living room area, Cooper sees Chase Campbell, the victim's roommate, pale and ashen, shaking. He is clearly traumatized from having the unfortunate luck to have been the one to discover the victim on his bed. He is being questioned by Officer Mathison now. Cooper walks towards them to listen.

"... he told me he was planning on getting lucky last night and that I should sleep at my girlfriend's place."

"Get lucky?" Cooper asks.

"Yeah, you know, hook up," the roommate said, blushing a little from having to explain this to another man.

"I know what 'get lucky' means, sir. I am interested in the details of how Mr. Ramirez was going to get lucky. Did he have a date with someone?"

"Sort of," murmurs Chase Campbell.

"Sort of? He either had a date, or he didn't."

"It's not really a date. What these guys do. They sort of, you know, meet up just to hook up. I don't know how much they actually do in terms of 'dating.'"

"When you say guys, do you mean men?"

"Men, women, non-gendered. Could be anything. I've seen Marco with all of them."

"Do you know who he was meeting last night?"

"No, sorry."

"Tell me what you do know. How did Mr. Ramirez meet this person he was hooking up with?" Cooper asks.

Chase Campbell tries to explain to Cooper the virtual dating life of his roommate. "He didn't have many friends. At least none that I have ever met, and we've been living together for almost two years. And no family that he ever spoke of. The only people he spoke to were online. He was always playing this game, *Dueling Swords*, and he always had his earphones on, talking to other players over the game. They all use fake names or aliases, so I don't think anyone knew anyone's actual name. They take on these online personas that are very different from who they really are. I know that Marco played under the name Knight Man. I don't know if any of the people he spoke to or met up with even knew him as Marco.

"Anyway, Marco has done this a bunch of times before. He would make plans to meet up with one of the players from *Dueling Swords*, and I had to sleep at my girl's place. That's what happened yesterday. All I know is that he told me he was meeting up with someone and I had to get out."

"And you definitely did not know who he was meeting up with last night?" Detective Cooper asked.

"No, man, like I said, people didn't use their real names."

"Did you get this person's online name?"

"No, he never told me that kind of thing. We sort of had a 'don't ask, don't tell' thing going. I give him space when he asks for it, and he gives me space when I need it."

"Do you know what bar he went to?"

"Yeah, um … The Rideout," Campbell replies.

"Can you please describe what happened this morning?"

"I got home this morning after being with my girl all night. It was quiet, but I figured Marco was sleeping after a late night. I didn't go into his room or anything, or even call his name. I was giving the dude space, you know?"

"Yes, I know. When did you realize something was wrong, then?" Chase Campbell is starting to get emotional. They may not have been best friends, but it's still traumatizing to be the one to find your roommate's dead, mutilated body.

"I went to the kitchen to make lunch and saw that we were out of milk. I was pissed at Marco, since he always finishes the milk and doesn't buy a new carton. He never goes out or gets the groceries, it's all on me, so I'm always yelling at him to pull his weight, to start getting us food and stuff. Anyway, today I noticed we were out of milk, and I was mad, so I called his name to tell him to get out of bed and go to the convenience store to get milk. He didn't answer. I knocked on his door, but he still didn't answer, so I just shoved open the door.

"That's when, well … you know … I saw him." Campbell's eyes start to water and his voice croaks. "Then I ran out of his room and called the police."

Cooper has heard enough from Campbell, and after a quick request to Officer Mathison to get more details, Cooper steps away.

He stares at the doorway, where the forensics team is hard at work, and considers what he has seen and heard so far. Everything reminds him of previous crime scenes he has seen. The details seem to correspond. The more Cooper sees here, in this decrepit apartment, the more convinced he is.

There is a serial killer in Toronto.

CHAPTER 13

Rose is fuming as she steps out of the tiny elevator and exits the apartment building. She has never felt so disrespected in her life. After all, she was just trying to help.

So typical, she thinks. In her experience, police detectives have always been smug and territorial; they would rather do things their way and take all the credit than to listen to someone else. This Detective Cooper is just like them. He looked at her as if she were stupid. She is *not* stupid.

So different than the first moment when he looked at me, with worry in his eyes. Her mind takes her back to that moment, lying down in the victim's apartment, opening her eyes to look into the face of an extremely handsome man. Those worried eyes are a truly remarkable colour, attached to a face with a strong, chiseled jaw with a cleft chin, something that Rose has always found incredibly attractive. And that sandy brown mop of hair, with thick untamed waves framing his face, the one stubborn curl falling into his eyes. In that moment, as she was coming to, she could not tell if she was awake or dreaming of this handsome saviour.

Rose, get it together! Why are you thinking about this? She scolds herself. She reminds herself that he is a smug, pretentious, know-it-all, who clearly has no respect for intelligent women. *He must be intimidated by me,* she thinks. *Good. He should be. I'll show him what I'm capable of, and he'll wish he had listened to me.*

Rose walks into her parents' house and sees Tyler sitting on the couch watching TV, eating chips and having a beer. "What, do you live here now? Don't you have your own house?"

"Emily kicked me out. I'm living here now."

"What?" Rose cries with concern.

Tyler laughs. "Oh my god, sis, you are just as gullible as ever! I came over to hide from Emily's book club. She has these monthly dates with her girlfriends where they pretend to discuss a book but really just get drunk and talk shit about their husbands."

Rose plops down on the couch next to him. She grabs the chips from him and says, "Sounds lame."

"Totally."

They sit in comfortable silence for a few minutes. Then Tyler ruins the moment by asking, "Want to play another round of hoops?"

"There is nothing I would rather do less, brother," Rose quips back. "Especially after the day I had today."

"I thought you were seeing MARS or whatever you call yourself?"

"LARS, and don't pretend you don't know that," Rose scolds. "I was with them, but then I saw in the news that someone was killed exactly like Will, and something inside me just drew me there, like this gravitational pull. I just had to go see. Maybe it was the same killer. Maybe they left a clue this time."

"Rose, it's been six years. They're not going to find the killer. You have to move past this." Tyler is both sympathetic and firm in his tone. "Bad things happen to good people, and the only thing you can do is try to move on."

"You wouldn't know, Tyler. You have the best luck in the world. You're athletic, and smart, and handsome, and people adore you. You have a perfect wife, perfect children, a perfect life. You don't know what it's like to go through this type of trauma."

Tyler thinks about this and is silent. For a brief moment, Rose thinks she sees something in his eyes, indicating that maybe he *has* experienced heartache or trauma. But as quickly as it appears, that look disappears and Tyler says, "You're right, my boyfriend was not murdered. But he was my friend, and my sister's boyfriend, so it did affect me, Rose. I miss Will too."

"You miss him?" Rose asks incredulously. "You don't know what it means to miss someone like this. To literally feel like your heart breaks in two every time you remember that the love of your life is gone. Every time something happens and you think to yourself, 'Will would love this," but you know what? You can't call Will to tell him, because he is dead!" Rose is crying now.

"You're right, you're right, I'm sorry," Tyler apologizes. "I cannot imagine what that is like."

"The worst part is that his killer is just ... out there. Living their life. I bet you they laughs when they think about all the things they have gotten away with. What if they've killed other people? That's why I just had to go today to see for myself—could it be the same person?"

"And was it?"

"I don't know, some self-righteous detective kicked me out of the crime scene before I could really look."

"Is he handsome?" Rose looks up to see her mother standing there.

"Oh my god, Mom, does it matter? He's an asshole!"

"You think every man is an asshole, Rose. The question is whether he is an attractive asshole."

"Are you really asking me about this man's looks? I saw him at a homicide crime scene. Finding a love match was not really on my mind, Mom."

"You never know how you'll meet a man, honey. My friend Betty's daughter Abby met her husband in line at a gas station! Would you believe that?"

"Cool, Mom. I'm sure their kids will love hearing that story," Rose says sarcastically.

"So, is he?" Isabelle asks.

"Is he what?"

"Attractive."

"Sure, he's good looking in the traditional sense," Rose acquiesces, while rolling her eyes.

"Good. I just want you to get married, settle down, have children, and be happy."

"Mom, I can be happy without being married or having kids."

"I know sweetheart, I just think you would be happier if you had a husband," Isabelle says.

"I think *you* would be happier if I had a husband."

"Trust me, Rose. I'm your mother. I know what's best for you." With that, her mother smiles and walks out of the room.

"Dude, you need to get a man just to get her off your back," Tyler says.

"Tell me about it."

CHAPTER 14

*H*as work always been this boring? Ugh. I must have liked it when I started years ago. It's just become so ... mundane. Wake up, hit the gym, shower, suit up, sit at a desk all day answering stupid emails and talking to stupid people. Every day, the same routine. No excitement. The tedium is driving me crazy.

I'm starting to feel numb. What is the purpose in all of this? I am better than this. The only time I ever feel anything at all these days is when I'm out on one of my adventures. The thrill of it all. The preparation. Watching my targets without them even knowing I'm there. The ultimate power and control I have. You might be surprised to hear this, but I like when my target struggles and fights back. The physical aspect of it is unlike any workout I've ever done. And, of course, I always win.

You'd think I was into karate or boxing growing up, but nope. I'm a self-taught fighter. Sure, I fought a bit as a kid, but parents or teachers would always break up the fights. That's why I liked playing sports. You were allowed to fight. In fact, you were encouraged to fight. Football and hockey were the best for that. Baseball and basketball are fun and everything, but they're too nice. I like getting down and dirty, getting in the mud, hitting people, dominating them. We used to spend extra time after practice working on my tackling and hitting. Taking control over the ball, the puck, the opposing team. I still love it.

Should I go hunting tonight for my next target? No, I can't. I just went on the weekend. It's too soon. I need to space them out. People might start to notice a pattern.

Normally the thrill of one adventure can tide me over for a while. I simply replay the killing in my head for months, reliving that moment, feeling the high each time I see it in my mind. It's like a movie that lives rent-free in my head.

But I don't know what's going on with me these days. Just watching the movie isn't doing what it usually does. I need to create a new one. I can't help it. It's like a drug, the power of standing over a man and watching the light extinguish from his eyes.

I need a hit.

Maybe I can just start the process tonight. Nothing serious, I don't need to commit to anything. I don't need to actually do it tonight. Just start the process. Start the hunt.

It takes a lot of time and effort scoping out the ideal target. Someone that is easily manipulated, easily influenced. Ideally someone who lives alone. That was almost a total disaster with Ramirez, he had never mentioned a roommate during our conversations. I can't believe I almost missed that. Anyway, it worked out fine, didn't it?

That was my first time finding a target online. I won't be doing that again. Lesson learned, am I right? I thought it was a good idea at the time, you know, adapting with the times. Everything and everyone is moving online. It was a risk, and you know how I feel about risks. Nothing good ever comes easy. Victory is sweetest when you've earned it. And I have earned each and every single one of my kills.

Anyway, it's way easier to find my target in person, watch him a little, make sure he isn't completely disgusting like that guy was. So I'll go back to that. Tonight.

My computer chimes, telling me I've gotten another email. This is the tenth email in the past five minutes. It just doesn't stop! Sigh. Back to reality, I guess.

CHAPTER 15

Detective Ben Cooper has been up most of the night. He has been trying to piece together the previous murders and how this one relates to the rest of them. There are no physical similarities; the victims range from dark hair to light, from brown eyes to blue. There does not appear to be a preferred race or religion. The only commonality between the victims is that they are men with a height range between fix-six and five-ten. Cooper suspects the reason for that is less to do with a pattern or preference and more to do with convenience. He imagines it might be tough for the killer to lift a six-foot-four, 275-lb man onto a bed or maneuver his body. Which means the killer himself probably is not a particularly strong man. Everything indicates that he is quite average.

Or the killer could be a woman. At this point, he cannot rule anything out. While serial killers statistically tend to be male, you cannot count out a female killer.

Cooper knows he has a long morning of paperwork ahead of him, in addition to the actual investigative work he needs to do. *No one tells you about the paperwork in the police academy*, he thinks. He spends more time doing banal paperwork than actually investigating. But that's the bureaucracy of police work, he thinks.

Needing a jolt of caffeine before tackling the tedious forms, Cooper stops at The Bean for a coffee on his way to work at Toronto Police Service – 53 Division. He patiently waits in line to place his order, in no rush to head over to the station. When it is his turn, he orders a large black coffee, then steps over to the counter to put in a bit of milk. Securing the lid over his drink, he turns and bumps into someone.

"I'm sorry …" he stumbles and apologizes, his coffee splashing all over him, burning his hands with the hot liquid. He looks up to see if he has splashed coffee on the other person and sees the woman from the crime scene—*What was her name again? Ruby? No, Rose something.* Ben notices that she is, simply put, gorgeous. How had he not noticed that before? She has long straight blonde hair and blue eyes that are the colour of the sky. Her slightly rounded face is soft and welcoming, although it quickly turns to anger when she sees him. He, in turn, shifts his response from apologetic to indignant.

"You! Why are you always showing up in places where you shouldn't be? Don't you know to wait your turn, let people step away before you elbow your way in?"

"Excuse me? Most people look where they're going before spinning around with piping hot coffee."

"I'm the one with hot coffee all over him, so I don't see why you're complaining," Cooper mutters in an exasperated tone.

Rose quickly switches the conversation: "How's the investigation coming along, Detective?"

"If you have questions, you can direct them to our police department, like all members of the public. I will not discuss an ongoing case with a civilian."

"Why won't you let me help you?"

"Because this is a police matter and is much more complicated than you may realize. This is not just a one-off murder that can be solved in a day."

"I know."

"You know?"

"I know. When I saw the news about a man found dead in his bed, with multiple stab wounds, it reminded me of … of another murder from six years ago. Will Sutton."

"I remember that case. Terrible. The guy had just proposed to his girlfriend, I remember there were rose petals everywhere mixed with blood."

"He had not proposed yet," Rose corrects Detective Cooper, with a forlorn look in her eyes.

All of a sudden, things click into place for Cooper. "Rose Davis. You were Sutton's fiancé."

"Almost fiancé," she corrects him again.

"I'm really sorry for your loss. Truly, I am," Cooper says earnestly. Now he understands why Rose is inserting herself into the investigation. Still, he can't allow that to happen.

"I need this killer to pay for what he has done to Will, and now to this second victim," Rose asserts.

"Fifth." It is Cooper's turn to correct Rose.

"Pardon me?" she stares at him, confused.

Cooper sighs. "This is the fifth victim that we are aware of with a similar killing pattern. Each time, a male victim is found in his bed, with multiple stab wounds, signs of struggle, torture and anal trauma. The physical object used each time in the sexual assault has been different, which is what has made this so tricky. I have been tracking this animal for about four years now, tying the cases together. My captain does not agree that there is a pattern indicating a serial killer, but with the discovery of Marco Ramirez yesterday, I think I can finally convince her to treat this as a serial killer."

"Then you have to let me help you," Rose demands.

Cooper is exhausted and frustrated. While he is sympathetic and feels bad for her loss, he does not have time for this right now. "No, I don't. I am perfectly capable of doing my job. Now, if you will excuse me, I have work to get to."

"I'm coming with you."

"To do my paperwork? Sure," Cooper laughs. "By all means!"

"That is the extent of your investigation? Paperwork? Wow, I'm glad to see our tax dollars hard at work. Let me know if you find the killer in your forms," Rose snarls. "I guess I'll have to do the real detective work myself."

Cooper is astonished by the nerve of this woman. He is simultaneously frustrated and in awe of her, her passion and persistence. He sighs and decides to appease her a little to get her to go away. "I'm going this afternoon to question someone. I'm not sure how far I'll get, but I promise, I really am working hard to solve this case."

Rose jumps on this opportunity and says, "Great! I'll stop by the precinct at 1:00, just after lunch, then we'll head out to question this person together. I'll see you in a few hours." And with that, she turns away from Cooper with a smug smile and saunters out of the coffee shop.

Oh boy, what am I getting myself into? thinks Cooper. He can sense she is trouble—in both the best and worst kind of way possible.

CHAPTER 16

Rose walks out of The Bean with her almond milk latte, still smirking, proud of herself for standing up to that detective.

Her phone dings, notifying her of an incoming message. It's from Paige. 'So? What did u buy me?'

'Haven't yet—but just bought a latte from that coffee shop I told u about. Does that count?'

'Drool emoji.'

'Paige, u're supposed to use the actual emoji, not just say drool emoji lol.'

'Whatevs. Go buy me a purse.'

'Can't. Looking into a case…'

'ROSE!'

'Can't help it lol.'

'U're going to be the death of me.'

'I know! Gtg'

'Love u.'

'Love u 2.'

She arrives at Division 53 police station at 12:45 p.m., nice and early. Detective Cooper is annoyed but not surprised to see her there. Together, they drive down in Cooper's police cruiser to the head office of VR Gaming.

"You're in the back," he says, motioning for Rose to sit in the back of the cruiser behind the bars. She makes a face at him and ignores him, getting into the front seat. As he pulls away from the parking lot, Cooper explains that they are going to see the head of the video game company that created the game Ramirez played and chatted with his killer.

VR Gaming has its headquarters in the heart of the financial district of Toronto. It is on the forty-second floor of a fifty-four-floor building. The building has a perfect view of Lake Ontario as well as the C.N. Tower. Rose actually worked in this building right before she was called to the bar; the law firm she articled at is on the thirty-eighth floor. The building's walls were made of dark tinted windows that reflected the water. The lobby is modern and simply decorated, all white and grey. There is a large security desk in the middle, with five elevator banks behind the desk.

Stepping into the main lobby of the tall building feels like stepping back in time. For a moment, Rose could picture herself stumbling out of this lobby, hailing a cab at 1:00 a.m., desperate to get home to Will and to crawl into bed next to him. She is roused from that daydream when Detective Cooper walks up next to her and gruffly says, "Let's go up," while mumbling under his breath as he walks away, "even though I still don't get why you're here and I wish you would go home and let me do my job."

"Did you say something?" Rose asks, having clearly heard him.

"I said let's go." He walks toward the elevator banks and presses the up button.

They take the elevator up to the forty-second floor. They are silent the entire ride up, acutely aware of the other's presence. Rose looks over at Cooper. She has worked with many police officers and detectives in her years as Crown counsel, but Detective Cooper is different than all of them. He is young and eager, but also relaxed and confident. Instead of a stiff suit, he wears jeans and a leather jacket. His cheeks and nose are lightly dusted with freckles. The softness of the freckles is a charming contrast to his chiseled jawline and cleft chin. Despite him being a total pain in the ass, she recognizes that he is gorgeous. Smart, too. As they ascend past forty-one floors, she notes that he subconsciously runs his fingers through his hair in a nervous habit. She thinks back to the first time she saw him, when she woke up to see his eyes looking back at her with concern. All she could see were those kind, deep teal eyes with a green halo around them. Her stomach did a little flip then as she came to. It does a similar flip now as she watches him.

Cooper catches her watching him and she quickly averts her gaze. The elevator dings. Perfect timing. The doors open to a beautiful foyer. Rose had been expecting the VR Gaming office to look like something from TV, where young hipsters are playing games and skateboarding around the office, walking around testing out VR equipment. Instead, the office is traditional and tasteful. The only indication that it is a video game technology company is the large sign over the receptionist desk instead of one of the long law firm names, like Dewey, Cheatem & Howe from The Three Stooges. Rose and her dad used to always watch that together when she was a little girl, and she still snickers at the thought of those three men, slapping each other and falling over themselves.

The receptionist greets them with an overly sweet and cheery "hello" and Rose instantly dislikes her. No one is genuinely that happy.

"We're here to see Jim Cullen," Cooper says.

"Do you have an appointment?" she asks pleasantly.

"No," Cooper says, flashing his badge.

The receptionist is clearly thrown off by seeing the detective's badge and she says, "hold on," as she clumsily reaches for the phone to call her boss. A minute later she tells them to have a seat in the waiting room and that Mr. Cullen will be out momentarily.

Momentarily turns out to be almost an hour. Rose and Cooper spend most of the time in silence, watching the hustle and bustle of people around them. Rose tries to chat with him, but Cooper remains quiet and professional, clearly not interested in engaging in conversation.

Finally, the receptionist approaches them and says to follow her. Jim Cullen's office is larger than Rose's entire condo back in Vancouver. The walls are covered in plaques and awards and pictures of Cullen with politicians, actors, and musicians. There is even a picture of him standing next to Canadian Prime Minister Justin Trudeau.

Cullen does not stand up when they enter, he simply indicates that they can sit down in the two oversized black suede chairs across from his desk.

"Detectives, how can I help you today? As I'm sure you are aware, I'm a very busy man, so let's not bother with pleasantries."

"Fine with us," Cooper says. "And I'm the only detective here, she is not." Rose gives Cooper a look that says, *was that really necessary?* "We need a list of your customers located here in the city who have purchased your game *Dueling Swords*."

Cullen laughs. When he sees that Cooper and Rose are not laughing with him, he asks, "You're serious?"

"Deadly," Cooper responds, deadpanned.

"That's not happening, guys. Sorry. That is our customers' private information. We guarantee customer privacy when they subscribe to our games, and we take that guarantee very seriously."

"Mr. Cullen, we are investigating a horrific murder that we believe could be one of a series of killings caused by a single man. We also believe that these murders are somehow connected to one of your games, sir, so with all due respect, we are asking that you help us out in our investigation. We need a list of all users who logged on to play *Dueling Swords* in the Greater Toronto Area two days ago on Monday from 3:00 p.m. to 9:00 p.m."

"Like I just told you, I cannot give you that information, doing so would be a breach of our customers' subscription agreement. And in fact, I have no legal obligation to give you that information."

"Legal obligation or not, you have a moral obligation to bring justice to the victims, to the families of the victims," Rose says with disgust.

"I'm sorry people have died, but that has nothing to do with me."

"You don't know that," she cries. She is getting extremely frustrated with this man's bad attitude and evident superiority complex.

"I didn't kill those people," Cullen says.

"Fine. But we do think the murder might potentially be linked to one of your games, so we are respectfully requesting that you provide us with the names of customers online in this geographic area during this specific time period."

"Even if I wanted to help you, I can't. We don't have the capacity at this time to pinpoint specific users at a specific time in a specific location."

"Isn't that what you do? Don't you work on creating new technological advances?"

"Yes, you're right, Detective. Technically we could do it. But we won't," says Cullen. "And we wouldn't. Imagine what would happen if that technology existed. It would it be a colossal invasion of our customers' privacy. It is a dangerous precedent that threatens everyone's civil liberties. It's like that huge fight a few years back, where the cops tried to convince the CEO of a big tech company to unlock the smartphone of a suspect in a mass shooting. It's a slippery slope. If we start invading the privacy of alleged murderers, who is next? Someone who committed armed robbery? How about unarmed robbery? How about someone who gets a speeding ticket? We cannot start intruding upon peoples' civil liberties.

"And if we do create this technology to pinpoint specific users at specific times and places, can you imagine what all these young new hackers and cybercriminals would do with that information? It could lead to the crime rate increasing. And that's not even mentioning what could possibly happen if this technology gets into the hands of other people, like our enemies.

"So can I help you? Maybe. Will I help you? No. Unless you have a warrant, do not come back here, or I will have you arrested for trespassing. Thanks for stopping by, I expect you can see yourselves out."

CHAPTER 17

I feel like I'm getting a bad rap here. I'm not a bad person. Sure, I do bad things sometimes. For example, I never change the roll of toilet paper when I finish it. No real reason why, I just don't do it. I don't like doing it. But that doesn't make me a bad person. It just makes me human.

What is bad, anyway? If I killed Adolf Hitler, does that make me bad? Or a hero? There is no question here: I would be a hero. People would celebrate me across the world as the person to end World War II.

Who is to say that the people that I have killed are good? And what is good, anyway?

Bad things happen to good people, and good things happen to bad people. These dichotomous words, good and bad, black and white, they don't make sense. They don't define me. I am grey. I am rainbow. I am every colour and shade and hue.

Most of the time I do what I'm supposed to do. I control my urges. But once in a while, the urge becomes so intense that I can't think of anything else. It becomes unavoidable. Inevitable. What's so bad about that?

Was this guy even good? Maybe I am good for ending his life, and my hurting him has preventing him from hurting someone else. Or *maybe he was suffering and was looking for an end. I provided him with that relief. Sure, the fact that it satiates my needs, my desires, is great. But look at it as a mercy killing.*

Ugh, there is blood under my fingernails. I better go wash my hands.

CHAPTER 18

Rose is drowning. She is swimming in the ocean and is caught in the undertow of the crashing waves. Suddenly her head is above water and she takes a breath of sweet, clean air, and she tries to call for help. Just as suddenly, she is thrown back under the water, fighting for her life. She tries to swim to the surface, but she cannot reach it. The salty water stings her eyes, her face, and her lungs.

Somewhere, deep in her subconscious, she knows she is dreaming. But it feels so real. She thinks, this is it. The end.

And then she wakes up, gasping for air. It was a dream. She is still panting a few minutes later, recovering from the sensation of drowning.

She looks over at her phone and sees that it is just before 7:00 a.m. She gets out of bed and tiptoes down the stairs to make a coffee, trying not to wake her parents. She adds a new filter and four tablespoons of coffee to the coffeemaker, making sure there is enough for her parents. Then she tiptoes up the stairs again to get dressed.

She puts on her running shorts, a sports bra and a loose T-shirt. Not the cute trendy matching sets of athleisure that she sees people wearing in The Village, but she's not all that fussy. If she can move in it, she will run in it. She washes her face with some cold water to wake herself up, brushes her teeth, then heads downstairs for the jolt of caffeine.

Her mother is sitting at the kitchen table, sipping a mug of coffee and reading the news on her tablet.

"Hi, Mom."

"Good morning, sweetie. Thanks for putting on the coffee. Can I pour you a cup?"

"Sure, thanks."

Rose grabs a banana and sits down at the table just as her mother sets down a fresh, steaming cup of coffee. The aroma immediately stimulates Rose's senses and she feels herself begin to perk up a bit.

"Can I make you some toast?" her mom asks.

"No thanks, I'm just going to have this banana then go for a run," Rose replies.

"You're going for a run?"

"Yes," Rose answers, knowing what is coming but still feeling annoyed. *Every time*, Rose thinks. *Every time I get dressed, there's a comment.*

"In that?"

"Yep."

"Really honey? You don't want to put on something a little cuter? What if someone sees you?"

"Then they will see me," Rose replies, refusing to take the bait for a fight that her mother is clearly dangling.

"Okay, then," Isabelle states, in a tone that is clearly judgmental, meant to say, *that is so* not *okay*.

Rose finishes up her banana and coffee, gives her mother a quick kiss on the cheek, and heads for the door to go for her run.

Truthfully, Rose hates running. She much prefers a Pilates or yoga class, something a little more low-key. But Rose finds that running really gets her adrenaline going. Especially first thing in the morning. She loves the feeling of pushing herself past the point of comfort. She loves the feeling of achievement when she is done, soaked in sweat, panting.

Rose also wants to go for a run because it is the best way for her to clear her head from the fog of her nightmare and to focus on the investigation. She puts on her earbuds and opens her phone to her various running playlists. She skims through and considers what she wants to listen to today. Top 40? 90s alternative? Motown? She settles on classic rock. Aerosmith, Springsteen, Kansas, Duran Duran, Journey, and of course AC/DCs "Thunderstruck," because what rock playlist would be complete without it?

Turning the volume up high, Rose sets out on her run. She heads south on Rosemary Road, passing the beautiful homes that line the street. She is trying to avoid the hubbub of The Village as much as she can; she is in no mood to stop and socialize. She takes Rosemary south all the way to Burton Road, at which point she makes her way to Spadina Road and continues heading south. She used to do this run all the time, running from her house to Casa Loma, just south of St. Clair Avenue, then back home. The run usually took her about an hour in total, but she notices she is not as fast as she used to be, and she expects today's run will take a little longer than that.

As she makes her way south, pushing herself and feeling her heart pounding with each step, she thinks about Marco Ramirez and the scene at the apartment earlier in the week. She thinks about Will. She knows that the two deaths are connected. She does not have any proof, but she has an indescribable feeling, like something crawling under her skin.

She thinks about the conversation she and Detective Cooper had yesterday with the video game CEO. She is convinced that he is hiding something. Her thoughts suddenly drift to thinking about Detective Cooper. She wonders if he ever runs. He definitely works out. She can see that he is muscular, but not too muscular that his arms bulge out of his shirt. He is perfectly toned. And that hair! She wonders what it would feel like brushing her own fingers through his sexy, tousled waves. What it would feel like pulling that hair in a moment of passion.

What is going on with you? Rose thinks to herself. She pulls herself from this silly daydreaming and tries to focus on the investigation. But then she is distracted by flashing lights up ahead, just to her right, on Walmer Road. She heads in their direction and confirms her suspicion that these are police cars. Rose draws near and realizes the commotion is outside a house. Just like when she saw the headline on CNN about Marco Ramirez's murder, once again she has this uncanny and ineffable feeling that she needs to go look. She knows she shouldn't. But she also knows that on some level, she has to.

Picking up her speed, Rose sprints toward the house, steeling herself for what she will find when she gets there.

CHAPTER 19

There are two police officers guarding the house on Walmer. They must have been instructed not to let anyone in. *I guess they learned their lesson from my last visit*, she thought, both impressed and annoyed.

Not that they can stop Rose.

Rose marches straight up to them with an undeniable confidence and sense of purpose. "Good morning officers, Crown Counsel Rose Davis, here to consult on the case."

The two officers eye each other. They had not been told that anyone was coming to consult but she seems pretty assertive and confident. Despite her workout attire. Rose jumps on their hesitation and strides right past them.

Rose discretely smirks and mentally pats herself on the back as she climbs the steps to the front door. She can be quite shrewd when she wants to be.

No one is on the main floor, so she heads up the stairs to the top floor. Just to the right of the staircase is a bedroom, where there is another police officer, as well as what appears to be a team of forensic investigators. She quietly approaches the door to the bedroom to get a peek, not wanting to announce her arrival.

She hears a sigh and then a frustrated voice, "I guess at this point I shouldn't be surprised anymore."

Rose turns around and sees Detective Cooper.

"This is him again, isn't it? The same killer?"

"You can't be here, Rose," Cooper states, stepping in front of her to block her entry into the room.

Rose looks past Cooper and sees the victim on the bed, with blood splatters all over the bed, the headboard, and the wall. She is overcome by an intense wave of nausea, as her thoughts immediately go to Will. It is like looking into a time machine, seeing him on the bed. She tried to shake it off and focus on the scene before her, analyze it with a critical eye. "This seems messier than the last one," she observes. "But is it otherwise the same? Stabbing and anal trauma?"

"Yes," Cooper answers her reluctantly and quietly. "It's the same cause of death and same setting." Mumbling more to himself than her, he goes on. "David Cruz, twenty-three years old. Found in his bed. Indications of wrists and feet being bound prior to death. Cause of death is stabbing through the heart. But this time, the body is torn to shreds. The knife marks are more reckless and aggressive. Looks like he used a tennis racquet again for the sexual assault, just like the first victim." Rose freezes, realizing that by "first victim," Cooper is referring to Will.

With a silent and strong resolve, she announces, "I'm going in to look."

"Absolutely not. Seriously, Rose, just go home." His eyes are kind but stern, imploring her to leave.

"Yes, I am. This is all part of our investigation. I need to see what happened. I need to see if our killer has made any mistakes this time."

"You can't be here, Rose, this is an active investigation. It is not *our* investigation, it is mine. You are not a member of the Toronto Police Services. You don't have the necessary gloves or boots on, you could disturb the evidence or leave your own DNA behind.

You have to leave before you are considered to be tampering with a crime scene."

"But I can help. Just give me a pair of gloves, I know what I'm doing."

"Please leave."

"This is not fair."

"Life isn't fair," Detective Cooper says, in a flippant tone that irks Rose.

"Life isn't fair? You're telling me life isn't fair? My entire life was ripped away from me, but this sick, twisted animal continues to torture and destroy the lives of other people. Like this dead guy lying here. Who are you to tell me that life isn't fair?"

"You need to leave."

"No, I don't. You know, you're lucky the media isn't here yet. If you force me to leave, who knows what I'll do. Maybe I'll have to call the local news to get information about this new murder," Rose says.

"Are you threatening me? You can't speak to me that way."

"I can speak to you however I damn well please," Rose declares, getting extremely frustrated. *What is going on here? Yesterday he was fine with me helping. What has changed?*

"No, you can't. If you do not leave immediately, I will have you arrested for obstruction of justice, tampering with evidence, and threatening an officer of the law." His kind eyes are once again angry, just like the first time she saw them.

"Ha! You wouldn't dare."

"Watch me."

Rose stares at him, daring him to follow through on this threat. "You don't have it in you."

And with that, Detective Cooper nods to the officer standing behind her, who had clearly come upstairs after hearing the shouting. The next thing Rose knows, her hands are cuffed together, and for the second time in one week, she is being escorted out of a crime scene.

CHAPTER 20

"I always thought that between the two of us, I would be the one in jail and you would be the one bailing me out."
"Shut up, Tyler."
"Little Miss Perfect, always working to make Mom and Dad happy. Hey, did you meet any fun criminals in there? Anybody you know? Do they know what you do for a living?"
"Tyler, I am not afraid to hurt you."
"Wow, one day in the hammer and you've already gone volent. Did you learn that from one of the prison gangs? Did you join the Latin Kings or the Aryan Brotherhood? Which one is more dangerous? If I've learned anything on TV, it's that you have to choose the one that gives the best protection. I bet you're all jacked from working out all the time, aren't you? Did you learn how to make a shiv out of a toothbrush?"
"Enjoy this moment, because you have thirty more seconds to make fun of me until you are forced to drop it, for life!"
Tyler pauses, before he says, "Don't show Mom your new teardrop tattoo." Rose gives him a filthy look. "Okay I'm done now!" and he continues driving, clearly enjoying this moment way too much.

"It's all that stupid detective's fault. He was threatened by me, so he tried to get rid of me."

"You mean the *handsome* stupid detective, Rose. Don't forget the most important part."

"I am really regretting calling you," she moans.

"I know," Tyler says, grinning.

On Saturday, Rose is getting ready to go to one of those combination mini golf and batting cage places with Tyler, Emily, Logan and Sloane. She is looking forward to spending time with the kids but is praying that Tyler doesn't mention her little run-in with the law yesterday. The last thing she needs is for the rest of her family to find out—she could only imagine what her mother would say!

While she waits for her brother to pick her up, she scrolls her Twitter feed, looking at all the references to the recent murders: "Twenty-three-year-old man found dead in his home," "Homicide rate increasing in Toronto," and "Murder victim believed to be linked to Ramirez murder." Rose is obsessed and reads every single tweet, along with every article she can find online mentioning the Ramirez and Cruz murders. She even searches back over five years trying to find comparisons to other murder victims. Some might call her obsessed; she calls herself meticulous and thorough. She wonders if the killer is reading all these posts as well, if they are following along with her. Do they like the attention? Or will it scare them, causing them to stop?

Her brother pulls up to their parents' driveway, with Emily, Logan, and Sloane all huddled into the car. Rose climbs in, taking a seat directly between her niece and nephew. They had picked up coffees from The Bean (iced coffees with milk for Rose and Emily, and plain black coffee for Tyler). Rose could not have been any happier. Sipping her iced latte, listening to her niece and nephew sing along with the radio at the top of their lungs, she starts to relax.

It is a beautiful late-April day. The sun is shining and there is a light breeze in the air. Rose smiles to herself thinking of the line from the movie *Miss Congeniality*, where a beauty pageant contestant is asked to describe her perfect date, and she replies: April twenty-fifth—because it's not too hot, not too cold. All you need is a light jacket! That is exactly the type of weather they are enjoying today.

When they arrive at their destination, Rose steps out of the car at the exact same time as Tyler and accidentally bumps into him. Tyler drops his coffee, wallet, and keys.

"Oh man, I am so sorry!" Rose cries. She looks at Tyler, who has coffee all over his pants, then she bursts into laughter.

"Really? This is funny?"

"No," Rose tries to stifle her laughter. "It is definitely not funny that your coffee spilled on yourself and it looks like you peed in your pants."

"Ha ha, Rose," Tyler says sarcastically.

She helps Tyler gather up the now almost empty coffee cup, his wallet, and his keys.

"Aw, Tyler! You still have the Superman keychain I bought you for your sixteenth birthday!"

"Of course I do, sis. You know I love Superman. And it makes me think of you—when you're not laughing at my expense!"

Rose snickers and says, "I'm laughing *with* you, not *at* you."

"Sure, sure", he says as he puts an arm around her and they start to walk toward the putting greens with Emily, Logan and Sloane.

"Auntie Rosie, watch this shot!" Logan cries, as he swings a ball into a moving crocodile's mouth, hoping it will stay open and allow the ball to pass through. It does, and Logan lets out a loud "whoop!" in celebration. Sloane goes next, and it takes her a few tries to get the ball through the crocodile's mouth, but she is a good sport and is happy just to be playing.

Tyler is next. "Wow, Tyler, for someone who claims to be an amazing athlete, you suck at mini golf," Rose teases.

"That's because mini golf isn't a sport."

"You mean a sport that you can play," Emily jabs. Tyler sneers at them all.

As they head toward the next hole, a trick shot over a bridge and through a tunnel, out of the corner of Rose's eye she sees Detective Cooper. "You have got to be kidding me," Rose murmurs quietly. She does not think anyone heard her, but Tyler must have heard something because he looks at her and asks her what is wrong.

"That horrible detective is here."

"The one you're secretly in love with?"

"No, the one I can't stand. The one who threw me in jail when I was trying to help him to solve a murder."

"Oh yeah, that one. The handsome one."

"I'm going to talk to him."

"That's not a good idea, Rose."

"Yes, it is. I'm going to give him a piece of my mind. He is an arrogant creep who thinks he knows more than everyone else. He needs to be put in his place."

"Rose …" Tyler tries to stop her, but it is too late. She is marching over towards Detective Cooper, pumped up, ready to scream at him.

There is no stopping her when she has made up her mind.

"What are you doing here?" Rose demands. "Why aren't you at the police station or questioning suspects?"

"Hello, Rose, lovely to see you too," Cooper sighs. He is wearing sweatpants and a sweatshirt and has a Toronto Blue Jays baseball hat on. A few of the longer brown waves peek out from underneath his cap. "It's a Saturday. I'm allowed a couple hours off here and there, you know. I came to the batting cages to let off some steam. I do some of my best thinking there."

"Well, I just did some great thinking in a jail cell, thanks to you," she barks.

"I warned you. You were disrupting my crime scene." Rose can see that he is slightly amused, one corner of his lips turned upward.

"Disrupting? I was helping! You think you're so smart, you don't need help from anyone?"

"Not from you."

"You're strong and powerful at a crime scene, but when you're here, you're just a regular person, not so scary now!"

Cooper stands up tall and puffs out his sculpted chest and abs, looking down at her, almost daring her to back away. "Are you saying I scared you?"

"Hardly," Rose scoffs. She puffs up her own chest and stands right up to him. It would be a powerful move if she were not so much shorter than him. He must be over six feet tall, while she stands at a mere five-three. They are inches apart. Rose can feel his breath on her. She glares at him, looks into his bright eyes and senses a mutual stubbornness. Neither one of them moves. *God, those eyes are something else. Look away.* She moves her gaze slightly down his freckled face and stares at his lips. His lips are slightly parted, as if he is going to say something, but he does not. His lips are full, the kind of lips many women pay for, and a dark pink colour. It almost looks like he is wearing lipstick. As Rose tries to avoid staring into his eyes, she notices that he has a tiny freckle at the bottom corner of his lower lip. She realizes she has never really seen freckles on lips, and frankly, it's pretty cute. Okay, that didn't work to distract her. She looks back up into his eyes and notices the look in his eyes has changed. They are not glaring at her anymore. They are staring at her. Staring into her. She notices her own gaze soften, no longer a glare. They are just staring into each other's eyes now.

After what feels like a lifetime, but is really only a few seconds, both Rose and Cooper break their eye contact and push away from each other. She is uncomfortable, sensing a change in their dynamic.

"Did you have something to say to me? Or did you just come to yell at me?" he asks.

"I, um ... I have to go back to my family," Rose says as she runs away, embarrassed.

CHAPTER 21

Rose spends the rest of the weekend hanging out with her parents like she did when she was young. They go for coffee and bagels on Sunday morning, then grocery shopping, and then they spend most of the afternoon in the kitchen, cooking for the week. Isabelle wants to make all of Rose's childhood favourites: baked chicken fingers and potato wedges, tacos, macaroni and cheese, spaghetti and meatballs. They also make chocolate chip cookies, and Rose's favourite dessert, cookies and cream cheesecake with a chocolate cookie crust. Rose can't wait to eat all of this. It's like she's eating her way through memories of her childhood. But even more than that, she is happy to be spending the time with her mom.

On Monday, with both her parents gone to work all day, Rose wanders around the house trying to decide what to do. Without her parents distracting her, some of the demons that Rose has been trying to suppress are starting to appear. Thoughts of Will, of Marco Ramirez and David Cruz, and of anonymous dead bodies start floating through her head. Memories of her last morning with Will. Images of bodies, with blood splattered everywhere. She feels like these thoughts are consuming her.

Listening to the advice of Dr. Hill, Rose decides to confront these demons. She will go for a run, but take a new route today, running past her old house, the one she shared with Will. The one where he died.

Rose vividly remembers the day she and Will moved into that house. She was in her first year of law school and he had just secured a job as a senior editor at a publishing house. Will was always gifted when it came to writing. Rose was so proud when he found a path that enabled him to pursue his passion for writing. He had found this house and surprised her by taking her to see it one day. It was a beautiful two-storey house on Rushton Road, in the Cedarvale area. She loved that it was still close to The Village and to her parents' house. She remembers laughing, saying there was no way they could afford that house. Will looked her right in the eye and said, "One day, you will be one of the top lawyers in Toronto and we will own multiple houses like this. I have faith in you. In us." Rose kissed him and they placed a bully offer on the spot, which was quickly accepted.

Rose changes into a pair of shorts, a tank top, and a tight zip-up hoodie, then laces up her running shoes. She grabs her earbuds and puts on a 90s pop playlist—Spice Girls, Backstreet Boys, Will Smith, and EMF. Rose takes her first step outside as she puts on the first song on the playlist: C+C Music Factory's "Gonna Make you Sweat (Everybody Dance Now)."

Instead of heading south like usual, Rose heads west toward Cedarvale. After warming up for the first couple blocks, she increases her speed. Fast, then faster, sweating out all the thoughts floating around in her head, until all she can focus on is the sound of her feet pounding on the concrete with each step.

Rose gets into a rhythm with the music, syncing her footsteps, her breathing, and her heartbeat to the music. She continues to push herself, seeking the adrenaline high she desperately needs. She's hoping that the endorphins will help counteract the anxiety that keeps nagging her as she nears her old house.

Finally, she is there, standing in front of her house. Jogging on the spot, so as not to drastically decrease her heart rate, Rose stares at the home she shared with Will. It has not changed at all. Rose can't help but feel as if Will is about to walk out that door any second. Almost as if she has willed it with her mind, the door opens and a man steps out. Rose lets out a sharp gasp. But it is not Will; it is the current homeowner. He catches Rose staring, and she bolts away from the house, her face burning with embarrassment and emotions.

Rose keeps running and running, as if she is trying to outrun herself. "All I Really Want," one of her favourite songs from Alanis Morrissette's album, *Jagged Little Pill*, comes on and she pushes herself as she listens to the lyrics. Just like Alanis, Rose is searching for peace, comfort, and justice. She is certain now that this is the path she is meant to be on. She turns away from the house and heads east back to her parents' house with a renewed sense of determined purpose. It's time for her to find out the deadly truth about who killed Will and to get justice for him, once and for all.

CHAPTER 22

Well, I guess there's no point hiding it anymore. Look at these headlines in the online newspapers and all over Twitter: "Serial killer on the loose in Toronto," "Ramirez, Cruz among other victims in serial killing spree," and my personal favourite: "Cause for panic: danger in Toronto."

People are freaking out. Because of me. Ha!

I was so scared of them figuring it out, of them tying the victims together. But honestly? I'm here for it. This is awesome. The whole thing has a new air of excitement. It's more dangerous now, knowing that someone is tracking my moves, trying to find me. It's just further proof that I'm better than them, stronger than them, smarter than them. They know I exist, but they won't find me. They won't catch me. Because I'm always one step ahead of them.

Did you ever sneak out of the house when you were younger? Or sneak a crush into your bedroom past curfew? This sort of feels like that. We used to sneak out of the house all the time as teenagers to go party with friends. The party was great, but the risk of getting caught, of getting in trouble, was what really excited me.

That detective might be a problem. Detective Cooper. He seems to be piecing things together, things that have previously gone unnoticed or been purposely ignored. He's smart. Not as smart as me, obviously.

But smarter than some of those other pigs that have been trying to catch me.

I had a dream last night about him, that detective. We met, shook hands, even had a beer together. And the whole time, he had no idea who I am. That I am the one he is looking for. It was amazing. In my dream we were just chatting away, and then before he had a chance to react, I grabbed him by the throat and whispered into his ear: "Just relax. It will all be over soon."

I can vividly picture the look in his eyes as he realized his mistake. As he realized who I am. That he was going to die.

And then that stupid alarm went off and I woke up. And now all day, I can't stop thinking about that dream. About that detective. What does the dream mean? I'm no Sigmund Freud, but I do believe that there is meaning in dreams. I think it was a prophecy. I will kill him in real life. I get excited just thinking about it.

But first: let's have some fun with him. Let's get in his head. Change things up a bit. That'll terrify them.

CHAPTER 23

Rose spends the next few days scouring the Internet for information on Marco Ramirez, David Cruz, and the other victims. By Thursday afternoon, her room looks like the hub of a criminal investigation unit, with scribbled notes sprawled all over the floor and walls. She is desperately seeking a pattern, a connection between all the victims. Something to tie them together, to make sense of these senseless crimes.

Grasping for straws, Rose realizes she and Detective Cooper never asked whether the other victims played *Dueling Swords*. They were so focused on Marco Ramirez, they did not take a step back and look at the overall pattern. Determined that she is onto something, Rose changes out of her sweats, puts on some lipstick, and heads over to see him.

The police station must have recently been redone. It is a modern building with glass windows everywhere. It looks out of place, amid the red brick buildings nearby. Rose walks up the steps leading to the entrance and approaches the front door. As she enters, she is shocked by how quiet the precinct is.

"I'm here to see Detective Ben Cooper," Rose announces to a man sitting in the reception area. The officer is in a uniform that looks like it has seen better days. It is worn out and looks like it is at least one size too small. The officer looks up at Rose with a disinterested look and does not say anything.

Unsure if he heard her or not, Rose repeats, "Detective Ben Cooper. I know he works in this precinct. I would like to see him." The officer continues to stare at her, and Rose can't figure out why he is not responding. She thinks, *Did I say something wrong? Maybe Detective Cooper does not work here? Maye this officer is deaf? Should I ask again?*

"I'm here to see …"

"Cooper, yeah, I heard you the first time," the officer cuts Rose off.

Confused, Rose stammers, "Oh, you did hear. Well, can you please show me to his desk?"

"Stay here," the officer grunts at her, then picks up his phone and whispers into the phone. Rose steps away from the desk and looks around her. There is a waiting room just to the left of the front desk. An old couple is sitting there silently, staring at the TV screen on the wall showing the daily news. There is also a woman sitting alone in a corner, crying. Rose stares at her sympathetically, unsure if she should say something to her. She decides against it and takes a seat on the opposite side of the room.

Finally, after what feels like an hour, Rose sees Detective Cooper walking up to her.

"Sorry to make you wait," he says, and his apology sounds sincere. "Wow, you got all fancy for me. I'm used to seeing you in workout gear. Or passed out on the floor."

Giving him a dirty look but otherwise ignoring this dig, Rose asks "Did any of the killer's other victims play *Dueling Swords*?"

Looking around, Cooper sighs. "Not here, okay? Come to my desk." And he briskly walks away. Caught off-guard by his abruptness, she follows him.

Walking past mostly empty cubicles and desks, Rose follows Cooper into a small office on the north side of the building. He has a beautiful view of the C.N. Tower. Cooper's desk is shockingly tidy. A few case files are sitting around, a couple loose pens, and some notes to himself sit on the desk, but otherwise it is organized and neat. Rose is impressed. Smiling a little to herself, she thinks, *Even Mom would be impressed.*

When they arrived at Cooper's desk, he explains, "We should not be openly discussing an ongoing investigation in public like that. Anyone could have heard you. You can't underestimate the importance of keeping some details private before announcing them to the public. Crazy people come out of the woodwork to claim responsibility, citing details of the crimes they read in the papers or tabloids. We try to control the messages that the public receive, especially at the beginning of the investigation."

"I didn't think of that, I'm sorry," Rose apologizes.

"I know. You don't know these things because you're not a cop. I know you think I'm doing a bad job, or I don't know what I'm doing. But I do. I need you to trust me a little here."

"I'll try. Now, about the other victims. Did they play *Dueling Swords*? Or other video games? Will didn't play *Dueling Swords*, but I think he played some car theft or racing games. Have you considered that that is the connection between victims?" She is worried that Cooper will snap at her. He seems to have calmed down a little, and they seem to be developing a bit of a rapport. She doesn't want to ruin it. But she also needs to pursue this.

Cooper sighs. "Yes, I have thought of that. David Cruz, the last victim, did not play video games, as far as any of his friends and family knew. And I was just trying to look at the other victim's files before you came. But we switched over our computer system last year, so the files are not currently on our online system. Which means I have to go back into the file storage room in the back there and find the physical folder," Cooper is indicating toward the back of the precinct.

"Great, let's go."

"Let's?" Cooper looks at her as if she just said they were going to the moon. "*We* are not doing anything. I am going to review these files. You are not."

"That's ridiculous and unfair. And don't you dare say to me 'Life's not fair' again, or I will make you eat those words."

"I promise I will let you know what I find. In the meantime, go home. Give me your phone number and I will call you if I find anything."

"You know, Detective, if you wanted my phone number you could have just asked me."

"Are you teasing with me?" he asks incredulously.

"Absolutely not," Rose smiles. "Now, where's the storage room? I'm coming. You could use a second set of eyes," she says as she starts walking toward the back.

Cooper grabs her arm and stops her before she gets past his desk. "You are not going back there." Rose stares at him, oddly aware of the touch of his hand on her arm. He notices it too, but he does not let go right away. She can feel the warmth of his hand on her, the tension between them. "I'm sorry, but you are not allowed."

"Are you joking me? Of course I'm going back there."

Cooper laughs. "'Joking me'? Did you actually just say that?" He thinks that's one of the cutest things he's ever heard. "It's 'joking' or 'kidding me,' not 'joking me.'"

Rose's face goes red from embarrassment. "You better be *joking me* that you are making fun of me right now, while I am trying to investigate a serial killer." The amicable atmosphere is starting to once again turn dark.

"Relax, I will look into this, I promise. But you cannot come with me back there."

Rose smiles and looks Cooper right into those gorgeous, blue-green eyes. With a determined voice, she says, "Watch me."

The file storage room is located in the lower level of the police station. Rose isn't sure what she was expecting, but she is impressed by the clean, methodical system in which the boxes of files are stored. Detective Cooper quickly and confidently walks around the room pulling the victims' files and placing them on a table in the back of the room.

Quietly, Rose and Cooper review the files looking for some type of connection to *Dueling Swords* or any other online gaming program.

After scouring the various files for well over an hour, in an exasperated tone, Rose exclaims "Nothing! What are we missing here?"

"We'll find it Rose, be patient. We're not giving up. But we really should leave. I could get in lot of trouble having you back here."

"There has to be a connection between these victims. Something tying them together, other than the fact that they were all stabbed in bed. I just need to think."

Cooper is quiet for a moment, almost as if he is debating whether or not to say what he is thinking. "What is it?" Rose prompts.

"We know the last victim, Mr. Ramirez, met up with his killer at a known LGBTQ+ bar, The Rideout. And Cruz was a proud homosexual who regularly frequented the bar. What if that is the connection?"

"The bar?"

"Yes. What if they have all been to The Rideout? Maybe the killer is a man fulfilling some homophobic fantasy of killing gay men."

"Will wasn't gay," Rose asserts.

"Not that you know of."

"He was not gay. He was going to marry me." Rose's tone is cold and sharp, making it clear that this was not to be discussed any further.

"Okay, maybe Will was the exception. But maybe it's worth considering, that there is more to this homophobia theory."

"Or maybe it's a woman, who just happened to be at an LGBTQ+ bar."

"It's possible. I can't rule it out yet. But I'm inclined to believe the killer is a man."

"A homophobic man."

"Maybe? It's worth looking into. But not right now. We need to leave before we get caught, Rose."

As Rose is about to respond, someone walks into the storage room.

CHAPTER 24

Detective Cooper grabs Rose by the arm and they duck behind one of the storage units in the back. They do not move a muscle, scared that the police officer who entered the storage room will hear or see them. They strain their ears to determine where the person is in the room, hoping they are far enough away that they will not get caught. Cooper failed to mention to Rose earlier that he had already received a couple warnings about playing fast and loose with the rules and cannot afford any further disciplinary action.

There is some rustling in the far end of the room, close to the front. They remain silent. In the quiet, all Cooper can hear is his breath, in sync with Rose's, and his heart beating. He realizes that they are sitting surprisingly close to each other. He notices that a few loose strands of hair have fallen out of her messy bun, now grazing her jawline and the nape of her neck. He has a sudden urge to reach out and tuck those strands of hair behind her ears, to feel the warmth of her neck, her shoulders. He feels a sudden, quick shiver run through his body.

After a few minutes, Cooper hears the door to the storage room open and shut again. They remain silent a few more minutes, huddled in the back, before they are confident that they are alone again. Cooper looks over and sees that Rose is watching him. He looks back at her, directly into her eyes. They sit like that, silently, for a moment.

Rose's phone dings that she has a text message and startles both of them. Cooper lets out a little yelp and he jumps to his feet.

"Relax, Detective, it's just a phone."

"Hard to relax when you're doing something you're not supposed to be doing," he points out.

Rose giggles and checks her message. It's from Paige.

'Solve ur case yet?'

'Working on it right now.'

'Stop what u're doing and go get drunk. U're on vacay!'

'Not vacay, remember? But not a bad idea. I should go to the bar.'

'Don't know what bar u're talking about, but cool. Go to the bar, girl. Get ur drink on.'

Rose jumps up and tells Cooper she's leaving.

Confused, Cooper asks, "Where are you going?"

"Home to change," she responds. "I'm going to The Rideout tonight. It's our best lead right now."

"Rose, I really don't think it's a good idea for you to go to a bar alone."

"Great, so you'll come. Unless you're not up for some undercover work?" she teases.

Cooper is astounded by this woman's boldness. This is a terrible idea. She should not be going. But he can tell she's made up her mind and she's going, and there's no way she can question a witness. At least not without him.

Rose must sense that he is relenting, because she gives him a wide grin and says, "See you there at nine," before marching out of the precinct.

Yup, Cooper thinks, as he runs his fingers through his tousled hair. *Trouble.*

A Deadly Truth

The Rideout is a flashy bar in Toronto's downtown club district and is one of the most successful long-running bars in the area. While geared toward the LGBTQ+ population, it is popular among both homosexuals and heterosexuals, and even offers special bottle service packages for bachelorette parties where the bride wants to grind with men without feeling guilty. The bar has bright lights on the front signage and two very large and very attractive bouncers at the door. The music inside is so loud that you can hear it clearly from across the street.

Rose steps out of her Uber at exactly 9:00 p.m. and she sees Cooper waiting for her. He is wearing black jeans and a tight black long-sleeve shirt, tucked in, with a deep V at the neck. His shoes are black high tops. He has put some hair product into his luscious sandy brown mop, which allows it to look neat while still embracing the natural movement of his thick waves. Rose can't help herself but stare, mouth agape. He looks incredibly sexy. She has never seen him so … well, stylish.

Rose walks over to where Cooper is waiting for her and gives him an exaggerated look-over, followed by an approving whistle.

"Why thank you ma'am, I was trying to look the part!" he laughs.

"Those pants don't leave much to the imagination, do they?" He looks down, blushing. "I'm talking about your wallet and phone," she laughs.

"Real funny," Cooper mumbles. "At least I'm wearing pants." He motions to her outfit. She is wearing a simple dress with long sleeves that stops mid-thigh. It is a deep emerald colour, which plays nicely against her blue eyes. The dress hugs her figure perfectly, emphasizing her curves. She is wearing short black booties with a reasonable heel. Her blonde hair is down and is the epitome of the "messy beach wave" style that is trendy. Her makeup is subtle but gorgeous.

"You're just jealous that you don't have these legs to show off," Rose quips.

Together they walk into The Rideout and are immediately hit by the intensity of the pulsing electric house music. The music is so loud she can barely hear herself think. It's the type of bass beat that you feel deep in your belly. Rose looks around and sees a sea of people dancing and gyrating on the dance floor. Actually, to clarify, Rose can see very little; it is very dark and crowded. But the little bit in front of her that she can see depicts a cross between a rave and an orgy.

They approach the bar and Rose tries to get the bartender's attention. She signals him a few times, but he barely glances her way and is instead focused on serving the numerous men waiting for their orders. Rose is frustrated and a little taken aback. She has never had this problem before. While she has never considered herself to be strikingly beautiful, she has always been pretty and has always received men's attention.

Cooper, noting her lack of success, says "Step aside, ma'am," with a sly grin. "I'll take care of this." He signals the bartender, who is in front of him in less than five seconds. Cooper winks at Rose, who rolls her eyes. He orders their drinks: a vodka soda for Rose, and a vodka soda, minus the vodka, for him.

After he orders, Rose looks at him and raises her eyebrows. "Minus the vodka?"

Cooper laughs. "Yeah, that's my go-to order at a bar. I'm not a big drinker."

"The reliable designated driver."

"Exactly. I just could never get past the taste. Most of the alcohols I've tried taste like feet!" Rose chuckles and agrees that some liquors are not too appetizing. Seeing that he has Rose's attention with this story and that he is entertaining her, he goes on. "In fact, I haven't had any alcohol since I was in the police academy. I was out at a bar with a bunch of the recruits and I ordered a vodka. I gulped the whole thing down quickly, then threw it right back up into the cup I was holding."

"No, you didn't!" Rose has tears in her eyes from laughing so hard.

"Oh yes! And then I did what any respectable man would do."

"Oh no …"

"I put the cup down and walked away, hoping no one would notice."

"That is absolutely disgusting!" Rose laughs and playfully swats at his shoulder.

"Not my finest moment, I admit. Which is why I stick to soda these days."

"A wise choice."

"I think so."

Rose takes in Cooper's charming, energetic disposition tonight. She is used to him mostly acting like an asshole—a sparring partner for her, an arrogant cop who thinks he's better than her. But Rose is starting to see that he might not be all that bad.

"Thank you for getting our drinks."

"It's my pleasure," he says. "It must be hard."

"What must be hard?"

"Being the most beautiful girl in the room but no men fawning all over you."

"Me?" Rose is genuinely confused.

"Yeah, you know. You're gorgeous, I'm sure you're used to men lavishing you with attention, throwing themselves at you, buying you drinks."

Did he just call me gorgeous? Rose thinks. She does not know what to say. She just stares into his mesmerizing eyes, feeling her face burning up. She averts his gaze and looks away with a shy smile. She can't help but feel an undeniable pull toward him. She has not felt this way in a long time. *I think I like him*, Rose thinks. *Shit.*

"I don't think we're going to get any information out of the bartender right now, he's way too busy. Let's go dance," Cooper says.

"Dance?"

"Yeah, dance. You know, where you move your feet, move your arms, shake your booty a bit. We don't want to look conspicuous. Come on." He grabs Rose's hand and pulls her out onto the dance floor. In the back of her mind, she can sense that the music is even louder here on the dance floor, but all she can hear is the loud thumping of her heartbeat, as she feels the warmth of Cooper's hand in hers.

Once they are buried among grinding bodies moving to the music, Cooper lets go of Rose's hand and starts dancing. He is feeling the music and enjoying himself. Letting herself go, Rose similarly gets into the groove and the two are getting lost in their dancing. She has not had this much fun in a long time. When an electro-pop remix of Donna Summer's "I Feel Love" comes on, Cooper grabs Rose's left hand in his right hand, spins her around in a circle and then brings her body close to his. She can feel the weight of his hands, now on her hips. So close to her ass, it wouldn't take much for them to reach it. But they stay planted firmly on her waist, where he presses her body into him. They get into a rhythm together, dancing and laughing. She can feel the heat resonating from his body and is overwhelmed by his smell: woodsy, with a hint of citrus notes, mixed with a little bit of sweat. It is intoxicating.

Rose is disappointed when Cooper signals to her that the bar is not as busy as it was before and that this is a good time to chat with the bartender. The pair walk off the dance floor and approach the bar. They both order just water this time, and as the bartender hands them their drinks, Cooper starts chatting him up. Thinking that Cooper is flirting with him, the bartender is caught off guard when Cooper flashes his badge.

"Detective Ben Cooper. I need to ask you a few questions about a man who used to come here on a fairly regular basis."

The bartender, let down, nods. Cooper shows him a picture of Marco Ramirez from his Facebook account.

"Yeah, I recognize him. He came here all the time. I saw what happened to him on the news. Horrible."

"Yes, it is. When was the last time you saw him?"

"I saw him that night. The night he died. I was working and he was here meeting up with someone."

"Do you remember who he was with?"

"A guy. Tall, brown hair. Medium build. I hadn't seen him before; he must be new. Maybe he's one of those closeted gay guys who is just starting to play around."

So it is a man, Rose thinks. *That narrows it down. Sort of.*

"Did the guy have any remarkable features? A tattoo? Piercings? An unusual mole?" Rose interjected.

"No," the bartender said, looking unimpressed with her. Clearly Cooper was getting further without her.

"Well, if you think of anything that might be of help, please let us know. Here is my number," Cooper hands the bartender his card and holds it there, touching his fingers. "Call me anytime."

"I will," the bartender says seductively, as Cooper and Rose walk away.

"Oh my god, you were totally just flirting with him to get information!" Rose asks incredulously.

"Flirting? For information? Me? I would never be so unprofessional." He pauses. "But do you think it worked?"

Rose shakes her head with a smile and says, "I'm not sure if it worked. Other than confirming that the killer is a man, that was a bust."

"It wasn't a total loss. At least now we know I'm the better dancer."

"No way! I'm way better," she insists, refusing to admit that he actually is a very good dancer.

"It's not a competition."

"You're right. Not a competition."

"But if it were a competition, I would win."

"In your dreams, Cooper."

"That is Detective Cooper to you, ma'am," he says with a grin. "Come on, I'll drive you home."

CHAPTER 25

*R*ose *is climbing up the stairs to her old house, giddy with excitement to see the man waiting for her in their bedroom. She traipses through the hundreds of rose petals strewing the floor, her body on fire with anticipation. She knows that when she opens the bedroom door, she will find Will sitting on the bed, engagement ring in hand. She has been waiting for this moment for months. Years. As she nears the door, she hears something. It sounds like a sputtering sound, like someone gasping for breath. Springing up the last few steps, Rose storms into her bedroom and sees Will on the bed, with blood everywhere. There is a man standing over Will's body, holding a knife over him. The man looks up as Rose enters the room, and Rose is shocked to see that it is Will holding the knife. When she looks back down to the bed, she sees that now the body gasping for air, reaching out to her for help, is that of Detective Ben Cooper. Blood is pouring out of him, oozing all over their pristine white sheets, onto the carpet. Rose is frozen in her place. She looks at Will, then looks over to Cooper. She lets out an unworldly scream.*

Rose's mother comes rushing into her bedroom, startled from her sleep by the shrieking. She gently nudges Rose to wake her. As she opens her eyes and sees her mother holding her, Rose pants for breath, trying to calm her body from the adrenaline of the nightmare and her screams. She feels tears drip down her face.

Rose is used to having nightmares, but she is not used to seeing other people in her nightmares. It is always her or Will being killed, rarely anyone else. She is at a loss and does not know what to say when her mother asks her what is wrong and what happened in her dream. She just whispers, "I don't remember." Her mother does not believe her, but for now, she just holds her daughter tight.

Rose takes her time in the shower, allowing the temperature to heat up to the point where her skin turns red and the water almost scalds her. Some people take cold showers to wake up, but Rose prefers boiling hot showers. She thinks about her nightmare and questions the new roles of the people in her life: Detective Ben Cooper as the victim, and Will as the killer. Rose admits that she felt something resembling excitement last night with Cooper. But she had dismissed her feelings last night at the bar as stemming from the alcohol. Was she wrong? Is Tyler right? Does she have a crush? Or does she see something in him that has lit a desire to help him, to "save" him? He doesn't seem like he needs saving.

Her thoughts are thankfully interrupted when Rose hears her phone chime with a message. She jumps out of the shower, wraps her hair in a turban and puts on her bathrobe, and checks the text message. It's Lauren, asking her to go get brunch. As much as a part of Rose wants to see Lauren, she can't bring herself to go. This happens to Rose sometimes, when she is in a wave of depression. She self-isolates and hides from the people she loves. She avoids the things that make her happy. Dr. Hill tells her that she needs to push past this penchant of avoidance and to try to reach out to people when she is down. But Rose can't seem to do it today.

Her phone chimes again. This time it's a phone call from her boss, Charles Mitchell. He is calling to check in on her and see how she is doing. She lies and says that she is doing great, that being home has helped her relax and de-stress. As always, Charles can sense that she is lying, and he encourages her to stay as long as she needs. So long as she actually rests. Rose promises him that she will and hangs up the phone.

Her thoughts wander back to Ben, trying to interpret his cameo in her dream. Is it just because they have been spending time together working on catching the killer? Rose is sure that must be it. Nothing more. Pretending that she has convinced herself of this fact, she turns her mind to the next steps of the investigation. She knows what she has to do.

Rose picks up the phone and calls Ben. She tells him that she is convinced that the connection between all the victims is the video game, and that Jim Cullen is hiding something.

"I need to see those files. I need to see if the other victims had the game. I don't need to see who was on at what time, I just need to know if the other victims played the game," Rose says.

"I know, but Cullen will never let you get close to them," he tries to reason with her.

"I know. That's why I'm going to sneak into VR Gaming's office tonight and log onto their system."

"You're going to WHAT?"

"I'm going to look through those files, see if the other victims are users. I have to do something."

"You can do something without breaking the law. Do you understand that you just told a police detective that you intend to break a law?"

"It's just a little minor trespassing."

"There's no minor or major trespassing! You're either trespassing or you're not. You're either pregnant or not. You can't be just 'minorly' pregnant."

"It's not a big deal, don't worry about it," Rose answers.

"You could get into serious trouble."

"Detective Cooper, are you worried about me?"

"No, I'm just trying to stop you from committing a crime, or worse, getting killed," he says.

"I'll be fine. If you're so worried about me, come. I'm going at nine." With that, Rose ends the call.

"Where are you going?" Rose sees that Tyler is standing in her doorway. She didn't know he was over; he must have come while she was in the shower.

"To do some investigative work with Ben."

"Ben? I didn't know we were on a first name basis with this detective."

"Detective Cooper. Whatever. It's work."

"Sure, it is," Tyler teases her. "You are so into this guy!"

"I am not!"

"You totally are! You're turning red! Oh boy, watch out everyone, Rose is in loooooove." He says the last part in a teasing, sing-song tone.

Rose says, "Tyler, I am not in love. I don't need a husband to be happy."

"I know," Tyler says with a very serious face. Rose looks up. Tyler has never agreed with her when she has said that before. In fact, no one she has said that to has ever agreed with her. She looks at him with expectant eyes. "But you don't need to fall in love. You just need to *make* love." Tyler starts making fake kissing sounds. Rose whips a stuffed animal at his head and he runs out of her room laughing.

It is closer to 9:30 p.m. when Rose quietly opens the door to the VR Gaming's office. It is dark and quiet, with no one in sight. She is relieved that she does not run into any employees who are working late, where she would have to pretend to be a new hire or maybe even the new cleaning lady. *I should have come in a uniform with cleaning gear*, she thinks.

While Rose's primary feeling is relief that she does not see anyone else in the office at this hour, she begrudgingly admits to herself that she feels a twinge of disappointment that Ben Cooper did not come. Not because she likes him, but just to have backup. *To be safe*, she tells herself. Although he would probably just try to stop her or tell her she can't do this. God, he drives her crazy.

Rose continues to quietly creep through the office, heading toward Cullen's office. She passes through a hallway with dark offices on either side. Suddenly, out of the quiet darkness, Rose feels someone touch her shoulder from behind her. She jumps and lets out a shrill gasp.

She turns around to find Ben Cooper laughing hysterically.

"What is wrong with you!" she demands, still gasping to catch her breath again. "What if someone hears or sees you?"

"I've been here for a while now, no one's around," Cooper responds.

"You came." Rose says, raising an eyebrow. It's a statement, not a question. "You were worried about me."

"Worried that you would wind up in jail. Again."

"I wonder why I was in jail in the first place"

"Hey, you can't say I didn't warn you," Cooper says with a shrug.

"You're a real prince."

"Yup, that's me. Prince Ben. Bow before me."

Rose ignores him and continues walking toward Cullen's office. The door is locked. As Cooper is about to suggest they leave and come back the next day during work hours, Rose pulls out a hair pin and starts jimmying the lock to open it. He stares at her, dumbfounded.

"Are you illegally breaking into the office of the CEO of VR Gaming in front of a police detective? You know it is literally my job to enforce the law, which includes no breaking and entering."

"Then close your eyes, Detective." The lock on the door clicks. "As far as you know, the door has been open the whole time." she opens the door and walks right in.

"Yep, eyes closed. That's a strong defense," Cooper mutters. Before he can say anything else, Rose is already rustling through the CEO's drawers and files.

"Do you think he's just going to have a drawer marked, "Usernames and Addresses," with a piece of paper for every single person who has ever played a video game? You know that's, like, millions of people, right? It's got to be stored electronically."

"Thanks, Detective. I didn't know that," Rose replies sarcastically. "I'm looking to see if he has a piece of paper with any passwords written down." She continues scouring through drawers and personal items.

"Who writes down all their passwords on one piece of paper? What if someone finds it and takes it?" Cooper asks.

"Precisely," Rose says, as she triumphantly pulls out a page torn from a notebook. She proudly holds it out to Cooper and says, "I told you I could be helpful." She sticks out her tongue at home.

"Real mature."

Rose takes out her phone and snaps a screen shot of the piece of paper with all of Cullen's passwords, then replaces it to the exact location it was when she found it.

"Now we just have to log in and find the list of users," Rose says. But before she can turn on the computer, they hear a noise. "Was that you?"

"No, I thought it was you," Cooper says, concern creeping into his face.

They stand silently, not moving, trying to listen for the sound again. After a few minutes, they hear it again. Someone is there.

Ben grabs Rose by the arm and pulls her under Cullen's desk. Thankfully it is one of those old-fashioned wooden desks that goes all the way to the floor, so it gives them enough coverage.

"I thought you said no one was here!" she whispers.

"Stay right here. I'm going to take a quick look." He slowly lifts his head so that his line of sight is just above the top of the desk. It is still quite dark and hard to see, but there is no mistaking it.

Someone is here. And that someone is heading straight toward them.

CHAPTER 26

Cooper quickly ducks back down under the desk.

"Wha-"

"Shhh," he silences Rose's question. He motions for her to be perfectly silent and still. They are crouched close together in this tiny enclave under the desk. Pressed up against her, Cooper once again notices the sound of their breathing and their hearts beating in unison.

"Detective Cooper, we keep meeting this way," Rose says mischievously.

"Shhhh!" Cooper whispers again, but she can see that he is smiling despite himself.

After a few minutes, it is clear to Rose and Cooper that the person who has interrupted their snooping went into a different office. They turn on the light in that office, stay for another few minutes, then turn off the light and leave. Rose and Cooper do not move for a little while longer, making sure they are in the clear.

When Cooper finally feels confident that they are alone again, he looks over at Rose and sees that she has her hands on his arm. She also notices her hands and suddenly feels very self-conscious. She backs out of the desk, stands up and announces, "We better go. We can probably log into the software from another computer, we got what we came for."

As they walk out of the building, he looks over at her and says, "You know you are crazy for coming here alone, right?"

Rose smiles. "I didn't come alone. You're here, aren't you?"

"You didn't know I was coming! What if you got caught?"

"I didn't. We're fine."

"Barely. What if someone there really is the killer? What if something happened to you?"

"Aw, are you saying you would miss me Detective?" Rose teases.

Cooper shakes his head, thinking, *this girl is totally crazy*. He starts walking toward his car parked around the corner. He looks back at her, still standing there, and asks, "Are you coming?" She runs to catch up to him.

They sit in comfortable silence in the car. Ben looks over at Rose, who is staring out the window at the dark sky and bright lights of the buildings as they pass by. Her golden hair is tied back in a braid, showing off her jaw line and high cheek bones. She catches him looking at her and gives him a wide grin. "What is it? Do I have something on my face?"

"Yes. A nice smile."

Rose rolls her eyes at him, "Oh my god, has that line ever worked on a woman before?"

Cooper laughs, "You tell me—did it work?"

"Yes, it did. Suddenly I am madly in love with you, Detective Cooper," Rose laughs.

"I think you are. You totally want me."

"Oh please, if anyone here wants anyone, it's you."

"Nope, I'm the wantee, not the wanter."

"Are those even real words?" Rose asks.

"I don't know. You're the smart lawyer, you tell me," he quips.

"I vote no."

"So it's settled then."

"Yes, it's settled. You want me."

He does not disagree. He looks over at her again with wistful eyes. She really does have a remarkable smile. The song "Motownphilly" by Boyz 2 Men comes on the radio, and Cooper starts to sing along to it. Rose joins in. By the chorus, they are laughing that they both know all the words to the song.

"One of the most underrated Boyz 2 Men songs, in my opinion," Ben says.

"You know, I kissed a boy for the first time to this song," Rose admits.

"No you didn't!"

"Yup. Matthew Greenberg. I was at my first co-ed dance party at my friend Anne's house. She had put together this amazing 90s playlist on a mix tape and played it on her stereo system. I remember he tried to be so smooth, but we were both so awkward. The second we were done, I ran off to tell all my friends that I had a boyfriend, only to turn around and see Matthew kissing Georgia Miller."

"No!"

"Yes! My first heartbreak," Rose says laughing. "I actually looked him up on Facebook a couple years ago, one night when my girlfriend Paige and I had too much to drink, and we decided to cyberstalk all of our exes. He's a teacher now. Married, with a kid on the way. I'm happy for him."

"No, I can't accept that. Matthew Greenberg, that's his full name? I'll find his address and give him a firm talking to. You don't go around kissing two girls in one night!"

"It's okay, I got my own revenge. I made out with his best friend Dan Hudson right after that." She gives Cooper a beaming, mischievous grin, remembering her scandalous act.

Then Rose suddenly asks, "Have you ever been in love before?"

Cooper is quiet for a moment, then says, "I'm not sure. I thought I was. But looking back, I think it was just infatuation. It's interesting what a bit of time and perspective can do to a relationship and how you view it."

"What do you mean?"

Cooper is quiet again, thinking how to put into words what he has been thinking. "When you're in a relationship, it's all-consuming. Whether the relationship is good or bad. You can't see past your small unit of two. You can lose yourself, lose who you really are. Then when things are over, you look back and realize you may not like who you were when you were with that person."

"Is that what happened to you?" Rose asks.

"Yes. I was a different person in my last relationship. I found myself questioning things, questioning people, questioning myself. I was insecure and jealous, and I have never considered myself to be a jealous person. This girl … she would draw me in then push me away, constantly making me second-guess her feelings for me. Yet she had this hold on me that I didn't understand. And I let her do that to me. I hate myself for allowing her to have that kind of power over me.

"I thought I was in love. But looking back now, I have to believe that that was not love. Love has to be better than that."

Cooper is surprised by how open and candid he is being. He has never said these things to anyone else before. He parks the car in front of Rose's parents' house and turns to face her.

"That must have been really hard to go through," Rose says.

"It was. It was a pretty dark time in my life. I started pulling away from my family and friends, throwing myself into my work. I was consumed by my cases, working well into the late hours."

"I do that too," Rose says. "Ever since Will. It's like I don't want to face my own life. I moved far away so I didn't have these daily reminders of the life I used to have, the life we were supposed to have together. I couldn't even go into our house where all of our dreams died with him. Instead, I throw myself into other people's lives. Trying to make them better. To get revenge for other people, to do what I couldn't do for myself and for Will."

"That must be very lonely."

"It can be. I have friends, don't get me wrong. But I prefer being alone, where I don't have to pretend I'm okay. Sometimes I just can't fake it. Sometimes, there is this heavy weight on me, holding me down, telling me to stay down, to give up. Every time I try to lift my head, to get up, to reach out, this heavy invisible hand gently pushes my head back down on the pillow, telling me to stop. And everything goes … dark. Not black, just dull, drab. Like there is nothing to look forward to, nothing to live for."

Cooper looks at her, sees she is once again staring out the window into the dark. "Do you always feel that way?"

"Not always. It comes and goes. It's better now. Or I'm just used to it now. I have an amazing therapist who helps me work through these things. I still have a very hard time reaching out to people and connecting to people. I have built this wall, this armour, to shield me from future loss or pain. I don't let people in. It's lonely, but I don't mind. I've sort of become indifferent to my indifference."

"I get that. Sometimes it all hits me. The job, the horrible things I see each day. I get overwhelmed by it all, how hard it can be."

"Yes, exactly! It's just too much sometimes. The thought of getting up each day, facing it all, over and over again, it makes me so tired. You know, every once in a while, I think about getting into a car accident just to get a break. Nothing serious, I don't want to break my neck or back. Just enough that I'll be in the hospital for a couple days, able to sleep and get away from the monotony of my life. Maybe just a limb. My left leg. A minor fracture. It won't be too painful and I'll still be able to walk with one of those boots. But I'll have to take time off work."

"You have really thought this through, haven't you?"

Rose laughs. "Maybe a little. I know, I'm crazy."

"I think you're amazing."

Rose turns to face him and gives him a sad smile. "I'm a work in progress," she says.

"We all are," Cooper agrees. He can see the sadness dissipate a little from that gorgeous smile of hers. He senses that the wall she has built up around herself is starting to crumble. He puts his hand on hers, light but deliberate. He feels a tingling sensation course through his body. He has a sudden, uncontrollable urge to kiss her. They are just inches apart, sitting in his tiny car. He knows that he could cover the distance in less than two seconds and feel the warmth of her mouth on his.

Before he could make a move, Rose gives a sudden dramatic gasp. "Is the infallible Detective Benjamin Cooper admitting that he may not be perfect? That can't be! Is hell freezing over?"

Cooper laughs. "You're a smartass and a badass? My dream come true."

"Better than being just an ass, like you."

"An adorable ass," Cooper corrects her. She reaches for the car's door handle and Cooper sees that he has missed his chance to kiss her. Rose smiles at him, shaking her head, and says, "Goodnight, Detective Cooper." She steps out of the car, shuts the door behind her and walks into her house. Cooper watches her every step of the way.

CHAPTER 27

When Cooper gets home that night, he reaches out to his friend Jon Ellis, a computer software engineer, to see if he can do anything with Cullen's password. Ellis was Cooper's roommate back in college and the two have remained close friends since. Cooper just stood as Jon's best man at his wedding a few months ago.

"Dude, are you, the annoyingly moral and upstanding officer of the law, asking me to hack into the computer system of one of the top gaming and technology companies in the world?" his friend asks, clearly amused by this request. "Why, sir, I'm offended you would think me even capable of such a task."

"It's just a little minor hacking."

"There's no minor or major hacking. You're either hacking or you're not. You can't be just 'minorly' pregnant," Jon says.

"That's what I said!" Cooper cries in an exasperated tone. "But here I am, asking you to do it. I'm too far in it now."

"I'll do it, but only because now you owe me. And I love when you owe me," Jon says.

"Call me when it's done."

Cooper sits back in his desk chair in his home office. He interlaces his fingers behind his head and leans back, stretching his upper back and shoulders. *What a day*, he thinks. This case is getting to him. He isn't sleeping well, his thoughts consumed by the horrible images from the crime scenes. He is trying to put all the pieces together, find a pattern in this maniac's behaviour. He is not hopeful that Rose's sleuthing earlier this evening will reveal any major answers. For years Cooper has been following these barbaric slayings, trying to build a profile and anticipate the killer's next move.

He thinks that they are on the right path with their theory of latent homosexuality. The killer is outwardly heterosexual and may even show homophobic tendencies. He probably tells himself that homosexuality is a sin, something against nature. But this is only to combat his own suppressed inclination toward homosexuality. Instead of accepting his true feelings, he chooses repression, denial, and anger, which can often lead to outward violence against homosexuals.

It is a profile that makes sense for this killer. He likely exudes confidence and charisma, but inside he is deeply insecure and uncertain. He feels anger toward others who can live their truth, while he suppresses his own identity.

Cooper gets up from his desk and turns off the light. He walks out of the main floor office and quickly tidies up, putting his shoes away in the closet and finishing up the dishes from his dinner earlier. He heads up the stairs, noticing the creak on the third step. *I really need to fix that one of these days*, he thinks, as he continues up. Cooper wanders into his bedroom and takes his clothes off, keeping on his boxer briefs. He wanders to the second bedroom, which consists of a lounge chair, a television, and a bunch of video game consoles. Cooper hasn't shared this with Rose yet, but he himself is a gamer. He is a huge fan of VR gaming, and *Dueling Swords* in particular. Cooper lays out his clothes on the chair, too clean for the laundry but too dirty to put away in the closet.

All the while, Cooper thinks about the killer. He realizes that he almost feels bad for this man, someone who hides his true self from the world. Someone who feels like he can't be himself. But that brief moment of sympathy quickly turns back into ice-cold hatred, as Cooper reminds himself of the horrific murders and the many lives he has destroyed. Including Rose's.

Cooper grabs his laptop and crawls into bed with it, reading and re-reading his case notes. His resolve to catch the killer intensifies as he spends the rest of the evening working, refusing to rest until this animal is stopped.

Sunday morning, Jon pulls through and sends Cooper an encrypted file with the names of all VR Gaming subscribers who play *Dueling Swords*. Cooper is disappointed to see that only two of the victims, Ramirez and one other, played the game.

As promised, he calls Rose and updates her on his discovery. She takes the news much better than Cooper had expected.

"Okay, back to the drawing board. Let's figure out the connection between these victims."

Cooper and Rose agree to meet up at The Bean to discuss the investigation. To be clear, Rose insists they meet to discuss the investigation; Ben's agreement is limited to meeting up with her at that time and location. He explains that he really should not be discussing an ongoing investigation with her, but she insists. He feigns reluctance but ultimately agrees to meet, admittedly because he just wants to see her. He walks over to The Bean, working out in his head how to discuss the investigation without violating any rules of professional conduct.

It is a dark, rainy spring day, and both Ben and Rose have to shake off their umbrellas and raincoats when they arrive at the café. They find a private booth toward the back and sit down. Rose has brought her notes that she has been collecting on the investigation. She has started a working file, the way she does with all her prosecution cases, and she wants to use her notes to build up the killer's profile.

The café has music playing quietly as background noise and Rose taps her toes along to the beat. They sip their coffee and nibble on a slice of apple pie while they work, listening to the melodic patterns of music and raindrops. They had initially sat down across from each other at the booth, but then realized that it was too difficult for both of them to look at the documents from different directions. Rose hops over to his side of the booth and Cooper is acutely aware of how close he is sitting next to her. Their knees are touching. Just like he did in the car, he thinks of how easy it would be to lean in and kiss her. *Focus, Cooper.*

Rose's words wake him from his spell. "We should check the sex offender registry, see if there are any similar cases that we missed."

"I already put in a request. They are working on it, but it takes time to comb through the records and cross-reference the names against the dates and times of murders. We also have to check the specific crime. Some people are added to the registry for less offensive offences. Like public urination."

"You're telling me you're not offended by public urination?" Rose raises an eyebrow.

"I'm offended by it, but I don't think it's necessarily a crime worthy of ruining a person's life by putting them on the sex offender registry."

"What kind of cop are you?" Rose asks, shocked.

"One who pees a lot and sometimes ends up having to pee outside!"

"Oh my god, are you one of those people that can whip it out and pee anywhere?"

"Not anywhere. I'm not a total creep."

"Just a little bit of a creep, then. So you're saying it's okay for a man to urinate in a children's playground?"

"No, that's definitely not okay. That's exposure, which is a criminal offence. I would never be okay with that. But there are levels of urination offending. You know, there's peeing in a playground around children, that's terrible. But then there's peeing in an alley, or a deserted parking lot, or outside an empty building that you didn't know was a daycare centre, and a kid just happens to walk by. The guy didn't mean to pee in front of a child, the kid just showed up."

"Detective Cooper, did you pee outside a daycare centre?"

"Only when it was empty, of course."

Rose laughs. "Creep." She nudges him with her shoulder, almost leaning on him. Ben leans into her. He loves the feel of her body against his.

Right on cue, the song "Creep" by Radiohead comes on at the café. They give in to the irony of the situation and start singing along to the music.

"You have a terrible voice, Detective Cooper," Rose teases.

"What? No way! I'm amazing. I got the lead role in my school play every year in high school," he says.

"Really?" she asks, credulously.

"Nope," Ben laughs.

"Smart ass," Rose hits him playfully with the back of her hand.

"You know it," he chirps. "You think you're a better singer than me?"

"I know I am."

"You wish."

Rose sticks out her tongue at him and turns back to her notes. Ben watches her subtly bob her head in time to the music, enchanted by her. She catches him staring and grins. He reaches out a hand to push back a lock of hair that has fallen out of her messy bun. The feel of her face in his hand causes a jolt of electricity to course through him. He can no longer control his urge to kiss her.

Keeping his hand on her cheek, he gently presses his lips to hers.

He pulls back and looks into her eyes. Then he gets the exact opposite result than what he expected.

She slaps him across the face.

"What was that for?" Ben asks, shocked, with his hand cupping his red cheek.

"Why did you try to kiss me?" Rose cries.

"I thought you wanted me to kiss you!"

"Why would you think that?"

"Because I wanted to kiss you too. There's something here, Rose. I can feel the heat between us."

"No, there isn't."

"Why are you denying it? I see the way you look at me."

"I do not look at you!"

Ben gives a soft laugh. "You do look at me, Rose. You feel this connection between us. I have never met anyone like you. You're smart and funny, and exasperatingly stubborn! You challenge me and push me to be better, to do better. You drive me crazy, and I can't stop thinking about you."

Rose stares at him. "Ben …" she whispers and looks away.

"Rose." He puts his hand to her face, similar to how he just cupped his sore cheek, and gently turns her face towards him. He looks into her eyes and she stares back. Her posture softens. His gaze shifts down towards her lips, hoping to see that heartwarming smile of hers. What he would give to make her smile right now. He leans in again to kiss her. This time, she does not slap him, but it is much, much worse. Before he can kiss her, she scoops up her investigation notes, gets up from the booth and starts to walk away.

Ben chases after her. "Rose! Come back," he cries. He catches her outside, reaches out for her and grabs her arm, gently but confidently. Rose looks at him, her red eyes moist. They are standing outside in the pouring rain. Rose's blonde hair is slick and sticking to her face and neck. Ben sees water droplets run down her cheeks and he is not sure whether those are raindrops or tears.

"Why are you fighting this?" He pulls her closer to him. She resists at first, but he tugs her again. She reluctantly takes a small step toward him, without fully succumbing to him. He gently wipes away her tears with his thumb.

"Because I can't do this. When Will died, a part of me died with him. I can't go through that again. You deserve to be loved, fully and whole-heartedly, with no restraint. I can't offer you that. My heart was broken and has never recovered."

"Rose, even a tiny shred of your love is more than I deserve. And I know your heart is broken, but hearts are amazingly strong. They're this little organ, and you think you have a finite amount of love that can go in it. But they're the most elastic muscle. Your heart can stretch and do amazing things. It can love Will but also love someone else, someone who can love you in return."

"I can't do that to Will."

"Will would want you to be happy. You don't have to choose between me and him. You can feel for us both, in different ways."

"I don't know, Ben," Rose says, but he can sense that she is relenting further. He takes a step closer to her. This time, she does not resist him or push away. Cooper gently brings her face to look at him. She is crying. "I don't know how to do this."

"I do," Ben says as he closes the distance between them, pulls her into his arms and kisses her.

The kiss is soft at first. Ben presses his lips to hers, feeling them out. When he sees that she is receptive to the kiss (and is not going to slap him or walk away again), his opens his lips slightly and gently slips his tongue into her mouth. Rose is surprised and begins to kiss him back with an overwhelming passion and hunger. Her body trembles at the feeling of his tongue on hers. It's a kiss unlike any she has ever had before. She can't stop touching him. His wavy hair, now wet and plastered to his face and in his eyes, his neck, his shoulders, his back. Her fingers wander to his chest and his toned stomach. *Oh my god, these abs! Is it possible to have a ten-pack? How many muscles are there?* She moves her arms to caress his arms, then back up to his chest. She realizes that he is touching her too. He grabs her ass and uses his hands to pull her into him and he grinds his hips into her. She feels him pressing up against her. Her stomach is full of butterflies—*no, not just butterflies, an entire kaleidoscope of butterflies.* She feels alive and on fire. They do not even notice the pouring rain soaking through their clothes or the strangers gawking at them as they pass by.

All the while, their lips do not part. She feels like she is in a daze. Her head is ringing, heavy with desire. She thinks she can hear bells.

All of a sudden, Ben pulls back. Rose worries that she has done something wrong. It's been a while since she has kissed a man. But as he reaches for his phone, she realizes that she was right, and she did in fact hear bells. Ben's phone was ringing.

"I have to get this, it's my emergency ring tone." He presses the talk button and says, "Detective Cooper." Rose looks expectantly at his face and she can sense it immediately. Something has happened. He quickly hangs up and tells her.

"They found another body."

CHAPTER 28

*T*hat was wild.

I've never done it with a woman before. I mean, I've done "it" with a woman before. I'm not gay. (Not that there's anything wrong with being gay, if I was. I'm just not gay.) But I've never done this with a woman before.

I saw her enter that swanky department store, Haddingtons, and she walked with a confident swagger, gently swaying her hips left and right. It felt like she was calling my name. I had just finished my errands and was about to head home, but I felt drawn to her. I casually strolled into the big department store and tried to find her amid a sea of young beautiful women carrying black and white Haddingtons bags. She was not at the makeup counters or the purse department on the first floor. I almost turned around and left. Maybe I just made this up. But something was luring me to her, so I kept looking. I had said I wanted to change things up a bit to confuse the cops. This could work.

I took the escalator up to the second floor and there she was. Surrounded by displays of beautiful shoes with names I had never heard of, but I knew must be expensive. My mom loves designer shoes. God knows why, it seems like a total waste of money. You're just paying for the name. We used to ask Mom why she cares so much about these fancy labels, and she just said, "Why wear cotton when you can wear Chanel?" As kids, we just laughed at her, we didn't get it.

This woman seems to like the really fancy, high-end designers too. I saw her in front of a table marked Valentino. I think I've heard of that one before. She had a pair of high heel pumps in her hands that had sharp metallic spikes all over it. I smiled. How apropos.

She tried the floor model of the shoe on, and started hobbling around with one high heel, looking for a mirror. Why do women have to look at their shoes in the mirror? Just look down, it's not like you can't see your feet. I watched her struggle with uneven steps to a full-length mirror and stood there, admiring herself, turning her foot in various directions to see how the shoe looked on her. I won't lie, it looked gorgeous on her. When she stepped up on that foot with the heel, her calf immediately tightened and her glutes flexed. Her ass looked like a tight, juicy peach ready to be bitten. Hey, I'm an ass man, what can I say?

She finally took off the shoe and placed it back on the table. I was disappointed to see her walk away. I quietly followed her as she strolled through the various sweaters and blouses, gently touching and caressing the hanging clothing as she strolled by.

After a little while, she made her way back down to the first floor and started to leave the department store. I sped up so as not to lose her. She exited Haddingtons and was headed toward the Starbucks right next to it.

I saw my opening and I took it before I had a chance to overthink it and stop myself. I got in line right behind her and started chatting with her. Casual, innocent banter. It was thrilling, knowing what I was about to do. I offered to buy her coffee for her and she accepted. I was a little shocked. Most women I know are feminists and refuse to have random strangers buy them coffee. Maybe she knew what I was doing, what I was hoping to do with her, to her. I flirted with her for a little while and then blatantly invited myself over to her place. Again, shockingly, she accepted. Who lets a random stranger into their home? She had no idea what I was capable of! This is what's wrong with our society today, people are so desperate for love and attention, they jump at any opportunity to receive it. No wonder crime rates are so high. People are stupid and trusting. She was stupid and trusting. And look where that got her.

It doesn't take long for us to start kissing once we enter her tiny apartment. It was familiar but different. Exhilarating. This was so unlike from all of my other adventures, and yet I felt the same excitement, the same intense desire to enter her, to annihilate her, to assume total power over her.

She is the one who took her clothes off and invited me into her bedroom. I mean, seriously? How stupid and trusting can you get? I watched her undress and then I asked her if she had any handcuffs or ropes. She seemed a little taken aback at first, but she was into it. She let me tie her up. Usually, the guys are already fighting me off and I have to hurt them or render them unconscious in order to restrain them. The fact that she was acquiescing to my touch, to my suggestions, was so foreign to me. I didn't know how I felt about it. It was as if we were sharing the power, as if she was trying to assert power over me. I didn't like it.

I tied her arms and legs behind her back, like I always do, but her eyes showed only desire. No fear. That was just not acceptable to me. I realized that I was no longer excited. I was furious. I had to change this. I had to take control over the situation. I looked around and found her underwear on the floor. I grabbed it and rubbed it against my face, sniffing it. Then I looked at her and stared into her eyes as I scrunched the underwear into a ball and shoved it into her mouth. I watched her eyes change from desire to concern. She tried to ask me to take them out, but I just ignored her and stared at her. She was probably wondering what I was doing or what I was waiting for. But then it happened, what I was waiting for. I watched as her eyes went from confusion to anger to fear.

I kept staring at her eyes as I slowly took my clothes off. Wordlessly, I left her bedroom and came back a minute later with my equipment. I was hoping for a baseball bat or tennis racquet, something I'm used to. She didn't have any of that, so I had to improvise. She watched as I silently laid everything out in front of her, and I quickly felt myself harden as I saw the look in her eyes when I placed down a sharp kitchen knife.

This is more like it.

CHAPTER 29

This time, Ben does not fight Rose when she demands to come with him to the crime scene. He rationalizes the decision to her (and himself?) by explaining that she has proven to be helpful and is already deeply involved in the investigation. But if he's being fully honest with himself, he just doesn't want to leave her.

They pull up to the victim's building on Bedford Road and push through the yellow tape to enter. It is a nice area, close to both Avenue Road & Davenport and Yorkville. Much fancier than the locations of the other victims' homes. Ben notes this as they enter the victim's apartment. It is small, only around 600 square feet, but is furnished with beautiful furniture, high-end appliances, elegant marble countertops, and elegant décor. Rose's hair is still wet as they enter, but they have taken off their raincoats and are starting to dry off. They dutifully put on paper booties to cover their own footprints and a pair of latex gloves. Like the previous crime scenes, the victim is found in the bedroom and is covered in blood. This victim was bound, stabbed and sexually assaulted. But this victim differs from the killer's previous victims in one substantial way: she is a woman.

"Are you Detective Cooper?" A cop is walking toward them. "I was told to expect you." The cop introduces himself as Officer McAllister. He is short and stout, with greying hair that is starting to have more salt than pepper. He has a thick beard that is almost white, and Ben estimates him to be in his late 60s. His gruff appearance is softened by kind deep brown eyes that show an appropriate level of compassion and respect for the victim nearby.

After shaking hands, McAllister gets straight to business and updates Ben on the crime scene. "Victim's name is Amanda Moore, twenty-nine years old. A neighbour called it in. The victim was supposed to meet her for some yoga or Pilates thing but never showed up. Supposedly very unlike the vic, so the neighbour came straight here after class. She knocked on the door a bunch of times, but no one answered. She has her own key to the place, they exchanged keys a year ago in case of emergency, so she let herself in. Said she had 'a feeling,' don't know what that means.

"Anyway, she found the vic around two-thirty this afternoon and called the cops right away. First arrivers got here around 2:44 p.m., and I showed up shortly after that. Forensics is doing their thing, but they are pretty sure that the vic was assaulted for an extended period of time before being killed. There is evidence of both vaginal and anal trauma and given the blood and fluids all over the vic and the gym equipment around her, I think it's pretty safe to say we have our weapon of choice. The only thing missing is the knife used for all those stabbings. The M.E. will conduct a more thorough review, but she is currently estimating T.O.D. to be between around 1:00 and 3:00 a.m."

"Any signs of defensive wounds?"

"None that I could see. Killer must have overpowered her quickly and tied her up right away. But it's clear he took his time after that."

"You'll make sure forensics runs every possible print in this room through the system?"

"Yes, Detective."

"The neighbour is back in her own apartment across the hall and has a couple officers with her taking her statement. We're getting a bunch of names of family and friends, anyone who could possibly have known the victim's whereabouts last night."

"Thank you, Officer," Ben says, patting him on the back and turning toward the crime scene. Rose audibly gasps as she sees the gruesome scene ahead of them. Ben instinctively takes her hand in a gesture of comfort. Amanda Moore is lying limp on the bed, her left arm and leg hanging over the edge haphazardly. There are blood splatters all over the room: on the floor, on the bed, and all over the walls. There are multiple stab wounds covering her torso and signs of vaginal and anal trauma. The victim must have been a personal trainer, or maybe just very into working out, as there is exercise equipment all over the room: dumbbells, stretch bands, medicine balls, poles, foam rollers, and a therapeutic massage gun. It appears, at first glance, that almost all those items were used to physically and sexually assault the victim. They are all covered in blood and bodily fluids. It is truly horrific.

The bedroom is teeming with forensics technicians examining the room as well as a deputy from the coroner's office. One of the technicians is carefully and methodically photographing the victim and the bloody exercise equipment lying around her. Other team members are bagging and tagging pieces of evidence where the photographer has finished capturing the scene. Everyone is quiet and somber.

"The media's going to have a field day with this," Rose murmurs.

"Trial by media, right?" Ben answers. "Our killer is getting more violent. More aggressive. Maybe he's even getting a little cocky," Ben suggests. "He's changing things up a bit. But why?"

Rose is silent as she walks around the bedroom, stealing glances at the victim amidst the forensics team. She studies the woman's walls, painted a muted beige tone that is both modern and warm. She peruses the victim's desk hutch and bookshelf, admiring the assortment of books, decorative items, and personal photographs of her with friends. Rose notes that there is no picture of a boyfriend. She looks at the nightstand beside the bed, seeing the typical collection of books, eyeglasses, random jewelry, and the victim's phone. She is desperately looking for clues, something to indicate why she was chosen as the killer's latest victim. *Why did he kill her? What is it about this woman that led to her fatal fate? Or was she just in the wrong place at the wrong time?*

Rose notices that Ben is watching her. Despite herself, and despite the circumstances they find themselves, her stomach does a little flip from excitement. She smiles briefly, then turns away when she realizes she is blushing. *Focus, Rose, focus.*

She bends down to look at the gym equipment but is quickly asked to back away. She goes back to perusing the victim's bookshelf. At one point, Ben gently brushes by her, gently touching her lower back. This time the flip in her stomach is more like an Olympic-level competitive gymnast's floor routine. She is so confused by the mixed emotions she is feeling: excitement for Ben and sorrow for this victim, mixed with guilt for feeling anything other than sorrow.

After a few hours, it is clear that the forensics team wants Detective Cooper and Rose to get out of the way and let them do their job. Ben offers her a ride home. Since she had walked to The Bean and then he had driven her to the crime scene, she accepts.

They are quiet in the car, somber, simply listening to the music on the radio and the pitter patter of the rain. They are both thinking about the latest victim. The fact that this time it was a woman has thrown them off. Their previous theory about latent homosexuality was clearly wrong. This means they need to go back to their files and look at everything all over again from a new perspective, trying to find a new profile.

Ben places his hand on the middle console beside Rose's hand. His fingers lightly graze hers. She smiles and gently rubs her pinkie finger against his.

The radio has been playing quietly, but when Billy Joel's "Piano Man" comes on the radio, Ben turns it up and starts quietly singing along.

Rose turns the radio station. Ben protests, "Hey! That's a great song!"

"I love that song, but life is way too depressing right now. Can we listen to something a little more upbeat?"

"What? A miserable lonely man singing about how he has given up on life isn't upbeat?"

Rose ignores him while she flips through the various radio stations. She finds a song by Alanis Morissette, "Right Through You," and leaves it on. The somber mood in the car is slowly starting to dissipate away as Rose and Ben fall back into their flirtatious banter.

"Really? Alanis? She is the queen of depressing, emotional music."

"Will used to say the same thing. That is actually a common misconception. I love Alanis. Her music is incredible. The tunes are catchy and the lyrics are brilliant and relatable. I remember discovering *Jagged Little Pill* when I was young, and I just listened to it on repeat. It wasn't until much later in life that I actually understood the meanings behind her words. But I enjoyed the songs at every age."

"Doesn't she just whine and talk about things that she calls ironic, even though they are not ironic at all, they are just bad luck?"

"Not at all! Her songs are deep, dark and gritty, but still have a sense of humour. They're relatable. "You Oughta Know"? Who hasn't felt that way about their ex finding someone new. "Head Over Feet" was one of my favourites, it totally described my relationship with my first boyfriend. And uh, "Forgiven"? Gives me goosebumps every time."

"You sure do know your Alanis."

"I do. Love her. Shush, listen to these words. They're sassy and clever," she pauses and winks at him, adding "just like me." They listen as Alanis Morissette talks about a man disrespecting her. When she sings about the man checking out her ass then going to play golf, Ben pipes up, "Wait, is that not polite? Checking out your ass then going golfing?"

Rose shushes him again and awaits Ben's reaction to the next line, which she sings along to: "You took me out to wine, dine, sixty-nine me, but didn't hear a damn word I said."

"Okay, I take it all back. She is a poet."

Rose laughs.

"Are you asking me to wine, dine, sixty-nine you?" Ben mischievously asks.

"Detective Benjamin Cooper!" Rose shrieks. "I am a lady! It takes a lot more than just dinner to get me into bed." Ben smiles and reaches for her hand, firmly grasping it in his. Rose feels her whole body tingle, taking in the intimacy of this gesture. Holding hands with a man. "But it's a good place to start."

"You like carbonara?"

There is something incredibly sexy about watching a man confidently move his way through a kitchen. Tonight, the experience is filled with sensual overtones. The various senses around Rose intoxicate her: the sound of acoustic covers of The Beatles playing softly over the speaker; the smell of salty pancetta crisping up in a pan as water boils in a pot on the stove; and the taste of the red wine in her glass, as she watches Ben masterfully chop up basil and parmesan to dust over the pasta. Rose is overcome with hunger, but whether that hunger is directed at Ben or at the delicious meal she is about to eat remains unclear.

Just like at the crime scene, she is trying to sort out her competing emotions. She is haunted by the crime scene they left just an hour earlier and the disturbing images she saw. She is furious at the killer for committing these heinous acts and at herself for not stopping him. But she is also happy, and excited, and aroused. She hasn't felt these feelings in a very long time, and so she tries to push away the negative thoughts and feelings and focus on the man in front of her.

Ben is humming and the two are chatting as he prepares dinner. Rose asks him how he is able to "turn off" after leaving a crime scene like that. He explains that over the years he has learned to compartmentalize. If he didn't, he would lose his mind, consumed by the horrors he sees on a daily basis.

As Rose considers his answer, one of her favourite songs, "Here Comes the Sun," comes on, and she closes her eyes and quiets her brain, allowing herself feel the music, almost in a trance.

Ben breaks Rose's reverie and asks, "Do you like to cook?"

"I love to eat. Does that count?"

He laughs, "No, it does not count."

Rose thinks. "I enjoy the process of cooking and I love watching people cook. But I'm not a very good chef, so I tend to just order in most evenings."

"You don't have to be good at something to do it."

"Why do anything if you're not good at it?"

"That's how you *get* good at something—with practice."

Rose remains quiet for a while, listening to the music again. John, Paul, George and Ringo are singing about a girl's smile finally returning to her face, after many years of sadness. *Just like me*, Rose thinks.

"What made you decide to become a detective?" she asks, changing the conversation.

"You know how little boys grow up wanting to be pilots and doctors and police officers? I spent my entire childhood pretending to be a cop. I thought it was the ultimate career choice: you get to help people and contribute to society, all while wearing a super cool uniform. I sort of just never grew up from that dream. Plus, you know, I'm not strong enough to be a firefighter," Ben says smiling.

Rose looks at him and laughs. "Somehow I doubt that."

"Dinner is ready."

Rose and Ben sit down to a small table, set with surprisingly tasteful dishes and matching cutlery. She twirls some pasta on her fork, catching crispy pieces of pancetta, and takes a bite. Her eyes immediately close. The combination of creaminess and saltiness tastes like a bite of heaven. Who knew the man could cook like this?

"My my, Detective Cooper, you are full of surprises. Are you trying to impress me?"

"Depends. Is it working?" he says with a wink.

Rose smiles. "Perhaps." And she is delightfully surprised that she means it. She is very impressed by Ben Cooper, both his skills in the kitchen and otherwise. She looks at him and stares at those remarkable eyes of his, bright teal with a dazzling green halo around them. As they share a meal in comfortable silence, she is overcome with a sense of peacefulness. She can feel the wall she has meticulously built and maintained over the years begin to crumble.

That brief moment of contentedness passes quickly as she feels a pang of guilt for thinking of a man other than Will. Ben astutely notices the change in her posture and can tell that she is thinking about Will.

"This is just dinner," Ben says. "We do not have to do anything that you are not comfortable with. I just want to be with you. I like you."

"I like you too. Which feels crazy to me. I never thought I would have feelings for another man. But this feels ..." She pauses as she tries to think of the word to describe how she feels. "Good.

It feels ... right." She decides, right then and there, to allow herself to feel happy without the guilt. To allow herself to be with another man. To start to live again. That's what Dr. Hill has been telling her to do all these years, right? And Tyler. And Paige. And LARS. Maybe they were all right.

"Good," he smiles and takes a sip of wine.

"That was a delicious dinner. What's for dessert, chef?" Rose playfully inquires.

"My talent stops at dinner. I cannot bake for the life of me. But I probably have some ice cream in the freezer, will that do?"

Rose looks at him with desirous eyes and a mischievous smile and says, "I have a better idea."

CHAPTER 30

Ben Cooper feels his heart skip a beat.

Rose confidently stands up from the table and reaches out for his hand. He obliges and places his hand on hers. He rises and she guides him away from the table. He looks down at her and thinks that he has never seen anyone so beautiful in his entire life. He wants to be with her, to be by her side, to protect her. But then he realizes that she does not need his protection. She is an unbelievably strong, independent woman. He thinks about all that she has been through and how she has taken care of herself. As this thought hits him, he remembers his first impression of her and smiles at how right he was: *This girl is definitely trouble and I am definitely in over my head.*

"What are you staring at?" Rose asks curiously.

"You," he says, as he leans in and kisses her softy.

He pulls back and asks, "Is that okay?"

"I'm not sure. You should probably do it again to be sure."

This time, they do not start soft or uncertain. Their lips immediately lock into a deep, passionate embrace and he loses himself in her: her taste, her smell, her feel. His hands are all over her.

Rose is running her fingers through his hair. She begins to explore his body. As her hands wander lower on his body and she reaches for his jeans, he feels an instinctive shiver throughout his body as he realizes what she is doing. As she starts to undo the button on his jeans, he fights to break from her embrace and pulls away to look into her eyes. "Are you sure? There is no rush. We can go slowly."

Rose presses herself back into his arms and continues kissing him. With her mouth on his, she mumbles the words, "I don't want to go slowly." She kisses the freckle on his lip and whispers, "I need you."

"Ms. Davis, what are your intentions here?"

"My intentions?"

He swiftly and confidently moves her face to meet his. "Yes, what are your intentions with my body?" he whispers, staring intensely into her eyes.

"My intentions are pure, I assure you."

"That's unfortunate. I was hoping they would be very impure," then he plunges his tongue into her mouth. He melts into her. He feels every inhibition fly out of his body and he starts greedily kissing her. He aggressively grabs her ass, pressing her body into him, thrusting his groin against her hips. She releases an almost inaudible gasp of delight.

Rose's hands creep up under Ben's shirt, and he takes her cue and rips it off, throwing it across the room. She undoes the fly of his jeans and they start to fall down. Laughing and stumbling, they make their way up the stairs. Rose jumps as the third step lets out its familiar creak, but Ben nudges her that it's okay, to continue. They enter his bedroom without ever taking their lips off of each other. As they approach the bed, Rose finally breaks off their embrace and pushes him down onto it. Ben's pants are at his ankles at this point and they laugh as she finishes the job and tugs them off. She stands before him at the foot of the bed. His hands are all over her, exploring the shape of her body, feeling her beautiful curves. Rose runs her fingers through his hair again.

"Wait a second," Ben says, pulling back, in a serious tone. "I'm down to my underwear here and you're still fully dressed. That's not fair."

"Life's not fair, Detective Cooper," Rose says, throwing his own words back into her face.

He groans and pulls her arms to join him on the bed. But Rose doesn't move. She stands at the edge of the bed, looking at him, enjoying the view. Then, wordlessly, Rose unbuttons her blouse excruciatingly slowly. Ben does not take his eyes off her, savouring each small movement, knowing each one brings her closer to him.

He wants her so badly.

Finally, after what feels like years, Rose removes her shirt, her pants, her bra, then finally her underwear. Ben continues to watch her, ready to explode with desire.

"Get over here, Davis," Ben demands, as he rips off his briefs.

She lays down on the bed and he crawls toward her. She is lying beside him, both of them now naked. "You are so beautiful," he says to her. Then they are kissing again. They are exploring each other with a hunger that neither has felt in a long time. It is both hard and soft at the same time, both dangerous and safe.

Rose crawls on top of Ben and is kissing every part of him. She moves from his lips across his cheek to his ear, where she nibbles on his earlobe for a brief moment, before moving down to his neck, then his chest. She continues working her way down his stomach toward his groin. Her movements are slow, maddening. She starts teasing him with her lips. He lets out a quiet groan.

Suddenly, in one swift motion, Ben grabs Rose and flips her off him and under him. He hovers above her for a moment. His pulse is racing, the tension is almost unbearable. "Is this okay" he whispers. "Very," she whispers, as she guides him into her.

Their lovemaking is everything all at once: passionate, intimate, animalistic, gentle, playful. Rose is feeling all the feels. At one point, when she catches him watching her in a moment of pleasure, Rose sticks out her tongue at him in a playful gesture and Ben gently nips at it with his teeth. In turn, she begins to nibble on his earlobe again. It drives him nuts and makes him thrust even harder inside her.

When they are done, they are covered in glistening sweat, surrounded in a sea of messy and strewn sheets. Rose is lying in Ben's arms, panting, while trying to calm her own heartbeat. She feels safe, happy.

"Thanks for inviting me over for dinner. It was delicious," she says playfully.

"I'm glad you came," Ben says wryly, and they both laugh.

Rose feels her eyes get heavy and sleep begin to wash over her. She fights it, not wanting their evening to end. She is terrified that she will wake up and realize that this was all a dream, a new form of a torturous nightmare that will devastate her when she is forced to face reality.

"We should go to sleep," Ben says, noticing her drowsiness.

"I don't want this night to end."

"It's okay. We'll make another night just like it tomorrow."

"What if this is just a dream," Rose ponders aloud. Ben pinches her on the butt.

"Hey!" she shouts. "What was that for?"

"See? Not a dream. This is real," Cooper says smiling. Rose can't help herself and she laughs.

"Go to sleep, Rose. I will be right here in the morning when you wake up."

She finally lets herself go and she drifts off into a wonderful, deep sleep.

CHAPTER 31

Rose has not slept that well for a very long time. It was one of those deep, luxurious, nightmare-less sleeps. In fact, she can't seem to recall having any dream at all. As she opens her eyes, she looks around and remembers where she is: in Detective Ben Cooper's apartment. In his bed, to be more specific, completely naked. Her anxiety washes over and she quickly shuts her eyes again. What if Ben is not there anymore? What if Ben does not feel the way she does and he left? What if this is really the nightmare and she imagined the whole evening?

Rose forces herself to take deep calming breaths, as she has learned to do to alleviate her anxiety. She wills herself to open her eyes, but she can't seem to force them open. Lying there, taking deep breaths, fighting her inner critic who is screaming at her that Ben must be gone, she feels a warm breath of air near her face. Then she feels the heat of Ben's body as he nears her. Her deep breathing quickens as it turns to excitement and then pleasure. Ben is kissing her neck, her jaw line, her eyes. Rose feels all her senses heightened as she keeps her eyes closed tightly. She reaches out for his neck, wrapping her arms around him, and bringing his lips to hers. But he does not acquiesce. He climbs on top of her and continues to kiss her neck, her shoulders, and her breasts.

Rose wraps her legs around Ben's body, allowing herself to feel the warmth and comfort of his gentle touch. She allows herself to fully surrender to him.

Ben must be able to feel her relax, as he moves his face directly in front of hers and whispers, "Open your eyes, Rose." She slowly opens her eyes and is greeted by those striking teal blue eyes with the emerald green halo around them. She smiles as she looks at him.

He finally lowers his lips onto hers and kisses her. Ben gently brushes his hands over her breasts, her stomach, lowering down to her legs. Rose can feel herself get excited. He is kissing her neck now and lightly tracing his fingers along the inside of her thigh. But he never goes all the way. He lies there, teasing her, fingers dancing all over but missing their mark. Her body is trembling now. He is driving her crazy.

After what feels like an eternity, Ben's kisses move lower across her body, over her breasts, her stomach, her hips. He lands directly between her legs, looks up at her and smiles. Rose gently nudges his head down and he gets to work. Rose can feel her hips rise to meet his tongue. She is writhing and breathing heavily, grasping his hair. As she comes, she cries out and yanks his hair.

He makes his way up again and is directly on top of her.

"Oh my god," she whispers, spent.

"Nope, my name is Ben," he replies and begins kissing her again.

Their lovemaking is different today. Last night, they were driven by an intense hunger and need for each other. They were wild. This morning, they are slow, deliberate, paying attention to every movement and every moan. They are learning each other and enjoying each other in the most intimate way.

When they are done, they lie in bed in a comfortable silence, their bodies still intertwined. Ben is gently brushing Rose's hair with his fingers. She can't remember the last time she felt so good.

"How was your wakeup call, ma'am? To your satisfaction?" Ben asks with an impish grin.

"Very much so. Although I thought I had put in an order for breakfast in bed," Rose quips.

"Your wish is my command." Ben jumps out of bed and throws on shorts and a pair of glasses. The glasses are a classic square shape with thick black frames. They are the kind of glasses that are super nerdy but, with the right confidence, can look cool and edgy. They look good on him.

"I didn't know you wear glasses."

"I usually wear contacts. Do you not like them? I think they make me look smart."

"Nah, I can still see your face," she teases.

"Very funny. Breakfast will be served in 15 minutes." Just before he leaves the room, he looks over his shoulder and says, "Feel free to not put on any clothes while I'm gone."

Rose smiles and spreads out on his large bed. She lets out a deep sigh, not aware that she was even holding her breath to begin with.

"I knew it!" Tyler shouts smugly. "I knew you were into him!"

"I don't know why I told you," she groans.

"Because you know I'm right and you love telling me I'm right."

"Sure," Rose says sarcastically. "Something like that." She calls her brother shortly after Ben drops her off back at her house. Thankfully her parents are both at work, so she does not have to answer too many questions about her whereabouts. She can only imagine her mother's reaction. If she thinks Tyler acting smugly right now is bad, just wait. Her mother will be truly triumphant.

Rose knows deep down that her family just wants her to be happy. But they seem to want that to mean happiness as they define it: marriage, two children, a dog, and a house with a white picket fence. Her parents are supportive of Rose's legal career, but they occasionally make comments regarding how she will have to find a new job once she has children. She ignores these comments to the extent she can and recognizes that part of it is their own upbringing, where women were raised to be wives and mothers. When Rose initially told her parents that she applied to law school to get her J.D. (Juris Doctorate), her mother told her what she really needs is her M.R.S. Rose has always been steadfast that she receive a good education and realize a solid career path before she even considered marriage and children. That is why Will waited until her graduation day to propose; he knew she would not have said yes until she had her degree and a job lined up.

But that never happened. He never proposed. So Rose has had six years to focus exclusively on herself and her career. It allowed her to become an excellent and successful lawyer. And she truly believed that that was enough. But now she isn't as sure anymore. Now that she has met Ben, she thinks that maybe there could be more out there for her.

Rose cuts herself off from her daydreaming and faces reality. She lives in Vancouver now. That is where she has built a home and career. She is just visiting Toronto. This is just a fling with Ben, it's not long-term.

She hangs up with her brother and goes to take a shower, but not before her daily obsessive scrolling of all news media outlets and social media posts relating to the murders. She has plans to return to Ben's later to go over the case files again. The latest murder of Amanda Moore has changed things and they agree that they should look at their investigation notes from a new perspective.

Rose returns to Ben's house later that afternoon and they begin poring over their notes. They slowly develop a new profile for the killer, moving away from a homophobic self-hating homosexual. They focus on the violence of the crime, the multiple stab wounds, getting more aggressive and messier over time, and the sports paraphernalia used for the sexual assault. That is another commonality between all the victims: sports equipment used to hurt.

Rose ponders out loud about a childhood trauma; perhaps the killer was abused as a child, maybe by a gym teacher or sports coach, and is recreating the attack now. Ben agrees that it is worth pursuing that angle. Did the victims play sports? Did the killer meet his victims through sports, aside from Marco Ramirez whom he met online? They begin re-examining the files again with this new perspective, looking into each victim's past. It is a time-consuming, laborious process, but Rose loves it. She is in her element, reviewing case files and crime scenes and finding evidence to support their theory.

Around seven o'clock, Ben prepares dinner for them. Roasted garlic chicken with lemon olive dressing, air-fried brussels sprouts, and smashed potatoes. Just like the carbonara the day before, it is divine. They sit close together at the kitchen table while they eat, brushing their legs up against each other. They can't stop touching each other, there is no denying the magnetic chemistry between them. And just like the day before, they skip dessert and head straight upstairs to the bedroom as soon as they are done eating.

This becomes their routine over the next few days: they spend the day alternating between making love, reviewing case files, discussing the investigation, then making love again. Every few days, Rose returns home to change into new clothes then heads back over to Ben's house. They spend their evenings watching movies in bed, sometimes focusing on the movie but usually focusing only on each other.

She feels like a teenager again. But along with a teen's sexual awakening comes the typical teenage insecurity: Am I pretty enough? Does he really like me? Do I look fat in these jeans? Rose's head and heart are constantly at war with each other, as she tries to manage her various clashing emotions: happiness, fear, unworthiness, and, of course, guilt.

She tries to exercise all the tools and skills she has been working on in therapy with Dr. Hill, including self-affirmations that she is worthy. She finds that this is not always helpful, as her inner critic (who is a total bitch, by the way) can convince her otherwise and make her question whether Ben actually likes her. She tries to fight this critic and see that it is her anxiety and depression talking, telling her she is not worthy. She reads the letter she had written to herself before coming to Toronto, as Dr. Hill's suggested. She tries to read it objectively and care for herself the way she would care for a friend. *Focus on the facts, Rose*, she thinks to herself. No one forces Ben to kiss her. No one forces him to sleep with her. He wants her. *Right?*

"I miss you. It's no fun watching trashy reality television without someone to laugh at them with," Paige says to Rose over video chat. It is early evening in Toronto, which makes it late afternoon in Vancouver.

"I miss you, too. But why are you watching television in the middle of the afternoon? Don't you have work to do?"

"Don't be judgy."

"You love me when I'm judgy."

"It's true. I do. But seriously, why are you not at work?"

"I asked to work from home today. Can't you tell I'm totally working?" Paige pans the phone to show her lying on the couch in pajamas with a box of takeout pizza beside her. Her work laptop was on the coffee table, unopened.

Rose laughs. "Yup, totally working."

"Um, Rose ... I hate to alarm you," Paige says in a serious voice. "But are you aware that there is a naked man behind you?"

Rose jumps and looks over her shoulder, only to find Ben coming into the room completely naked. He had been in the shower and clearly decided that this was a "clothes-optional" evening, as it usually is with them.

Rose looks into the phone and says with a conspiratorial smile, "He's not naked, he's wearing glasses! Gotta go, girl!"

"What! You can't leave me like that! Details!" Paige shouts.

"Another time. I'm going to be busy for the next hour. Bye, friend!"

Tonight, they are watching the 2012 remake of *Les Misérables*. Rose keeps asking, "Why do they all have English accents when the movie clearly takes place in France? The title itself is French! It's about the French Revolution!" Ben shakes his head and laughs. He is totally smitten by this woman. She is so beautiful. She doesn't seem to see how gorgeous she is: her long golden locks, which are currently tied in a knot at the top of her head, her sky-blue eyes that are tearing up as Fantine succumbs to her death, and her voluptuous body that is pressed against his. Ben knows Rose is insecure about her curves, but he finds them incredibly sexy. She has curves in all the right places. To him, she is perfect. And he can't seem to wrap his brain around the fact that she seems to like him too. How did he get so lucky?

She catches him staring at her and throws a piece of popcorn at him playfully. Ben smiles and wraps his arm around her, pulling her into the crook of his arm. He kisses the top of her head. They are both aware that they are living in a bubble and that the bubble is likely to burst at some point. But until it does, they succumb to their bubble and let it carry them away.

Charles Mitchell checks in again, asking Rose when she will be returning to the Crown Counsel's office in Vancouver. She has tried to not think about the fact that she will have to leave Toronto soon. He had said she could take a leave of absence, but not an indefinite one. For now, Rose simply tells him that she will not be returning this week.

Rose does not tell him about Ben or about their investigation into a psychopathic serial killer. But Charles, intuitive and sensitive to his protégé's moods, can sense a change in Rose. He notices that Rose, for the first time, sounds happy. He does not push her and encourages her to stay as long as she needs. Her position will be waiting for her when she returns.

But just before he hangs up, Charles adds: "We miss you here. People say I'm no fun again. I need you to come back to make people like me again!"

CHAPTER 32

The next Sunday, Rose kisses Ben goodbye (and then she kisses him again, and again, and again) and leaves his house to go have brunch with her girls. She has been chatting with Anne, Lauren and Stella by text, but she has not seen them in person in a few weeks.

They are meeting at Café Miles, a trendy restaurant in Yorkville that seems to only serve avocado toast and overnight oats. It's obnoxious and pretentious but delicious and Rose's friends love it there. They promise her that she will love it too.

Rose decides to walk to the restaurant, which is only about a half-hour walk from Ben's house on Oriole Gardens, just north of St. Clair Avenue West. She can feel the warmth of the sun soothe her body and her soul. She takes a moment to enjoy the beautiful spring weather, to feel the warm breeze dance across her face. As she passes Davenport Road, she gets a weird sensation that she is being followed. She looks around but does not notice anyone or anything out of the ordinary. She continues to walk, but the nagging sensation that she is being watched does not go away. She stops and looks around again. *You're imagining things, Rose*, she tells herself, as she tries to shake off that weird feeling. She speeds up her pace to a brisk walk, eager to be surrounded by the safety of her friends.

She arrives at the restaurant right on time at eleven-thirty and sees that she is the last to arrive. After hugs and kisses, the four women sit down at a table and immediately order coffee and mimosas. Lauren refrains from the alcohol, but she clinks a champagne glass that is filled with orange juice as the four of them toast.

Just as Rose takes her first sip of her drink, Stella looks at her and blurts out: "You had sex!"

Rose almost spits out her drink. "What?"

"Oh my god, you totally had sex!" Stella cries, a little louder this time.

"Ssshhhh!" Rose tries to quiet their shrieks, but she gives it away immediately by blushing and smiling.

"Tell us everything and do not spare a single detail," demands Anne.

"Seriously," concurs Lauren. "This pregnant girl has not had sex in six months, I'm way too nauseous, so let us live vicariously through you!"

"His name is Ben," Rose begins, and immediately the three other women are shrieking again with excitement. Rose shushes them again and begins to share every naughty detail with her besties.

"You totally like him!" Anne cries.

"I do," she squeals, covering her face with her hands in embarrassment.

"Rose, this is huge. This is the first man you have shown any interest in since Will."

"I know," she says. "It feels weird. But also, right. Does that make sense?"

"It makes perfect sense. You are allowing yourself to feel happy again, it's incredible. We are so thrilled for you," Stella says.

"Girl, you better not let this one go. He sounds like a keeper," says Anne.

"I would kill for Jared to cook for me!" cries Stella. "The only thing he knows how to make is toast. And he usually burns it!"

"He's too perfect," Lauren says, always the cautious and level-headed one of the bunch. "What's the catch?" asks Lauren.

"He's not perfect, he's a total pain in the butt. He's sarcastic, has a twisted sense of humour, and he thinks he's smarter than everyone around him," Rose says.

"So he's exactly your type, is what I'm hearing?" Anne laughs.

"Pretty much," Rose admits with her own laugh. "He can't bake, does that count? You know how I feel about dessert: it's the most important meal of the day!"

"He hasn't made you any desserts during all these feasts he prepares? No fancy cakes or eclairs or some other swanky French dessert?"

"Nope."

"Boot him. That's unacceptable."

"It's okay, I brought over a bunch of cookies that my mom made," Rose says.

"Ooh, I love your mom's cookies!" Stella says. "But were there brownies?" The girls all laugh. Stella loves Isabelle Davis's brownies.

Rose is grinning from ear to ear. The only people that could have pulled her away from her happy little Ben bubble these three women sitting here. Not for the first time, she thinks about how nice it is to be home and how glad she is that she is here with her best friends.

Ben is nervous. It has been a week since the last victim was found. It felt like the killer was amping up, increasing the frequency of his kills. *Has he slowed down again? Did he realize that we are onto him? Does that mean that we* are *onto him? Maybe we're getting too close.* Ben knows that won't be enough to stop him. This guy is going to act again. Soon. He can feel it. But how can he stop it?

It is Sunday evening. Ben is lying down on the couch in his living room, staring at the laptop on his lap. Rose is sitting on the plush blue lounge chair to the right of the couch. It has become her favourite place to curl up with a book or, like today, old case files.

"Penny for your thoughts?" Rose's voice pulls Ben out of his anxiety-driven daydream. "Where does that saying even come from? A penny for your thoughts? Why would someone pay you for your opinion? And why is it that someone would pay one cent for your thoughts, but when you give your own opinion, you are giving your two cents? You would think that would cost less, since nobody asked you."

Ben has come to expect and adore these questions. Rose is full of questions. Do you think someone dug out that tunnel, or the earth collapsed and it came up naturally? Who do you think was the first person to eat curdled milk and think *hmm, this is delicious, we should call it cheese*? Why do we call a red onion red if it is clearly purple? If there is no dog in hot dogs, why do we call them hot dogs? And if there is no ham in hamburgers, why do we call them hamburgers?

"I don't think a million dollars would be enough to cover all of the thoughts in that brilliant brain of yours," Ben says.

"I'll give you a taste right now for free: I think you're thinking of the killer. You're nervous that something is going to happen soon. You want to catch him before he can hurt someone else, but you are worried that you won't." Ben is silent, scared by how accurate her thoughts are. She continues: "Either that, or you're thinking about me naked. Hard to tell." Ben can't help but laugh.

"Can't it be both?"

"Multi-tasking? Very impressive, Detective. I didn't think you had it in you."

"What is that supposed to mean?" Ben asks, sitting up.

"Oh nothing. Just that men typically are not able to do two things at once. Usually, they are thinking about work or sex. There isn't room for much else to consider, let alone considering both at the same time."

"I'm hurt," Ben feigns anguish.

"All I'm saying is that men are usually pretty simple."

"Not me."

"No?"

"Nope. I'm deep. Complex. I have layers, like Shrek." Ben pulls Rose over to sit on his lap on the couch. He brushes his fingers through her golden hair.

"I did suspect you were an ogre when I first met you."

"What? I was perfectly charming!"

"You were rude and brazen! You even had me arrested! And I'm pretty sure I caught you staring at my boobs on more than one occasion."

"I can neither confirm nor deny that any of that is accurate." He brushes a loose strand of hair off her face and lets his hand linger on the side of her face. His thumb traces her cheekbone and he pulls her face toward his. He gently brushes his lips along her jawline, making his way toward her lips. His lips barely touch hers and he holds them there, less than an inch apart. Rose moves to kiss him and he pulls back a little, teasing her.

"You know, it's not like you made the best first impression," Ben says. "First you pass out at my crime scene. Great start to any relationship. Then you come to and start trying to take over the scene, barking orders and telling me what to do."

"I thought you like being told what to do," Rose teases, taking his hand and slowly guiding it over her chest and down her stomach, stopping at the button of her jeans.

"Only in the bedroom," Ben says as he begins to undo the buttons. She guides his hands further down, underneath the denim fabric.

"What about on the living room couch?" she whispers, her breath warm in his ear.

"I think we can make an exception, just this one time."

CHAPTER 33

*T**his is my favourite part. When I'm locked in and ready to spring into action, and this guy has no idea. He is going about his day, doing errands, going home.*

I'm not really prepared for this one. I mean, I'm always prepared, to some extent. I always have a fresh pair of gloves in my car and some type of binding, like rope, duct tape, or a bungee cord. It's easy to keep an ample supply of those, since they're so handy. I could be using them for any other purpose, like cleaning, working on the car, painting, gardening, all that.

I just happened to be out doing my own errands, minding my own business, and then I saw him. He was perfect. I tried to ignore him. I walked right by him and even left the store to remove the temptation. But then he walked right up to me and got in line behind me as I waited for my coffee at Starbucks. And that was it. I knew it had to happen. I knew I had to have him.

I started chatting him up in line, talking about coffee. We declared our addictions to caffeine. We laughed at people who ordered fancy drinks, like a half-caf, no foam, no whip latte with oat milk and a sprinkle of cinnamon. Just get a black coffee, like a normal human being! We were enjoying ourselves. He laughed at my jokes. He was nice.

I invited him to sit and drink our coffees together. He agreed. Again? Seriously? People need to be way more wary of the strangers they meet. We spent the next hour chatting and shopping together. I was hoping he would want to continue our time together, but after a while he said he had to go. Well, I couldn't let that happen, right? I had plans for us. For him.

I tried to get him to invite me to join him, but he said he was going to meet up with a friend. I asked if I could join him, but he refused. He started getting jittery, slowly taking a few steps away from me. Which meant I had to get even closer to him, since he couldn't get away. We did this little dance a few times, him taking a couple steps away from me, me taking a couple steps closer to him. He looked like he was about to call security so I backed away. I told him it was nice to meet him and that I was hoping maybe I'd run into him again.

Which I did, of course.

I let him finish up his errands and then head toward the exit of the mall. I stayed a safe distance behind him, I couldn't let him see me. I watched him make his way across the parking lot, heading towards the bus station just east of the mall. I continued walking in his direction. Head down, I reminded myself. He can't see you. No one can see you.

Now I'm closing in on him. He doesn't even look around. What an idiot. You would think someone would know they were being followed. She did. I could tell that she sensed my presence. But of course she couldn't see me. Not this dummy, though. He was too focused on his plans, meeting up with his friend. Although I'm not convinced he actually had plans. Maybe he was just trying to get away from me? That pissed me off. If he did have plans, he won't be making it to them.

In fact, he won't be making any plans ever again.

The anticipation is almost killing me now. I start to feel a rousing in my pants. This guy has no idea what's about to happen, but I do. And this thought, this knowledge that I hold the power over him, that

I get to determine whether he lives or dies, is thrilling. It's exhilarating. It's a drug. No, it's better than a drug.

There is a quiet, shaded area at the southeast corner of the parking lot, which he has to walk through to get to the bus. It's perfect. I pick up my pace and catch up to him. Just as he is about to exit the parking lot area, I call out his name. He turns around, shocked to see me. I am already wearing my gloves. But before he can say a word, I swing back my arm, weapon in hand, and force it down on him with all of my strength. I can hear the crack of bone shattering as the weapon connects with his head. He collapses to the asphalt. Quick and easy. I am smarter than him. I am stronger than him. He is weak. And now he is mine.

CHAPTER 34

"The mall?" Rose asks, in shock.

"The mall," Ben confirms. They had been cuddling in his bed, covered in a post-coital sweat, when Ben got the call about another victim. He had asked to be notified of any homicides involving multiple stab wounds and sexual assault. They quickly throw on clothes and jump in the car and are racing toward the mall to get a look at the crime scene.

"Do you really think this is our guy? The past victims have always been found in their bedroom. How do we know it's the same killer?"

"We don't. But it's worth going to check this out."

"Okay," Rose agrees. "If it is the same killer, then he's changing his pattern again. Has something changed? Is he trying to throw us off his scent?"

"I don't know. If it is our guy, this can't be good."

They sit in silence the rest of the way to the mall.

They arrive at Roncey Mall, just east of the trendy hipster Roncesvalles area, to see at least half a dozen police cars and an ambulance parked at the far southeast corner of the parking lot. The police cars' lights are flashing but the ambulance has its lights turned off. It must have sped over hoping to take the victim to the hospital, only to discover it was too late. Ben notes how fortunate they are that it isn't raining, which could wash away pertinent forensic evidence.

Ben uses his ID badge to push his way through the crowds beginning to form and past the police cordon. Rose is right on his heels, and she feels an intense wave of nausea when she sees the crime scene. The victim is lying on the cold asphalt. The police have set up bright lamps to illuminate an otherwise dark, abandoned corner of the parking lot. Other than the victim, there is nothing but random pieces of trash, left by shoppers who were too lazy to clean up after themselves. From where Rose is standing, she cannot see any potential weapons nearby, no baseball bat or tennis racquet.

She is not convinced that this is their killer. Ben is.

"He's escalating," Ben says simply. The scene is horrifying. Even from ten feet away, the first thing Rose sees is a pair of eyes, frozen and unstaring, yet looking right at her. The eyes show a mix of sheer terror and great pain. Even without seeing the rest of the body up close, she could tell that this murder was the most horrific one yet.

The eyes belong to a body that is lying in an unnatural position. The victim is lying on his stomach, his head is turned to the left, facing the mall. His neck is turned past ninety degrees. He has cuts and bruises all over his face, with blood pouring from his nose and mouth. He is naked from the waist down. The victim's legs are spread at a wide angle, his right leg bent and almost parallel to his waist. His hip must have been broken in order to get to this angle. His arms are tied behind his back. So far, all this killer's previous victims have been found restrained in a hogtied position, or they were released but the body still showed evidence of both arms and legs being tied back. This victim is different.

His legs were never bound, rather they were pushed upward at an agonizing angle. Restraining a man of this size without tying his legs requires great strength, indicating the killer is quite strong.

The victim has been stabbed numerous times. Rose can see blood pouring from multiple different entry points of his body, forming a pool around him. She turns her attention to the right of the body, where she can see something shiny, covered in blood. She takes a step closer and moans, "Oh god." Ben is right. It's him. Continuing with what appears to be the killer's obsession with sports paraphernalia, the shiny object Rose notices is a golf club.

"A kid's," Ben says. Rose looks over at him questioningly, and he elaborates. "The golf club. It's a kid's club. Look at it, it's smaller than an average club. Looks like a thirty-two inch nine iron."

"Why would he use a kid's golf club?"

"Beats me," Ben mutters. "Does this guy have kids?" Rose wonders aloud. The profile they have spent weeks building is challenged. They now have to consider the fact that he may not be an unattached gay man who just plays video games all day, but rather a father. Maybe it was the kid who was playing video games? Or was their killer a child? That can't be possible, given the strength required to commit these acts. But maybe a teenager could...

"Let's move away from the latent homosexuality/homophobia theory. What is the killer's motive? Why is he doing this? What drives him?" Ben asks aloud.

"Does there have to be a reason? Maybe the guy's just a total psychopath," Rose suggests.

"No, psychopaths don't usually have this type of strategic pattern. Our guy is doing this for a reason. He is choosing these victims for a reason. He's also escalating the violence and aggression and shortening the amount of time between kills. Something is triggering him. Maybe someone?"

"The investigation? Maybe he realizes that we're onto him? That we have noticed the pattern, that we are connecting him to all the previous murders?"

"Maybe. There's also a struggle for power here. The ropes indicate he likes to be in control. Maybe he is otherwise a submissive person? And these murders are his chance to take control, to be the dominant one. Someone who on the outside appears normal and nice, but has a deep, dark inner urge to dominate, to control, and to hurt. He gets to choose whether his victim ends up alive or dead. He's probably chasing that power, that adrenaline high, of being in control."

"So we're looking for someone submissive and weak?"

"Maybe. Or maybe the opposite. I don't know. We're looking for someone who feels the need to dominate and overpower people. I bet he has been the victim of an abuse like this. Maybe he was sexually assaulted as a child. Or he saw someone, maybe a family member, be assaulted. And now he is living out his childhood trauma, but on the opposite end. Maybe he thinks this is what makes him 'masculine' and 'powerful.'"

"Aside from that archaic and patriarchal description of masculinity, you might be right. Do you think he was assaulted by sports equipment? Do you think that's why the victims have been assaulted with a tennis racquet, a baseball bat, a golf club, and other sports objects?"

"Maybe. It appears too much of a coincidence to be just a weapon of convenience. Unless the guy just happens to be a total sports freak and always happens to have equipment on hand. But what are the chances of that?"

Ben sees Officer McAllister walking toward him. "Fill me in, Officer," Ben requests.

"The victim was discovered by a homeless man rummaging through the mall's trash bins, trying to scrounge up food. He's over there with a colleague of mine, who is taking his statement. He seems pretty shaken by what he saw, so I don't see any reason to consider him a suspect. Although you never know, which is why my guy is talking to him. The guy is also clearly intoxicated, slurring his words. We're doing our best with him."

"What can you tell me about the victim?" Ben asks.

"Name's Christopher Pattinson," McAllister says. "Twenty-four years old. Found his ID and his wallet with all the money still in it, so we don't think it was a robbery gone wrong. Cause of death is knife to the heart. The medical examiner will confirm whether the rest of the stab marks are pre- or post-mortem, but I suspect they were pre. This guy must be a whacko. He tortured this kid for a long time."

"Defensive wounds?"

"None that we can see so far, but we'll have the M.E. take a look."

"I wouldn't hold your breath. This guy is strong. None of his previous vics showed any signs of self-defence," Ben says.

Rose can hear Ben and McAllister discussing the investigation, but she can't focus on their words. Once again, she has this weird feeling that she is being watched. This has been happening a lot to her lately. She keeps getting the eerie feeling of being stalked. This case is getting to her. She just keeps staring at the victim in front of her and the horrifying image of the child-sized golf club a few feet away. It was impossible to conceive that this animal, who destroyed her life, could be a father. *The father of a lucky kid*, Rose thinks. *Those are nice golf clubs.*

"He has money," Rose blurts out. Ben and McAllister stop mid-conversation and look over at her. She continues: "Golf is an expensive sport. The clubs, the clothes, the balls, the membership. If this guy is buying golf clubs for a kid, then he must have money. My brother golfs and likes to show off how much money it costs. His son, Logan, even asked for a set of golf clubs for his birthday next month, and they are not cheap. Plus, there's a wad of cash in the victim's wallet, which the killer could have easily taken." Rose pauses, as this reality hits her. "This guy has the means and the resources to not only commit horrible crimes, but to get away with them. Even if we catch him, he'll probably get the most expensive lawyer and somehow get off scot-free."

"One step at a time, Rose," Ben tries to soothe her nerves. "That's why we're here. We will build a solid case so that no lawyer, no matter how good they think they are, can get an acquittal."

She does not answer. She knows that it doesn't matter how strong a case is. With enough money, you can get away with murder.

Rose and Ben head inside the mall, which is closed off and considered part of the crime scene. They head in the direction of Albatross Golf, assuming the golf club came from there. The manager of the store has been called in for questioning and Ben is eager to get started. There is also a general sports store, Dave's Sporting Goods, on the other side of the mall, and Rose overhears Ben direct some of the other officers to talk to the store manager there. Another group of officers is on their way to speak to the security desk and try to get video footage of the mall, focusing specifically on the two sports stores, and the parking lot.

Ben is interviewing the store manager and asking about the customers from that afternoon. "We're looking for a man, tall, at least six feet, medium build. Brown hair. Do you recall anyone fitting that description in the store yesterday?"

"Officer, you just described seventy-five percent of our customers. Was there a tall guy with brown hair in the store yesterday? Yeah, there was. In fact, there were tons."

"Sir, I would like to remind you that this is a homicide investigation, and you should watch your tone with me," Ben says, clearly getting agitated. "Can you figure out who a certain club was sold to? Based on thr serial number or something?"

"We can tell you all the people who have purchased that kind of club, but we can't track down a single golf club to a specific customer. But do you know how many golf clubs we sell every day?"

"A lot?"

"Yeah, a lot. Look," the manager says, "I'm sorry I can't be more helpful. But unless you have more information or details, I have nothing to offer you."

Ben, clearly frustrated, starts to respond, but stops as he hears a crackly on his radio. "Detective Cooper, get over to the security desk immediately. We have video footage." Ben looks at the store manager and says, "We're not done here, don't leave." Then he grabs Rose's hand and they start racing toward the security desk.

"We don't have footage of him in the mall, too big and too many customers," the officer who had been reviewing the footage explains. "We quickly took a look around the various sports stores, Albatross Golf, Dave's Sporting Goods, what have you, but pretty much every customer was a tall white guy with brown hair. So instead, we focused on the parking lot footage to see if we could find him approaching the victim or even catch him in the act." The officer pauses and can't seem to find the words to continue.

"And?" Ben urges, impatiently.

"We see him approaching the victim."

"You got him!" Rose cries.

"Yes and no," the officer responds. "We have footage of him in the parking lot, but you can't see his face. It's dark and he's far away. We weren't even sure this was our guy, and not just some random stranger talking to another man, until … well, just watch for yourself."

The video is long. Just under fifty minutes in total. At times they speed up and watch it on fast forward because it is too repulsive to watch in real time. Rose has never seen anything so horrific in her life. The killer walks right up to the victim and immediately whacks him in the side of his head. She can see the blood begin to pour from the wound as the victim's body collapses to the ground, unconscious.

Once on the ground, the killer ties the victim's arms behind his back then rolls the body over, so he is facing up. For a moment, the killer just stands there, staring at the victim. Rose gets the sense that he is trying to take it all in, as if he is trying to savour the moment. She shudders. Then she sees the killer reach into the set of golf clubs he is holding and takes out the driver. The killer assumes a golfer's stance, as if he is about to tee off, then in one quick smooth movement, he pulls back and swings with all of his might at the victim's knee, shattering it immediately into pieces. The pain wakes the victim, and his body jerks involuntarily. The killer quickly moves to the victim's other side and does the same thing to his other knee, immediately immobilizing the victim.

Rose can see the victim writhing in pain. She is sure he is begging the killer to stop, to leave him alone. But the killer doesn't. He keeps at it, beating this man to a bloody pulp. He swings the golf club over and over, hitting the victim in multiple areas of his body, torturing him. He takes a final swing at the victim's face, which whips to the right, facing the camera directly. Rose watches the grainy footage. She can't see the guy's face clearly, since it is so far away, but she knows what it looks like: defeated, broken and bloody, pleading for mercy.

The killer steps back and throws down the golf club, and if Rose had not seen the crime scene in person, she would have thought he was done. But she knows better.

The killer pulls out a knife from his pocket and menacingly walks toward the victim. He is enjoying himself, Rose can tell. He sits on the victim's chest and smoothly slides the knife across the victim's face. Blood begins to seep out of the incision. The killer then gets to work, savagely slashing the victim, a combination of stabbing and slicing. He is wreaking havoc on this man's body, shredding it. He is enjoying this. He is having fun.

Just when Rose thinks things could not get more disturbing, they do. The killer rolls the victim over and pulls his pants off, then his underwear. The killer switches his weapon of choice back to the golf club, this time the nine iron, and he swings at the victim's legs, spreading them apart and up toward his chest. At this point it's not clear whether the victim is even conscious anymore. The killer bends down and admires his handiwork. He then pulls back the club and jams it into the victim's asshole. As he begins sodomizing the victim with the club, Rose runs out of the security office and throws up into a garbage bin. She has never seen anything so disgusting in her life.

When she returns, still shaken and nauseous, she sees that the killer is standing up and cleaning himself off. He must have picked up his knife again after traumatizing this man's body, because there is a knife protruding from the left side of the victim's back. The killer stripped off his shirt and pants, down to just underwear and a t-shirt, and folded his clothes up into a bag. He then took the time to get a cloth and wipe down the golf club, making sure there were no prints left at the scene. He stands over the body one final moment, picks up his knife and bag of clothes, and walks away.

CHAPTER 35

Look at them, terrified. Of me. I can see it in their faces. I watch them walk into the detective's house. She seems upset. She is shaking. I bet they are thinking of me. What I've done, and what I will do next. Who will be my next victim? How many bodies are lying around for them to discover?

It's a game. A treasure hunt. We used to love going on treasure hunts when we were younger. Dad would hide a bunch of toys throughout the backyard and give us a map with clues. We would run around the yard digging them up, squealing when we found something, excitedly making our way toward the big prize, where "X" marked the spot on the map. It felt like we were getting a new toy every time, even though they were just things Dad grabbed from our rooms. Mom hated it, she said we were ruining her garden. Which, of course, made us laugh even harder. I remember the excitement when we found the final big prize, eyes lighting up, dirt flying everywhere as we dug out the buried treasure.

Should I start burying my targets? That would throw everyone for a loop. But nah, it's too much work. Where would I do it? How would I get the bodies there? And I do not feel like shoveling and getting dirty, I'm not six years old anymore.

No, I have a good system in place. No point messing it up. Although I do love the idea of messing with that detective's head. Can you imagine? I watch him now. They are sitting on his patio, holding hands, drinking beers. They are quieter tonight than they normally are. I wonder if they sense my presence. It is exhilarating, watching someone who cannot see you. Knowing things that they don't know. I've been watching them for a while now. Laughing in The Bean, holding hands when they walk, sloppily undressing themselves and tumbling into bed, trying to forget about the outside world.

I see them stand up and start to head back inside. Once they're in and the door to the backyard is fully shut, I slowly and quietly change positions, heading to the northern side of the house, following them through the windows. They take turns changing into pajamas, brushing their teeth, washing their face. It seems so dull, so mundane. So ordinary. That's it? Are they calling it a night?

He climbs into the bed first, while she finishes getting ready for bed. He is playing on his phone, waiting for her. Playing a game? On social media? Maybe he's on Twitter, reading all the latest posts about me, the crazy theories about who I am and why I'm going on these adventures.

Finally, she comes out of the bathroom wearing a robe. She climbs into bed beside him, and gently takes his phone away. Can you believe it? If someone took my phone out of my hands while I was on it, I would be so pissed. How dare she try to control him, to tell him what to do? But you know what the craziest part is? He likes it. Seriously. He lets her do whatever she wants. Whatever happened to male dominance? I bet he likes being told what to do. He's weak.

I watch her climb on top of him, allowing the robe to slip off her shoulders, though her arms are still inside the robe. She leans down to kiss him, and they stay like that for a while. She breaks off all of a sudden and looks around. She looks out the window, straight in my direction. She can feel me there. I take a small step back to ensure my coverage, but I'm confident that I am well hidden.

The detective doesn't seem to notice because he just continues on. He sits up and pulls her hair to one side, then he starts kissing her neck. He slowly slides the robe off her back, his fingers tracing her skin. Thankfully she is distracted by him and turns away from the window, bringing her focus back to him.

I watch as she starts writhing on top of him, moving up and down. Their pace is slow at first, then quickens, then slows down again. They last a long time, close to thirty minutes. Good for him, I didn't think he had it in him. Once they finish, they collapse onto the bed. I can't see their faces, but I'm sure they are panting, exhausted from the exertion. I bet they are drifting off into slumberland now. What a nice little break for them, a short hiatus from thinking about me.

But they won't forget about me. I will make sure of it.

CHAPTER 36

You know how sometimes you can feel someone's presence in a roo without being able to see them? Rose knows she is asleep but she feels a presence in the room. She gasps as suddenly she feels the weight of a hand pressing down on her chest. She opens her eyes and sees a dark figure standing over her with a knife in his hand, shushing her to be quiet. She tries to scream, but no sound is coming out. All she can hear is a whoosh of soundless breath trying to escape her. The hand on her chest begins to press down harder and the figure slowly lowers his other hand holding the knife toward her. Petrified, Rose tries to scream again, and this time lets out a piercing shriek.

"Rose!" She is still screaming when she realizes that she is sitting up in bed, wrapped in the protective arms of Detective Ben Cooper. She begins sobbing, and Ben just sits there holding her, caressing her hair. He doesn't ask her what happened, he doesn't try to stop her crying; he is just there.

Rose's sobs subside and Ben guides her in some deep breathing exercises. She is beginning to calm down, but she is still deeply disturbed from her nightmare. She can't seem to shake the feeling that there really was someone in the room with them, that it was not a dream. It was so real. She can still feel the weight of the hand on her chest.

Unable to fall back asleep, Rose gets up just after 5:00 a.m. and goes for a run. She needs to clear her head. As she hears her feet pounding on the pavement, and she listens to Tupac's "Changes," she thinks about the killer. They need to start from scratch, look at all the victims from a new angle. What if this isn't a single, creepy man who is committing these gruesome crimes? What if he's a charming family man? Someone you would say hi to on the street, someone friendly, unassuming? Maybe the connection isn't video games, or homosexuality, or any of the other ideas they have been focusing on. But that begs the question, what is the connection between all these victims, and why is this man hurting them?

And more importantly, who is next?

Rose also can't help but wonder: if they were so wrong about his profile, what else are they wrong about? Can she even trust her own judgment anymore?

This thought haunts her as she nears Ben's house and starts to slow down her pace. Again she still feels the unwelcome presence of someone watching her. She is terrified. She quietly runs into the house and sees Ben lying in bed. Still in her sweaty workout clothes, Rose climbs back into bed and clings to him, hoping that the warmth of his body pressed against her, the sound of his deep, sleepy breathing, and the feel of his heartbeat where her head rests on his chest will help ease her terror.

"How are your nightmares?" Dr. Hill asks over video chat. This is just the second time they have spoken since her return home, and Rose has a lot to fill her in on.

"Still happening," Rose answers.

"Are they increasing in frequency? Intensity?"

"Yes. All of the above. Almost every night now. And they're getting super-realistic." She describes last night's dream. She still is feeling the effect of it, the feeling of a presence in the room, the weight of a hand on her chest.

"Your anxiety is increasing."

"Yeah, because there is a killer on the loose."

"Are you worried he's going to kill you?"

"I'm worried he's going to kill again, period. It doesn't matter who."

"That's understandable. But it's not your job to find this person."

"Not my job? What is that supposed to mean?"

"Exactly that, it is not your job. You are not a police officer. You are not responsible for finding killers."

"I am Crown counsel, I'm responsible for putting killers away," Rose says determinedly.

"Yes, once they're caught."

"Sure. But sometimes I help with the investigation. Think of the Lewis case. I helped."

"Helped. But it wasn't your job. Rose, you are not responsible for doing everyone else's job. Sometimes you can trust other people to do their job."

"I do trust people, but that doesn't mean I can't be involved in the investigation."

"Be involved, as in helping? Or as in putting yourself in dangerous situations, to the neglect of your own safety and wellbeing, to find a serial killer?"

Rose thinks about her little jaunt at VR Gaming's office and doesn't answer.

"Because you can do it better?" Dr. Hill prods.

"Not better, per se. I just I need to do this. I need to find this killer."

"You need the killer caught? Or you need to catch him?"

"Is there a difference?"

"Yes, I would say there is. You want the serial killer to be found and stopped, but more than that, you want to be the one who solves this. And why is that?"

"I don't know."

"Is it because of Will? Because you think this serial killer you are hunting is the one who killed Will?"

"I guess. What other reason could there be?"

"You tell me."

Again, Rose is silent and does not respond.

"Rose, you are taking too much on, expecting too much of yourself. Just like you always do. Don't put this on yourself. Don't torture yourself, pushing yourself to do something that you do not need to do. I know you, Rose. You focus on your files, work to get a conviction against every single killer that comes across your jurisdiction. But you don't have to take on everything. You don't have to be the one fixing everything and solving all crimes. You have nothing to prove."

"I don't take on everything," Rose says defensively.

"Really?" Dr. Hill asks, raising an eyebrow.

"Fine. Point taken. But I'm not doing it alone. I'm working with this guy, Detective Cooper. And I trust him. I know he's working hard and is as invested in finding this serial killer as I am."

"That's good. I'm proud of you. You asked for help when you knew you needed it."

"Well, I didn't ask for help, so much as force myself into the investigation. In fact, Ben arrested me for barging in on a crime scene, and …"

"Arrested? Rose! You need to stop putting yourself into dangerous situations!"

"It's fine, it's all been sorted out. My brother bailed me out and I have forgiven Ben."

"Ben. You've called him Ben twice now. You're on a first name basis with this detective?"

Rose instinctively blushes and smiles. "I guess you could say this is a little bit more than a professional relationship." She describes Ben a little more and Dr. Hill can tell that she is clearly gushing over him.

"I am so happy for you Rose."

"Turns out you were right about coming home. It has been good for me."

"Yeah, I get it right every once in a while, don't I?" Dr. Hill smiles. "Our time is almost up. I want to conclude by telling you how proud I am of all the progress you have made on this trip. Just being able to identify and label some of these feelings and anxieties is the first step to being able to cope with them. But I want you to keep working on those affirmations we talked about a little while ago. 'I am strong. I am worthy. I am enough. I am loved, just as I am.' I want you to repeat these affirmations to yourself every day."

"Thanks, Dr. Hill. I'll try. I am enough. I am loved, just as I am. It sounds like a self-help book. You should write one! Teaching us all to love ourselves, just as we are. You can call it "Just As You Are.""

"Great idea, I'll start working on it now," Dr. Hill laughs. "I look forward to catching up with you again in a couple weeks."

Later that morning, Rose goes home to her parents' house to grab some fresh clothes and relax a little until Ben is done work that afternoon. It is Wednesday at 11:30 a.m., and she is surprised to see her mother's car on the driveway. She works in communications at a pharmaceutical company and is usually at her office all day.

"Mom?" she calls as she enters the house.

"In the kitchen!" Isabelle calls back.

Rose drops her purse and enters the kitchen. Her mother is still wearing navy suit pants and a white silk blouse with a tie around the neck. Her navy suit jacket is draped around one of the kitchen chairs. Isabelle has her head in the fridge and is staring at the contents.

"Hi Mom, what are you doing home in the middle of the day?"

Isabelle closes the fridge, still empty-handed, and turns to Rose. "Hi honey, I had a meeting nearby, so I thought I'd come home to have lunch first. It's nice to see you here, I feel like we haven't seen you in days."

"Yeah, sorry about that, Mom."

"Don't be sorry, sweetheart. I just want you to be happy," Isabelle says. And Rose knows that she means it.

"Thanks, Mom."

"Can I make you some lunch?"

"That would be great, thanks."

"Any requests? I was just looking through the fridge searching for inspiration."

"How about one of your famous Isabelle BELTs?" Rose suggests.

"Coming right up," Isabelle says with a smile. This used to be Rose's favourite lunch; her mom made it for her all the time. It's a take on a BLT, but with a fried egg thrown into the sandwich. Rose loves taking the first bite and piercing the runny yellow yolk, which drips down her fingers and onto the plate. She watches the familiar movements of her mom fussing about in the kitchen and preparing lunch for them. It feels comforting. It feels like home.

"When can I meet this detective of yours?" Isabelle asks, a poor attempt at sounding casual.

"He's not *my* detective, Mom," Rose says, "but I will speak to him and see if he wants to come over one day."

"How about tonight?"

"Tonight?"

"Yes, tonight. Why don't you invite him over for dinner? What does he like? I'm thinking Caesar salad, miso black cod, and smashed potatoes."

"Sure, that sounds good. I'll call him later to confirm. But please try not to embarrass me too much in front of him."

"I would never," Isabelle says defensively. Then she adds with a wry smile, "I'll leave that to Tyler."

The smell of bacon wafts out of the pan and fills the room. Rose helps her mom by slicing the tomato. "This is going to end up being one of those wild family dinners, isn't it?" she asks, pretending to be annoyed but secretly excited for Ben to meet her brother and the rest of the bunch.

"Oh yes, most definitely. What would Ben prefer, pecan pie, coffee cake, or brownies?" Before Rose even has a chance to respond, Isabelle says "Never mind, I'll make all three."

Rose laughs. This is so typical of her mother. Always taking on too much, never asking for help, and going overboard. It occurs to Rose that this is something she does, too: she takes on too much and refuses to ask for help. And then by putting the pressure on herself, she ends up feeling overwhelmed and stressed, and resentful of other people who do not have the same weight on their shoulders.

Rose says as much to her mother now. "It's like my therapist was saying to me this morning, you don't have to do everything. Let me help."

"Nonsense, sweetheart, this is my job as your mother. To care for you, to feed you, to love you." She takes the bacon out of the pan and uses the grease from the meat to fry up the eggs.

"Mom, you have spent your life caring for us and loving us. And we are so grateful for this, don't get me wrong. But what about you? How do you care for *yourself*? Dad's great and all, but he's not the type of person to smother you in gifts and praise and attention."

"I care for myself," Isabelle answers. "Don't worry about me, honey, I'm fine."

"I know you are, Mom. But isn't it hard, always being fine? Never needing help? Always putting things on yourself? I find it so hard. I'm trying to work on that in therapy."

"I hope you don't talk about therapy like this with your new boyfriend."

"Actually, I do," Rose says, a little defensively. "Why wouldn't I?"

"Because that's your private business. You shouldn't air your dirty laundry. Men don't need to know about all of that." Isabelle finishes plating their sandwiches and carries their plates to the table.

"Mom, it's a part of me. I *am* my dirty laundry. I am trying so hard to accept that side of me. I have clinical depression and anxiety. Some days, I am really sad. Some days, I'm happy. Some days, I am so worried about everything, I question my career, my family, my weight, my intelligence, everything. My anxiety can drive me to the point of insanity. I am not perfect. But I'm learning that that's okay, I'm still loveable."

"Of course you're loveable, Rose. You are a wonderful person. I just want you to be happy. I hate to think that you are sad. I'm sure it's all my fault somehow, isn't that what all therapists say? Blame it on the mother?"

"No, we don't just blame everything on you. And I know you just want me to be happy. But you need to accept that sometimes I'm not. And that's not because of you. I have very low moments sometimes, triggered by my anxiety and depression. But it's not your fault. It's no one's fault. This is a chemical imbalance in my brain, something that has been in our family for years. You tried to hide it from me, but I remember Grandma being depressed a lot when I was younger," Rose says, referring to Cohen's mother.

"You knew? Isabelle asks, surprised. "How?"

"It wasn't the best kept secret, Mom. I have eyes, I could see. Also, one time when I was thirteen or so I was at their house looking for Grandma's slippers, which she had asked me to get, and I found a box of things from one of her stays at a mental health clinic."

Isabelle is silent for a moment. "Did you see the Javex pig?"

"Oh my god, the pig!" Rose cries, laughing. "What was that? It terrified me!"

"Your grandmother did all sorts of art therapy and that was one of her projects. They used old bottles from cleaning solvents to make all sorts of animals." Isabelle laughs along.

"That's hilarious. Terrifying, but hilarious."

"I'm sorry, sweetie," Isabelle says, turning the conversation serious again. "We tried to shelter you from the pain. We tried to give you everything you could possibly have wanted. I really tried my best raising you and your brother."

"You did an amazing job, Mom! You loved us so deeply, so intensely, and we really felt that love. You never wanted us to feel any pain. So we rarely did. And I know you meant well, but in the end, it put so much pressure on me to be *good*, to make you happy, to make your job of raising us easier. So I worked my butt off getting nearly perfect grades. I made friends. I played sports, until I didn't. I did everything you wanted me to do, and I tried to be the best to make you proud. And I think it worked.

"Until I realized that I am not the best. I am not the *most* beautiful person in the room, I am not the smartest or the funniest. And I have a hard time handling that. I have never really had to cope with failure. I am not equipped to do so. Which just triggers my perfectionism, this intense drive to do my best and be the best. To win every case I try."

Rose realizes that she is rambling a little and stops herself to look at her mother. She is not sure how she will respond to this. She could be hurt, as if Rose is accusing her of something. That is not her intention. Rose loves her mother so much and had a wonderful childhood. But there are effects from this childhood that have crossed over into her adulthood and her ability to cope.

Isabelle's eyes are red. "I am so sorry. I really thought I was doing my best to raise you."

"You did, Mom!" Rose says, rising to give her mother a hug. "You were an incredible mother. You still are!"

"I tried so hard. You know, I don't talk much about my own childhood, but it was very hard. We didn't have much, and my parents were constantly screaming at each other. My dad would hit my mom in front of me, and I couldn't do anything to stop him. Growing up all I wanted was to make a happy, loving home. I tried hard to make sure you kids had everything I never had. I didn't let you see the times I struggled. The times I fought with your father, or when I was sad, or stressed, or worried, or sick. I didn't want you to ever experience that type of conflict."

"I know, Mom. And you had such good intentions. The problem is, you hid your own anxiety, trying to make sure everything was perfect. You still do! You still don't want people to see any of my 'bad' sides, like my mental illness. But times have changed, Mom. It's okay to be your real self these days! People embrace flaws. People love your flaws. The flaws are what make us human."

"I accept you for all of your flaws, Rose. I just don't think you need to showcase them to the world in such a public way."

Rose sighs. She thought she was getting through to her mom, getting her to do some self-reflection and work on herself. But Rose sees that her mother is limited in acknowledging her own flaws and past mistakes. Maybe it's generational, maybe it's personal to Isabelle. Rose understands that her mother will never truly understand her. But she does her best and she tries, and she loves Rose unconditionally. That is all that she can really ask for right now.

"Okay Mom," Rose says and puts her arm around her mother. "Let's eat. Our BELTs are getting cold." Isabelle changes the subject to what Rose will be wearing that night for dinner with Ben. She suggests a dress. And lipstick, of course.

Rose decides to stay at her parents' house until dinner. She calls Ben and invites him to join, and he eagerly accepts the invitation.

Rose is nervous. She has not shared her family dinner routine with another person since Will. How will Ben fit in with her family? Will they like him? Will he like them? She is most nervous for Ben to meet Tyler. She idolizes her big brother and it would be devastating for her if the two men do not get along.

She spends the afternoon practicing self-care the best way she knows how. She does an online yoga class, then takes a long hot bath. She even takes a nap around 4:00 p.m. At times she feels twinges of guilt that she is not doing more to help the investigation today. But she keeps reminding herself what Dr. Hill often tells her: you cannot give to others unless your own cup is full.

Around 6:30 p.m., Tyler, Emily and the kids show up. Rose is downstairs in the kitchen helping her mom with the potatoes. They are listening to the soundtrack from Hamilton on Broadway and singing along to the lyrics. Both Rose and Isabelle have always been huge musical theater lovers. They had been discussing going to New York to see Hamilton live. They used to go on girl trips to see Broadway shows all the time when she was a teenager.

Sloane comes running into the kitchen and throws her arms around Rose. "She's still not used to having you around. She's so happy, she talks about you nonstop at home and at school," Emily says to her.

"The feeling is mutual," Rose says, as she smiles at her sweet niece. "Now tell me about school today, missy!" Isabelle turns the music off to allow Sloane to have everyone's undivided attention.

Sloane goes into a long story, with many random and irrelevant digressions along the way, about one of her classmates losing a tooth at school. Rose watches her animated, theatrical niece and laughs.

Tyler, Logan and Cohen are all in the living room watching hockey. Of course. The four women are in the kitchen, chatting around the table while Isabelle puts the final touches on the meal. The doorbell rings.

"I'll get it!" Rose and Sloane shout at the same time. They stare at each other in a deadlock, and it feels as if time has stood still. Rose is nervous about the family meeting Ben and wants to be the one to let him in and initiate him into the family. But Sloane has made it very clear that she is the protector of her family and she insists on "vetting" Ben before allowing him into their lives. Rose starts to get up and sees Sloane rise from her chair quickly, daring her to move. Sloane is quick, much quicker than Rose. She will probably get to the door faster than Rose if they do not come to a reasonable agreement. But before she could suggest a truce, she hears the door open and Tyler's booming voice greeting Ben.

"Detective Benjamin Cooper, nice to finally meet you! So you're the guy that has been stealing all of my dear sister's time. Have you been using those handcuffs of yours to restrain her to your bed?"

"Why would he do that?" asks Logan innocently, protectively worrying that this man is hurting his beloved aunt.

"He wouldn't!" shouts Rose as she shoves Tyler aside, who laughs as he rejoins the rest of the boys on the couch in the living room. Rose greets Ben with a kiss on the cheek. He is wearing his typical jeans, this time with a collared shirt tucked in. He is also wearing his glasses, which he told Rose earlier is an attempt to look smarter and more impressive.

"You look incredible," he whispers to her as he walks inside the house. They are standing alone in the foyer, the calm before the storm. "God, your ass in those jeans. You should wear those jeans every day."

"Thank you, Detective." She does a little twirl, showing off her curves in her tight jeans.

"Let's go take a quick detour to your room," he whispers softly into her ear. She laughs and gives him another kiss, this time on the lips.

"Don't make me beg, Davis."

"We don't have time! Dinner will be ready soon."

"I can be done in three minutes."

"I wouldn't brag about that, buddy." Laughing, she wraps her arm around his elbow and escorts him into the living room where everyone is waiting. "Guys, this is Ben. Ben, this is my crazy family."

As Ben warmly shakes everyone's hand, Rose overhears Cohen whisper, "Welcome to the lion's den."

"Dad!" Rose shouts, both laughing and horrified.

"Am I wrong?" he asks, feigning innocence.

"I've been to a few circuses in my time, don't worry about me," Ben says. "I've been known to tame the lion where necessary."

"I bet he even has a whip and everything," Tyler says in a loud whisper with a sly grin. Rose punches Tyler in the arm.

"Tyler, don't embarrass your sister so early in the evening." Isabelle admonishes her son as she saunters into the room. Her hair is tied back perfectly and her clothes are spotless, despite working feverishly in the kitchen whipping up a feast for the past two hours. "Hello Benjamin, welcome to our home."

"Lovely to meet you, Mrs. Davis," Ben says. "You have a beautiful home."

Ben looks around at the elegantly decorated living room. Rose never pays much attention to it, she is used to it all, so she forgets how striking her home can be to newcomers. The walls are filled with various forms of artwork, a combination of oils, paints, and prints, both traditional and modern. The soft grey L-shaped couch is offset by a lush purple lounge chair in an unusual, architectural shape. Sitting in the middle of the furniture is a light blue leather ottoman, with an acrylic tray sitting on it, displaying a short stack of coffee table books.

Behind the grey couch is a console with framed photographs of Rose and Tyler as children, pictures from Tyler and Emily's wedding, and more recent photographs of Logan and Sloane. The centerpiece on the table is a large, beautiful ceramic and gold-plated abstract sculpture.

"Please, call me Isabelle," she says with a warm smile. "Dinner will be ready in twenty minutes, everybody. Rose, why don't you offer our guest a drink and help him get settled?"

Rose pulls Ben to the couch and they sit down as Emily hands them each a glass of wine. Ben lazily drapes his arm over Rose's shoulders as he chats with her family.

Thirty minutes later, well into their second glass of wine, they sit down to dinner. It goes surprisingly well. The initial teasing of Ben quickly turns to relentless teasing of Rose, including an embarrassing recollection of her wetting the bed when she was six.

"I don't think it's necessary to share these stories, Ben won't be interested," Rose says, desperate to change the subject.

"Oh, I think it is *very* necessary, and I am *very* interested," Ben says with a large grin. "And feel free to grab some photo albums too, I'm a visual learner, so I think it would be helpful for me to have some photographic evidence as well to support the stories."

Rose nudges Ben's ribs with her elbow. She prevents the albums from coming out, but that doesn't stop everyone from endlessly teasing her. She is a good sport about it, and everyone is laughing and regaling Ben with funny stories of their childhood. He has tears in his eyes when he hears about Pink Pussy and lets out a little snort, which makes everyone laugh even harder. Rose can see this being a regular occurrence, having Ben over for dinner. She has a good feeling about him. She looks at him and smiles, and he reaches out and squeezes her knee under the table.

What starts as innocent quickly turns naughty. Ben's hand starts slowly moving up her thigh. As everyone at the table chats and jokes, Ben's fingers are very busy, finding their way under the hem of her dress. Rose gives him a look, and he smirks at her but doesn't stop. His fingers gently trace her inner thigh, moving upwards, then stopping just short of her underwear. A calculated tease. He moves his way back down to her knee again, and Rose is mixed with a sense of relief and disappointment. But not for long. His fingers continue their wandering and gently make their way up her leg. His fingers lightly brush over her underwear as they continue back down, and she lets out an audible gasp of surprise.

Rose's face turns beet red as Ben tries to stifle his chuckling. She clears her throat. "Sorry, that was a little spicy for me."

"The cod?" Isabelle asks, incredulously. "I didn't use any spices when preparing it."

"Black pepper maybe? Yes, a bit too much pepper," Rose stammers. But then she senses her mom getting offended that the food isn't perfect, so she adds, "But it's delicious! Really, your best ever."

That seems to satisfy Isabelle and everyone at the table goes back to their conversation.

"You are bad!" Rose mouths to Ben.

"You are loud!" he mouths back. She giggles. He leans over and whispers in her ear, "Let's see how loud you can get after dinner."

Rose puts down her fork and announces, "This was great Mom. How about some dessert now? Ben needs to get back to work, he has a very busy night of work ahead of him."

"Have you warned your new boyfriend about our post-dinner battles?" Tyler asks.

"Battles?" Ben inquires.

"Not battles," Rose explains with a smile. "More like friendly competitions."

"There is nothing friendly when it comes to this family competing," Emily says to Ben in a conspiratorial tone.

"We usually play a game or two while Mom cleans up dinner, before we have dessert. You know, earning your victory makes dessert taste better," Tyler says.

"Tyler, that is not the saying! Earning it makes the *victory* taste sweeter. Not dessert!" Rose corrects him.

"Same difference!"

"I will not debate the English language with you right now. Anyway, we don't have time for a game tonight. Ben has work to do. Let's just have dessert so we can go, is that okay Mom?"

"Sorry, Rosie, I need to clean up and finish baking the desserts. Go play your little game then come back on for dessert in half an hour."

"Great!" Tyler jumps at the opening. "As our guest of honour, Detective Cooper, you can choose. I usually suggest basketball or hockey, but Rose here usually tries to get us to play some boring game like chess."

"Chess is not boring!" Rose says defensively. "It can be a brilliant, sexy game." She pauses, then: "If you're smart enough to know how to play."

"Oh no, you did NOT just go there, Miss Valedictorian!" Tyler cries. "I'm smart. I just did things other than study through school. I partied and played ball."

"Alright, break it up you two," says Ben. "Do I need to step in with the handcuffs?"

"I prefer the whip," says Rose with a wink.

"If I get to choose, then I choose basketball."

"Yes!" shouts Tyler, as Rose mutters "traitor."

"Hey, I gotta side with the family members! I'm still trying to get them to like me. I already know I've got you fooled." Ben reaches for her hand and kisses it, while looking into her eyes romantically. Rose swoons. Then, in typical Ben fashion, his eyes narrow and he sticks out his tongue, giving her hand a huge, sloppy lick. "Let's go, bedwetter!" and he slaps her ass as he walks by her, headed toward the basketball net in the back.

That night, after a particularly vigorous session of lovemaking, Rose and Ben lie on their sides, wrapped in their sweaty sheets, facing each other. Ben is lazily tracing a finger over her arm and back. Rose looks like she is deep in thought.

"What are you thinking about?"

"Eggs."

"Eggs?"

"Yes, eggs. In *Beauty and the Beast*. You know the opening number, where a woman screams desperately that she needs six eggs, and someone responds that's too expensive?"

"No, but sure, I believe you. What about it?"

"I was wondering why eggs are so expensive. They live in a provincial town in France, which, as a side note, is yet another example of a movie that takes place in France but no one seems to have a French accent, other than a candelabra. Anyway, you would think there would be plenty of chickens around to provide eggs. So why is there an egg shortage?

"And it just occurred to me. Gaston! In the song "Gaston", he talks about eating four dozen eggs when he was a child, and now as an adult he eats five dozen eggs. That's a lot of eggs! No wonder this poor woman is desperate. She just wants to make an omelet for her children, and Gaston is out there chugging eggs like it's his business."

Ben looks at her with an amused grin. "That's a lot of eggs."

"Right?! Why, what are you thinking about?"

"I was thinking about the fact that your cheeks get really red during sex."

"What?" Rose laughs. "No they don't!"

"Yes, they totally do! They're so red right now."

"Now they're probably red from embarrassment!"

"You have nothing to be embarrassed about. You are the most beautiful woman I have ever seen."

"Even when I'm all sweaty and red-cheeked?" she asks.

"Especially when you're all sweaty and red-cheeked! Especially when I'm the reason for those cheeks," Ben says, playfully attacking her cheeks with quick, wet kisses.

"Tell me about your family," Rose blurts out of nowhere.

"My family? They're amazing. And almost as crazy as your family."

"Wow, that's saying something!"

"I know, right? And I love them to death. My parents are retired and living in Monkland Village in Montreal."

"I didn't know you're from Montreal. So do you speak French?"

"Oui, madame."

"Ooh la la, how fancy! Do you speak to your parents often?"

"I call them at least once a week. And I try to visit every few months."

"You have sisters, right?"

"Four of them. All older than me, I was the surprise baby that came 7 years after my youngest sister was born. I remember asking my mom if I was a mistake, and she told me that I was an accident, but not a mistake."

"Four girls. Tell me you had more than one bathroom growing up. I cannot imagine four teenagers fighting to get ready every day."

Ben laughed. "We had two bathrooms, one for our parents and one for us. It was a complete disaster. It felt like the Hunger Games, everyone trying to get rid of the other to take their turn."

"Sounds deadly."

"They only got violent a few times," he laughs. "But we're all still close. They may be very different from each other, but they are all strong, independent women. And they are very protective of their baby brother."

"Do you think they would like me?"

"They would adore you. Who wouldn't?"

Rose smiles at him. His wavy hair is falling into his stunning eyes.

Then Ben surprises both of them and he props himself up on an elbow. Nervously, he tells her he really likes her and is worried she doesn't feel the same way. Rose responds by propping herself up to meet his him and asks, "Are you joking me?"

Ben chuckles, remembering how cute it is that she says that. He says, "No, I'm not joking you. You are this incredible woman: strong, smart, funny, gorgeous, and stubborn as all hell! I can't seem to figure out what you're doing with a guy like me."

"I feel the same way," Rose says. "I worry that you're not actually interested in me, that you're just bored and I'm an easy solution to your boredom."

"Let me start, Ms. Davis, by telling you that you are *not* easy! It took me two weeks to get you to be in the same room as me, let alone kiss me!"

Rose laughs a little and admits, "True, I did make you work for it."

"You sure did. But just like your brother said, earning your victory makes it taste even sweeter."

"He was talking about dessert!"

"The theory applies here, too."

"Still. What if you're just sleeping with me out of pity? Since my fiancé was the first of the killer's victims. Maybe you're keeping me around for information? Maybe you think I'm a suspect? Maybe you …"

Ben interrupted her and said, "Maybe you're just an incredible person that I enjoy being with?"

"Maybe. Hopefully."

"I promise not to go kissing other girls tonight, like Matthew Greenberg."

Rose laughs. "How do you remember that story?"

"I love your stories. I want to learn everything about you."

She pauses. "I like you." She feels both physically and emotionally naked, completely vulnerable for the first time in years.

"I like you, too."

"I mean, I really like you. I like everything about you. Which I don't really understand, because you're stubborn and a smartass and you drive me crazy."

"Thank you for that, I do my best," he teases, before he softens his tone again. "It looks like we're both struggling with the same insecurity here. So why don't you and I agree to accept that we are both amazing and sexy individuals who are worthy of all the love and attention in the world? And we don't question each other's interest again. Can we do that?"

"I think we can do that," Rose says, and gives him a gentle kiss on his nose.

"We are both amazing. Well, maybe I'm a little more amazing than you."

"It is not a competition, Detective."

"Absolutely not. Because if it were, I would win."

"No way, I'm more amazing than you."

"If you insist," he sighs. "But I have a better voice," Ben teases.

"In your dreams, Cooper. I'm so good, I'm basically Beyoncé."

"Does that make me Jay-Z?"

"Well, you do have ninety-nine problems ... but a bitch ain't one of them." Laughing, Rose gets up to start putting pajamas on.

"Where do you think you're going, Beyoncé?" Ben jumps up and grabs Rose by the arm, turning her to face him. He lifts her off the ground, and she throws her arms around his neck and wraps her legs around his waist. She says, "To put on my PJs."

"You are not putting a single thing on." Ben kisses her deeply. Rose kisses back, slipping her tongue into his mouth, feeling her desire for him grow. She moves her hands to run her fingers through his tousled hair. Ben moves his hands lower down her back and grabs her ass. He falls back onto the bed, holding her tight on top of him. Rose pulls back and sits up straight, straddling his naked groin.

"I don't think you're ready for this jelly," Rose sings, writhing on top of him.

"I am very ready, my bootylicious beauty," Ben says in a breathy voice as he thrusts into her.

CHAPTER 37

"We got him," Ben tells Rose as he throws on jeans and a hooded sweatshirt over a grungy T-shirt. With no time to put in contacts, Ben puts on his glasses and quickly grabs his phone and wallet. They had been cuddling in bed, blissfully unaware of their surroundings, when Ben got the call.

"What?" Rose cries.

"We got our killer," Ben answers excitedly. "Forensics ran a slew of tests at the Pattinson crime scene at the mall. They found a partial print on the golf club and ran it through all their databases. That was Officer McAllister, he got a hit on the sex offender registry. I'm heading into the station, stay here. I'll call you as soon as I can." Ben throws on his leather jacket, kisses Rose goodbye, and runs out the door.

His mind races as he drives to work. Is it possible? Did they just get lucky? A part of him worries that it's too easy, too convenient. The killer has never left a print before, did he really just get sloppy? As a million questions float in his mind, Ben pulls into the parking lot of the police station and races up the steps. McAllister is in one of the interrogation rooms, which has been converted into an epicenter of sorts for this case. They call it the war room. Files, photos, and papers are strewn everywhere, with random words written on a whiteboard, nouns and adjectives thrown together in an attempt to create a meaningful profile: homosexual, stabbings, crime of passion, aggression, sports equipment. In the centre is a relatively new word, with a large question mark beside it: kids?

McAllister is sitting at the long table, switching his gaze back and forth from his laptop computer to the files splayed out before him. He is using his finger on the computer to keep track of his place on the screen. He looks like he hasn't slept in days. In fact, he hasn't.

"Tell me everything," Ben demands. McAllister immediately fills him in. "I heard right before I called you. They ran the partial print found on the kids' club through every database we could think of: Interpol's AFIS, CODIS, IRCC, and of course the Provincial and National Sex Offender Registry Databases. We got a hit this morning on the RCMP Sex Offender Registry. His name is Stuart Cassidy. History of sexual assault, aggravated sexual assault, and procuring sexual activity."

"Can we tie him to any of the other victims?"

"We're checking now, cross referencing old files, trying to see if we had any other prints or partial prints. Maybe Cassidy wasn't registered yet when they happened, or maybe some cop screwed up and didn't properly run the prints."

"Anything so far?"

"Waiting to hear back from my guys. In the meantime, I'm checking his incarceration dates. This guy has been in and out of the pen more often than a heroin addict in and out of rehab. He just got out again after doing two years for aggravated sexual assault."

"When did he get out?"

"March 28," McAllister answers.

"That lines up with the Ramirez murder. And it explains why he was quieter before but ramping up the frequency now. Any indication that he has since left town or gone back to jail?"

"Negative."

"What about the Will Sutton murder? June 6, 2015."

"Hang on," the guy says. McAllister types feverishly and then sits back. "He had just gotten out of prison two days before."

"This could be our guy," Ben says excitedly.

"Want to know the best part?" McAllister asks. "He works at Albatross Golf in the Roncey Mall. That puts him at the scene for two of the latest murders."

"Let's go pick him up."

It takes just over five hours for them to find a judge to sign the warrant. From there, it takes another hour to plan their raid.

By 9:30 p.m. that evening, Ben, McAllister, and four other cops are climbing the stairs to the third floor of the apartment building in Parkdale where Stuart Cassidy lives. They knock on the door and wait for a response. None comes.

Ben bangs on the door and announces himself, "Detective Cooper with Toronto Police Services. Mr. Cassidy, are you in there? We would like to talk to you." They hear some shuffling inside the apartment, but the door remains closed.

Ben shouts out a final warning then nods to one of the officers to kick down the door. He leads the way into the apartment. The smell is the first thing that hits them. It reeks of garbage, rotten eggs, sour milk, and stale body odour. The apartment is very small. There is a modest kitchen with a white laminate fridge and freezer combo. There is no dishwasher, and dirty plates and take-out containers litter the little bit of counterspace that exists on either side of the sink. A single bar stool sits near a short, narrow island that protrudes from the left side of the kitchen area. To the right of the kitchen is what must be the family room, although it is clear that no family lives here. There is a small couch and a beanbag that is being used as an ottoman, aimed toward an old television set. The television is on, set to an infomercial where a man appears to be shouting about the virtues of the knife he is waving around. To the right of the family room is a bedroom, its door closed.

Holding his gun out and letting it lead his way, Ben approaches the couch, while McAllister heads for the bedroom, motioning the other officers to split up: two check the kitchen, one goes with Ben, and the other joins McAllister in the bedroom. There are pornographic magazines and DVDs splayed out on the couch next to the remote control, both heterosexual and homosexual in nature. Ben expects to find a lot more of each on Cassidy's computer and phone.

McAllister signals that the bedroom door is locked. Ben joins him at the door and knocks, announcing himself again. "Stuart Cassidy, this is Detective Ben Cooper with the Toronto Police Services. Please come out of your room with your hands up."

They are met with silence.

Ben shouts again, "Mr. Cassidy, you have one last chance to open this door before we break it down with necessary force. I will count to five. one … two … three …"

Right as Ben calls out the number four, they hear Cassidy announce that he is coming out. The door opens, and Cassidy walks out, hands above his head. He is wearing blue plaid pajama pants and a white undershirt, both of which look like they have not been washed in days, if not weeks. He has the stubble of a beard that hasn't been washed or trimmed in a long time. His mousy brown hair, which is thinning at the top, is disheveled and in desperate need of a haircut.

All in all, he looks like your stereotypical criminal.

"Stuart Cassidy, you are under arrest for the sexual assault and murder of Christopher Pattinson," Ben begins, as he steps behind Cassidy and begins cuffing his hands behind his back. "You have the right to retain and instruct counsel without delay.

You also have the right to free and immediate legal advice from duty counsel …"

Ben is pacing back and forth in the tiny room, repeatedly checking his watch between sips of strong, bitter coffee. He is in the room next to the interrogation room where Cassidy is sitting, shackled to a single metal table bolted to the ground in the middle of the room. The chair opposite Cassidy is unoccupied, while Ben makes him wait and sweat it out a little bit. From his experience, the longer you make a suspect wait, the more anxious they become and the more vulnerable to questioning.

Cassidy has been sitting here alone for almost three hours. He is sweating and showing signs of stress: eyes darting left and right, legs shaking, and fingers tapping the table. He knows he is being observed behind a one-way mirror and he stares through it every so often, trying to see the people behind the mirror watching him.

"Should we start talking to him?" McAllister asks. Ben shakes his head, indicating not yet. He types off a quick text message to Rose, letting her know that Cassidy is still in the holding room and they haven't begun their interrogation of him. She has been anxiously messaging him asking for updates. He tries to keep her in the loop, giving her general updates without divulging any confidential information, which would be in violation of police regulations.

After another hour or so, Ben decides that he has waited long enough. He enters the interrogation room wearing jeans and his grungy shirt. He purposely removed his jacket and stayed in his plainclothes in an attempt to remain casual and lower Cassidy's defenses.

Ben is silent and waits for Cassidy to say something. They sit in silence for ten minutes, staring at each other, each one daring the other person to go first. Eventually, Cassidy does.

"I didn't do it," he says.

"Do what?" Ben asks.

"Whatever it is you think I did."

"So you don't know why you're here?" Ben asks. Cassidy shakes his head. "I arrested you for the sexual assault and murder of Christopher Pattinson. Although I'm pretty sure he was not your only victim."

"I don't know what you're talking about," says Cassidy, disinterested.

"Chris Pattinson. Found dead in a parking lot last Sunday morning."

"Oh yeah, I heard about that. Real shame," Cassidy says.

"Where were you Monday night?"

"Monday? I dunno. Most nights I'm usually home alone in my apartment, drinking and watching adult films. Hell, that's every night," he says with a deep, throaty cackle.

"Do you have anyone that can attest to that? Anyone who saw you?" Ben asks.

"Nope. Don't need to. I was home alone, remember? No one saw me." Cassidy laughs again, thinking that this guy clearly doesn't know what he's doing.

"Does the name Amanda Moore mean anything to you?"

"Nope." Cassidy sits back in his chair, as far as his shackles will allow him, and continues to deny knowledge of any of the murders. Each time Ben brings up a victim's name, he has the same cocky response of denial.

"How about Will Sutton?"

"Listen, officer," Cassidy begins, but Ben cuts him off: "Detective."

"Okay, listen, Detective," Cassidy says, enunciating the word with malice and mockery. "I don't know what you're talking about. I don't know what you think I did, but I'm innocent!"

"The same way you were innocent all those other times?"

"Of course! I'm a model citizen. Honest to goodness, I never hurt no one." Even Cassidy himself wouldn't believe him with the tone he is using.

Silently, Ben lays out pictures from the crime scenes on the table: Pattinson, Moore, Cruz, and Ramirez. Will Sutton's body lying in bed. Ben has a hard time looking at pictures of Will's death, knowing that that was Rose's bed. It's not jealousy he feels, thinking of Rose with another man; it's just deep sadness for her loss.

He does not say a word and simply watches Cassidy's face, looking for a reaction, any sign that he has seen these crime scenes before, that he had been there before.

Cassidy says, "Real tragic, but I never saw none of these people before in my life." Ben does not believe him. Cassidy's words say one thing, but his eyes say another. He can't turn away from the pictures. He just stares at the bloody corpses, almost as if he is enjoying them. As if he is reliving them.

Ben focuses on Pattinson's death, since they have Cassidy's prints on the murder weapon. "So you never saw this man before?"

"Never."

Ben points to the golf club next to Pattinson's body, the murder weapon that ties them to Cassidy. "What's this?"

"Looks like a golf club. Guess you don't get around much, huh, Officer?"

"Detective," Ben corrects him again. "Do you play golf?"

"I like to play mini golf. But I'm not allowed at any courses anymore. Something about my record. You should speak to your boss about that."

"You work in a golf store, correct?"

"Yeah."

"You know a lot about golf clubs?"

"Some."

"What kind of club is this?"

"Looks like an iron. But real small, maybe a kids' club."

"It is, in fact. It's a thirty-two inch nine iron. Do you know if you sell these in the store where you work?"

"Yeah, we sell all sorts of golf clubs."

"Do you own any golf clubs?"

"No, I ain't ritzy or anything like that."

"Maybe you've taken one home from work. I'm sure you were just borrowing it. After all, there are so many golf clubs there, no one would notice if one went missing, right?"

"No."

There it is. A tell. Any time someone lies, they usually have their own tell, something that gives away the fact that they are not telling the truth. When Cassidy just said no, his eyes shifted to the left ever so briefly. Most people wouldn't notice it. But Ben is a trained detective, and a damn good one at that. He can usually tell when someone is lying.

"Yeah, I bet you have. Nothing wrong with borrowing something, as long as you return it, right?"

Cassidy is silent.

Ben presents a photo of Christopher Pattinson, one he had gotten from Pattinson's mother. "Do you recognize this man?" Pattinson's bloody corpse was so disfigured and slashed that it is hard to see his face in the crime scene photos. But here, in this picture, you can see his face plain and simple.

"No."

The tell. His eyes darted to the left again. Ben knows he has him.

"Yes, you have. You've seen him before. Maybe he came into the store one day while you were working," Ben suggests. Cassidy is silent, so Ben goes on. "Maybe you helped him out. Helped him find a nice new set of clubs? Or maybe an outfit for his mom, for Mother's Day. Was he nice to you?" Cassidy still does not say a word. "Was he rude? Dismissive? After all, you were just a lowly worker, there to serve him."

Cassidy finally speaks up: "Those fancy pricks, they think they're better than everyone cuz they got money. That don't make you better than me, pal." Ben can see the aggression in him.

"It must be so frustrating. People thinking they're better than you. Pushing you down, treating you like you're nothing. Like you're trash."

"Those assholes are the trash. They deserve what they got. All of them!" Cassidy shouts.

We got him, Ben thinks with a smile.

"Hey D.J., choose some music for us tonight. And make it festive, we're celebrating!" Ben shouts from the bathroom upstairs as he steps out of the shower, dripping water all over the floor.

Ben gets home that afternoon, after interrogating Cassidy for almost eighteen hours straight. He is exhausted, but he is grinning from ear to ear. He tells Rose all about the raid on Cassidy's house, about the interrogation, and how Cassidy ultimately confessed to killing Pattinson. He didn't admit to any of the other murders, but Ben left him with Officer McAllister to get more information out of him. Ben is sure that they will have full confessions for all the murders by the end of the day.

"So that's it?" Rose asks as he takes off the filthy clothes he has been wearing for almost forty-eight hours straight.

"That's it. We're done. We got him. We caught the guy who has been raiding the city hurting people. We did it, Rose. We got guy who killed Will."

She bursts into tears of relief and collapses into Ben. He hugs her tightly. It is then that he announces they are having a celebratory dinner tonight. To honour those who have died and to celebrate their lives. To celebrate new beginnings. He gives Rose a long kiss then tells her he is jumping into the shower.

Now Rose is in the kitchen chopping up vegetables for a salad. She put on a black cropped T-shirt and a flowing, floral skirt. They are eating dinner outside on the patio tonight. Ben will be grilling steaks on the barbecue and Rose is in charge of the salad. She puts down her knife and pulls up her phone to choose their evening tunes.

Ben has a speaker system set up so that music can play throughout the house, with a set of speakers even on the patio. They like to play music during their dinners. Some nights they listen to soft soothing tunes quietly in the background; other nights they play fast-paced pop songs from the 90s, singing along and dancing while they eat.

Rose looks through her music library on her phone, considering what playlist to select. Ben wants something celebratory, but Rose does not particularly feel like celebrating. She knows she should be happy; they caught their killer. That is what she has wanted for over six years now. To catch the horrible animal that has been killing people, the one that took her Will away from her. This is great. But She doesn't feel the sense of relief she thought she would.

Maybe she's just exhausted and overcome with emotion. Maybe she will feel the happiness once the shock has worn off.

She tries to convince herself that that must be the problem. She's just overwhelmed. And yet she can't shake this weird feeling inside her. Something feels ... off.

Cassidy has been in and out of prison for the past ten years. He has a history of getting caught. The serial killer they have been tracking is smart. He has killed on numerous occasions, never leaving any evidence behind. Until now. Until that golf club. How did he make a mistake this time? He has been so careful. So good. Did he not wear gloves or wipe off his prints like previously? Unless it wasn't his print on the golf club. Cassidy worked at Albatross, it makes sense that his prints would be on a golf club. Sure, it makes less sense that this specific club was taken from Dave's Sporting Goods, not Albatross. Was it stolen? Did he buy it? Cassidy doesn't have any kids that Rose is aware of, so it seems odd that he would have taken a children's club either way. Rose wonders if maybe Cassidy went to check out the competition or compare prices. Maybe he didn't take the club at all, maybe he just picked it up then put it back down. Who's to say that the print on the club is the murderer's print?

This all just seems too easy. Too convenient.

But the evidence clearly points toward Cassidy, Rose reminds herself. Between the print, the history of sexual assault and aggravated sexual assault, and convenience of location, it all points to Cassidy as the killer. Plus, he confessed to murder on interrogation.

Maybe, Rose wonders, she is just feeling weird because it's over now. She has dedicated years of her life to finding Will's killer. To putting bad guys behind bars. What is her purpose now? With the case solved, she will have to let go of the anger that has driven her for six years. Let go of the grief. Let go of Will.

Maybe what she feels is guilt of letting go of Will. Not completely, he will always be in her heart. But she is now sharing her heart with another man. She admits to herself that it is more than just a fling with Ben. She loves him. They haven't said it to each other yet, but she feels it. And she thinks Ben does too. Rose feels both wonderful and terrible simultaneously. Is she betraying Will?

Rose hears the creak of the third step and looks up as Ben makes his way downstairs and into the kitchen, fresh faced and smiling. He is wearing grey sweatpants and a white T-shirt, simple but incredibly sexy. She can see his toned body through the shirt. He comes up behind her and wraps his arms around her waist. He kisses her neck. Rose can smell his intoxicating scent. She remembers the first time she was close enough to smell him. Woodsy, with a hint of citrus. She knows now that he uses a citrus lavender shampoo. She inhales deeply and feels the butterflies in her stomach. She loves this man. And in that instant, Rose knows that she can love him without fully letting go of Will. And that she should not feel guilty about this love. Will would want her to be happy. And she is so happy with Ben.

"Hi," Ben says.

"Hi," Rose responds. She wriggles around in his arms to face him and kisses him deeply.

"What was that for?" he asks, delightfully surprised.

"For you," she says with a smile, then turns back to her phone to select the playlist for their dinner entertainment. But before she can choose one, Ben surprises her by putting her phone down and scooping her up into his arms. He carries her to the kitchen table, where he throws her down on top of it, brushing aside the plates and cutlery Rose had meticulously set out.

Shrieking with laughter, Rose cries, "What are you doing?"

"I need you. Now." He lifts her skirt up and yanks off her underwear in one smooth movement. Within seconds, he has plunged deep inside her, on top of the kitchen table. She cries out in pleasure and shock.

CHAPTER 38

I run into my car, needing a private place to rant where my yelling will be shielded. The second I shut the car door, I let out a primal scream, shouting, "What the fuck! How could they be so stupid?" I pound the armrest of my seat, the side door, and my steering wheel. I hit it so hard, the car's alarm starts to go off. I quickly turn off the alarm and force myself to take deep breaths to calm down. I don't want to attract any attention.

But I am fuming! Do those idiot cops really think they have found their killer? Do they really think that pitiful man could do what I have done? How dare they. And these headlines plastered all over the news? "Toronto Police have caught serial killer," "Serial killer off the streets." "Dangerous killer caught, local detective deemed a hero," and "Man in custody admitting to multiple homicides over the years." Insulting!

This patsy doesn't have the strength to overpower another human being like I do. He doesn't have the brains to plan the murder out like I do. And he doesn't have the brains to be careful not to get caught like I do.

He is not a killer. He is just an ordinary man. Not extraordinary like me. I'll show them.

I didn't get the chance to plan this one as thoroughly as some of the others. I feel a sense of urgency to prove those pathetic cops wrong and show them how dangerous I really can be. But I don't think I need to plan as much as I used to. I know what I'm doing. I am strong and powerful. No one can stop me.

I go back to The Rideout on Saturday night. Last time I was here I noticed a ton of losers looking for a fleeting moment of attention. So sad. I figured I can go there, look around, and find someone to have a little fun with.

The tricky part is figuring out how to get them home. That Ramirez guy was easy. I slipped him a little Rohypnol in his drink at the bar and he was quick to invite me back to his place. At that point, the drug had taken its full effect and I barely had to hold him down while I restrained him. But that young kid from the mall, he was a lot tougher. I didn't have any of my stuff, so I had to knock him unconscious first with a good strong blow to the head.

I sit at the bar and take a look around me. It doesn't take more than two minutes to find my next target. He is looking down into his drink, lost in his own world of thought. He seems sad and lonely. Maybe recently dumped? Those are my favourite, so easy to manipulate. They just want to feel whole again and get lost in some love and attention. Plus, no one really misses them when they're dead. I stand up and walk over to him, then slip into the seat next to him. As expected, it was almost too easy to get him chatting. I was right about his relationship. He was just dumped. I'm always right. That is why I'm so good at this and I don't get caught. I know how to pick them.

I slip some Special K into the guy's drink when he's not looking. I'm all out of my usual stash of Rohypnol, but it won't be a problem. While I try not to use ketamine, since it can more easily be traced back to its source, I have used it before and it worked great. I just need him a little calmer, a little looser, and a lot woozier. I learned that after my third adventure. Best to let the drugs do their job.

It doesn't take long before he invites me back to his place. I always make it seem like their idea, even though I know from the beginning that is where we will end up. It makes them feel more relaxed while also more in control. He lives in a small apartment nearby, so we walk there. It's been about half an hour since I slipped the ketamine into his drink, and I'm not sure what's going on, but this guy seems fully with it still. Usually, the guys are falling over themselves by now.

We enter his apartment, and he seems a little unsteady on his feet, but not as much as I want him to be. It looks like I will just have to use my brute strength to restrain him. Like I did with the guy at the mall.

He offers me a drink and I accept. As he walks over to a bar cart and reaches for a glass, I throw an arm around his neck and try to knock him unconscious by cutting off his windpipe. He's strong. Stronger than I thought. As he struggles against my arms, all of a sudden, I see his arm swing above his head and behind and I feel a sharp pain on my forehead where he smashes a glass on my face. Shit. I can't forget to wipe up this blood when I'm done.

The sudden movement and pain in my face causes me to loosen my grip and the guy wrestles free. He stands a few feet in front of me and we stare at each other for a moment, neither one of us moving. He has nowhere to go. I am blocking the way to the door. The longer he waits, the more I am able to recover from his surprise attack and regain my strength. He lunges for me and instead of fighting him, I go with it and allow him to roll on top of me. I am thrown to the ground, and my back and head crash to the ground. It hurts, but I am still fully conscious. And this is where I want him. He thinks he has me knocked down, but I am able to quickly roll over, using the momentum of his body thrown at me and pin him down. I start throwing punches at his face. I almost lose control, but then I stop and restrain myself. I have to make sure not to kill him yet. The party isn't over that quickly.

I force myself to stand up and take a step back. In our struggle, all of my stuff has been thrown around: my cellphone and keys and wallet and strewn all over the floor. I make another mental note to make sure I clean all of this up before I leave.

God, my head hurts. That asshole made me bleed. He will pay for this.

CHAPTER 39

Rose and Ben are enjoying a slow, quiet morning in bed. Ben is reading a newspaper on his tablet while Rose reads a trashy romance novel. They are barely dressed. Ben is wearing his grey sweatpants again while Rose is wearing just his white T-shirt and her underwear. They can hear the birds chirping outside, as the warm May weather breezes into the house through an open window. Spring is a short-lived season in Toronto. It usually goes from a horrendous cold winter to torrential rain, a couple weeks of sun, then scorching hot summer. Those couple weeks of warm spring sun are Rose's favourite. Magnolias are blooming in front of the house across the street, and Rose can see the beautiful flowers from the window. Put simply, life is good.

Shortly before noon, Ben's phone rings. "Ignore it," Rose pleads. She doesn't want to ruin their peaceful moment. Ben ignores it.

And then it rings again. This time, it is the emergency line from the station.

"Shit," Ben mutters. This can't be good.

"It can't be. We got him," Rose says. But Ben can hear the uncertainty in her voice. She tells him about the reservations she had about Cassidy being their guy. She is mad at herself. She should have listened to her gut. She should still be looking for the killer.

Ben and Rose pull up to the red-brick apartment building, just minutes away from Trinity Bellwoods Park. It had been McAllister calling, telling Ben about the call he got that morning. His name was Justin Turner. Adult male, found in his bed, in a similar pattern to their serial killer. Ben makes a mental note that this one is close to The Rideout and wonders if that means anything.

Ben flashes his credentials as he enters Justin Turner's apartment. McAllister is there talking to an officer, who is furiously jotting down notes. McAllister stops midsentence as he sees Ben and heads toward him. He looks distraught and appears to be embarrassed.

"Detective," McAllister says as approaches.

"Officer," Ben nods at McAllister. "What do we know so far?"

"Justin Turner, aged twenty-eight. Neighbour called it in, Turner was supposed to watch his dog this morning, but he never answered the door. He got worried, so he called the building's superintendent, who let the neighbour in. The neighbour and super found the body. Forensics just got here, it looks like cause of death is knife wound to the chest. But before that, he suffered multiple stab wounds all over his body, severe trauma to the skull, as well as several punches to the face, you can see substantial bruising and swelling around the eyes and mouth in particular. He was also brutally sexually assaulted. We haven't confirmed, but we can probably assume that he was assaulted with the hockey stick lying on the floor beside the body. I hate to say this, but this looks a hell of a lot like the previous pattern with the other eight victims."

"Can forensics narrow down time of death?" Ben asks.

"Between 11:00 p.m. and 1:00 a.m. last night."

"And I assume Stuart Cassidy is still locked up following our arrest? He hasn't made bail or anything yet?"

"Your assumption is correct."

"Which means we got the wrong guy," Ben says.

"We got the wrong guy," McAllister agrees.

Ben puts on his gloves and starts to walk around the apartment. The open-concept apartment has a small living room area to the right of the kitchen. Although calling it a kitchen is a generous description. It is a fridge and a small countertop area with a sink and cupboards above the sink. Separating the two spaces is a large bar cart with various bottles of liquor lined up along both the top and bottom shelf of the cart. There is also a silver tray with glass tumblers. Ben looks at the bottles. He doesn't know much about alcohol, but it is clear that the victim spent a lot of money on his liquor collection. The victim has everything from whiskey to gin to tequila. He clearly preferred to drink his money instead of saving it for a nicer apartment.

Ben wanders away from the main living area and heads toward the bedroom where the victim is on the bed lying face down, with his hands and feet pulled behind his back in a hogtied position. His face is turned slightly to the left. Well, what's left of his face. His skull has been bashed in and there is blood everywhere. He recoils at the sight of the victim's exposed skull, the bones splintering and caving in above his left temple. His body is covered in bruises, abrasions, and knife marks shredding his torso. Like the other victims, there are signs of anal trauma. As if that isn't enough to convince them that this was their serial killer, there is a bloody hockey stick lying next to the victim.

There is no other word to describe it than barbaric.

"He's mad. He's sending us a message."

"How do you know?" McAllister asks.

"The M.O. is the same, but this looks particularly bloody and aggressive. Like the killer is trying to take out his anger or prove a point."

"What kind of point?"

"That you got the wrong guy," Rose whispers. Ben is so caught up in the scene he almost forgot Rose is with them.

"All of the stab wounds, were those all from the same knife?"

"I'll ask the coroner's office to confirm, but I think so. I haven't heard otherwise. Why do you ask?"

"There are shards of glass on the floor over there, under the bar cart. Any sign of wounds from the glass? Also ask them to pick up every piece of glass they find, see if we can get any fingerprints or blood …" Ben stops in the middle of his train of thought as he sees Rose bend down near those few shards of glass. She is on all fours, crouching close to the glass, looking under the bar cart.

"Rose, be careful. You don't want to cut yourself."

"Or mess up our crime scene," McAllister mutters, wondering why Rose is even there with them.

She stands up holding something, what appears to be a shiny object. She is staring at it, all colour draining from her face that is now a ghostly shade of white. She looks terrified.

"Hey, put that down where you found it," McAllister demands. "You have to let forensics survey the entire scene and mark off all the evidence. You can't tamper with the scene."

Wordlessly, Rose puts the object down and walks out of the apartment. Ben kneels down to see what she found. It is a keychain, broken off from the main set of keys. It is blue with a yellow triangle that has a bright red "S" in the middle. Superman's logo.

"McAllister, get forensics to run this immediately for prints. We may have just caught a break."

"Will do, Detective." McAllister sees Ben charge after Rose. "Where are you going?"

"To see why that keychain got Rose all spooked."

Ben catches up with her as she races down the stairs toward the apartment building's exit. "Rose! Wait up!" he shouts, but she does not slow down or stop. He picks up his pace and hops down the stairs, skipping multiple at a time. He finally catches up to her and grabs her arm, stopping her in her tracks.

"Where are you going Rose? What's going on? Why did you run off like that?"

"I have to go Ben, please let me go," she pleads.

"It's okay Rose, I know you're upset that the killer is still out there. I'm disappointed too. But we got him now. For real this time. You did it. You found that keychain. We'll run it for prints on an urgent basis, we'll have the guy in jail by tomorrow," Ben tries to assure her.

"You don't need to run it. Don't waste your time," Rose says in a deathly quiet whisper.

"What do you mean?"

"I know who the killer is," she states, matter-of-factly.

Shocked, Ben asks, "You do?"

"Yes. And you know him too."

CHAPTER 40

"What are you saying, Rose?" Ben asks incredulously. "That keychain. It's my brother's. I gave it to him when he was sixteen."

"Tyler?"

"Yes. He has always loved superheroes, and I bought that for him when he got his drivers' license. I was so proud of myself, it was the first time I bought something with my own money that I earned."

"That was years ago, Rose. He probably doesn't have it anymore. Nobody still has the same set of keys since they were sixteen."

"Tyler does. I noticed it a few weeks ago, that he still carries it around," Rose says.

"That still doesn't mean it's his keychain. Superman is one of the most popular superheroes of all time, it could be anyone's," Ben says, trying to reassure her. But she can hear the doubt in his voice. "We won't know until we run prints. Let's not jump to any conclusions."

"You're probably right," Rose says, trying to sound more convinced than she feels.

"Let's wait to see if the prints get any matches."

"They wouldn't. My brother's never been arrested or done anything bad in his life. His prints won't be in the system."

"You never know."

"I'm going over to his house to talk to him," Rose tells him.

"What?!" he shouts. "Absolutely not."

"I need to. I need to talk to him, to ask him. I'm sure this is all a horrible misunderstanding. I'll ask him, we'll laugh about it, and probably just get drunk. It's fine, Ben, really."

"Rose, you cannot go talk to your brother right now. If he is the killer we've been looking for, it is way too dangerous for you to go near him alone."

"He's my brother, Ben. I've been alone with him millions of times, my entire life. He won't hurt me."

"Please. Just trust me here. I can't risk you getting hurt."

"I won't get hurt, it's Tyler, he would never hurt me," Rose says stubbornly.

"Then you'll potentially be interfering with a criminal investigation. I can arrest you."

"Really? You're going with that again?"

"I'll do it Rose. I'm serious. I need to know that you're safe." She can her the desperation in his voice.

"Okay."

"Okay?"

"Okay. I won't go talk to him."

"Thank you. Just wait. We can decide how to do this. Together," Ben says, as he wraps his arms around her. She doesn't push him off, but she does not relent in his arms.

Rose is silent for a moment, then she tells him, "I'm going to go home to lie down."

"I'll drive you back to my place. I'm going to finish up here, then I'll see you back home later."

"No, I want to go to my parents' house. I just need to think about things a little. I'll meet up with you at your place later."

"At least let me drive you."

"It's okay, I can take an Uber."

"Are you sure?"

"I'm positive. You have work to do here."

"I'll see you later," Ben says. He leans down and gently kisses her. She kisses him back, but her heart isn't in it.

"See you," she says.

Rose grabs an Uber and heads to her parents' house. She spends the car ride thinking about everything. About Tyler. About their childhood together, about how close they are. About Emily, and Logan and Sloane. There's no way Tyler could be a killer.

She thinks about Will. Tyler loved Will, they got along great. He wouldn't have done anything to hurt him. The more she thinks about things, the more she is convinced that Tyler is not the killer. It has to be someone else. There's just no way. When she gets home, she calls Tyler and asks him to come over. She tells him she wants to talk about a birthday gift for Logan.

Rose paces the house as she anxiously waits for Tyler to get there. Her heart is racing and she is starting to sweat. Her regular level of anxiety is through the roof, she can only imagine what Dr. Hill would say to her right now. Calm down, take deep breaths. Dr. Hill often recommends a cognitive behavioural therapy technique, where Rose imagines the worst-case scenario and plays that out in her head to see that she can prepare herself for any outcome and see that things won't be so bad. Except in this case, the worst-case scenario is that one of the most important men in her life, Tyler, killed her fiancé (well, almost fiancé) and is a serial killer who has killed almost ten people. That they're aware of. These thoughts amplify her intense anxiety instead of soothing it. *We have to start trying some new techniques, Dr. Hill,* she thinks to herself.

She wanders into Tyler's childhood bedroom. She tries to see if there are any signs or clues that could tell her whether Tyler could really be capable of something like this. But all she can see are the shelves full of trophies and prizes and team pictures from years of playing hockey, basketball, and baseball. She opens his closet and sees the *Sports Illustrated* swimsuit edition posters on each door, with Heidi Klum and Elle Macpherson smiling at the camera, which Tyler always thought no one knew about. This room looks like a typical teenage male's bedroom: chock full of sports paraphernalia and unfulfilled hormonal urges.

Oh god, Rose thinks, *sports paraphernalia.* She can picture the crime scene photos, each one having a bloody piece of equipment found next to the victim's body. But that must be a coincidence, she tells herself. Tyler will get here and he will exonerate himself. He will show her his Superman keychain, still intact on his keyring. He will have solid alibis for all the dates of the murders. He will shake his head at her momentary insanity for questioning him, and they will laugh it off. She is sure of it.

A part of her feels guilty, doing the exact thing that Ben told her not to do. But technically she isn't breaking her promise, per se. She isn't going over to his house. He's coming here. *I am such a lawyer, finding loopholes based on semantics,* she thinks. She just really needs to talk to Tyler. He's one of the best men she knows. He has stood by her, supported her, and taken care of her for her entire life. He held her as she wept after Will was killed. There's no way Tyler could have been the one to hurt Will, to have caused Rose that type of pain.

And anyway, Tyler was at Rose's law school graduation when Will was killed. He couldn't have killed him and then made it to my graduation. Could he? Rose tries to remember the details from that day. The medical examiner had said that Will had died that morning. In theory, Tyler could have killed Will and still made it to her graduation. Oh god.

Stop it, Rose. This is your bother. He would never, she reprimands herself. *There has got to be a logical explanation for all of this.*

To distract herself while she waits, Rose sets up some tea and snacks for her and Tyler. She fills the kettle with hot water and grabs a handful of fresh mint that her mother just planted in their garden. Whenever Rose was sad or anxious growing up, her mother would always calm her down with fresh mint tea. She also checks the fridge and decides to put together a charcuterie board with a variety of cheeses, crackers, dried fruit, and some almonds.

Rose realizes this is exactly what her mother would do, focus on creating something beautiful, something perfect from the outside, to avoid facing the terrible thoughts in her head. She always criticizes her mother for doing this, for putting on appearances to make things seem right when they are so *not* right. But now that Rose is doing it herself, she realizes that it has a soothing effect. Maybe Isabelle wasn't always trying to cover up and bury her sadness or anxiety so no one would see it. Maybe she was trying to relax and feel better herself, so she could take care of everyone around her and let *them* fall to pieces.

Rose realizes now that she has never seen her mother fall apart. She feels a deep appreciation of her mother for always being the strong force in everyone's lives. But she also feels sad for Isabelle for not feeling like she could relax and be a mess. She should just feel whatever feelings she feels, without guilt or remorse or trying to make it go away. No one is perfect.

But this charcuterie board is pretty close to perfect. Rose is putting the final touches on the beautiful arrangement when she hears the front door open and the familiar voice of her brother.

"Hey, sis," Tyler calls as he closes the door behind him. She takes a deep, calming breath. It's time to find out the truth.

"In here," she calls from the kitchen.

"You look like Rose and you sound like Rose. But this kitchen is screaming Isabelle Davis. What's going on here?" Tyler asks, looking at the elaborate setup and grabbing a piece of smoked gouda. Rose didn't realize how far she had gone, how unlike her this all was. She is just so anxious.

"Oh, it's nothing. I was in the mood for a snack and figured I'd make enough to share," Rose says dismissively.

"Hey, I'm not complaining," Tyler says, sitting down and helping himself to a cracker and slice of brie. "We never have this kind of stuff at home. The kids just want string cheese and cheese slices, which, by the way, I'm convinced actually have no cheese in them."

Rose laughs. She used to love those cheese slices. They make a delicious grilled cheese because they melt so easily.

"So what did you want to talk about, sis?"

She has been thinking for an hour now about how to start this conversation with her brother. She doesn't want to accuse him of anything outright. He's most likely innocent, so it could make things super awkward between them if he knows she has been thinking these horrible things about him. Somewhere between pacing the house, picking mint from the garden, and cutting slices of cheese, Rose comes up with an idea.

"I want to surprise Logan and deliver a bunch of balloons for him to wake up to on his birthday tomorrow."

"That's a great idea, he'll love it."

"Can I borrow your keys? I don't have a key to your house, and I can't use Mom and Dad's, since they don't even know which key goes to your house, their keychain is full of so many random keys!"

"Why don't you just knock on the door quietly and we'll let you in?" Tyler asks.

"I don't want to be a bother," Rose says dismissively.

"Just call me and wake me," Tyler suggests.

"I'm planning to come really early before I go for a run tomorrow morning. I don't want to wake you. Just give me your keys and I'll slip in and out quietly, no one will ever know I'm there."

Tyler is silent for a moment. As if he is thinking of another excuse to not give Rose his keys? Is Rose reading too much into this? Why won't he just give her the keys?

Realizing he is out of arguments, Tyler says, "Sure, I'll give you the house key. But I'm keeping the car keys, you're not taking everything from me!" He is trying to laugh it off, but Rose sees he is a little nervous. Tyler digs into his pocket and starts playing with his keychain under the table. He is struggling to pull off the house key.

"Don't be weird, just give me your keychain and I'll grab it! You never could figure out how to use key rings."

"You have the advantage of long nails," Tyler says defensively.

Rose grabs the keychain from Tyler and looks at it. She sees his car keys, his house keys, and a few other random keys. She seems an empty key ring. She does not see Superman.

"Hey, where's the Superman keychain I got you?" Rose asks, trying to sound nonchalant. "You said you never take it off."

"It must have fallen off, I guess," Tyler answers.

"When?"

"I don't know. I guess a couple days ago?"

"Did you not notice that it had fallen off?"

"I did notice. I just didn't think it was a big deal, I guess. Why do you care so much?"

"Have you looked in your house? Maybe it's in your room or the kitchen somewhere?"

"Uh, maybe? This is getting weird Rose, it's just a keychain. Why do you care so much?"

"Why are you so flippant? It's not just a keychain, it is the first present I ever bought you, that I worked very hard to earn the money to purchase for you, and now you just lose it and you don't seem to care?" she screams, pacing the room. She knows she sounds hysterical but she can't stop herself.

"What is going on, Rose? Is this really about the keychain?"

"How did you get that cut on your forehead?" Rose asks, pointing to an abrasion on the right side of his forehead, close to his hairline. It looks recent.

"This?" he asks, putting his hand to his forehead. "It's nothing, I bumped my head getting into the car."

"But that wouldn't give you a cut, it would give you a bruise. This looks like the skin broke, like something cut you."

"Maybe my door is sharp, I don't know. You're being really weird."

"It looks like a cut from a piece of glass." Tyler doesn't say anything, he just looks at Rose. Rose goes on. "Like you got hit in the head with a glass which shattered, a shard slicing your forehead."

Tyler remains silent, staring at Rose. And then the weirdest thing happens. She didn't expect this response.

He smiles.

"You know," he says. Matter-of-factly. It's not a question, it's a statement.

"Know what?" Rose asks, needing him to say it.

"You know how I got this cut on my head. You know how I lost my Superman keychain." He sounds proud.

"I don't know anything, Tyler. Why don't you tell me," she prompts.

He leans back in his chair and sighs, "That prick, Justin. He was strong. Stronger than I expected. He put up a real good fight."

Rose just stares at him in shock. She doesn't know what to say. She looks at her brother, a man she has known her entire life, and she doesn't recognize him anymore. His face has turned dark. His eyes have lost their playful nature and are more serious. Dangerous.

"What?" he asks.

"How could you? I don't understand."

"You have no idea, Rose. You don't know how hard it is, everyone always looking at you, watching you, expecting you to be perfect all the time. It's exhausting."

"So that's an excuse to kill people? Because people think you're great?"

"That's not what I'm saying. It's exhausting, being everyone's puppet. Sometimes I just need to control my own life! My own actions! Take back my power."

"This doesn't make any sense, Tyler."

"It does, Rose, it makes perfect sense. You just don't get it. You spend your life following rules, doing what you're told. But at some point, you get to decide your own rules. You want something? You take it. Show people who's in control." Now he is the one who is hysterical.

"You're powerless in everyday life when you follow the rules. But at night, when you get to be free? When you can do whatever you want? God, it's like nothing else, Rose. I'm telling you. Go anywhere you want, flirt with whomever you want. You control them. It's such a rush. And it's so easy, you have no idea. These people, they're idiots! They're desperate for someone to control them. They're pathetic."

"Why do you have to control them?" She does not understand anything he is saying.

"Control is the nature of human beings. There is always a dominant and a submissive. You can be either. You can be powerless in your own life, be a submissive, let others tell you what to do. Or you can be strong and powerful. You can take what you want. Be dominant. Show them your control."

"But why do you have to kill them?"

"I didn't mean to, not at first. The first time, I was just asserting my power. I didn't mean to kill him."

"Will," Rose whispers as tears stream down her face.

"I'm sorry, I really didn't mean to kill him. But if I'm being honest, it felt good! It was a total rush. I had never felt a high like that in my life. It's incredible, Rose! I tried to stop, I tried not to do it again. But it's like a drug. I needed a hit. I needed to dominate, to show people that I was in control. Earn the victory, and it tastes sweeter. Rose, I have earned each of these victories."

"How can you call them victories? They are murders!" Rose gasps as the words come out of her mouth, and she hears herself say, "You are a murderer!"

"You have to have control and power to win. Dominance on and off the field, that's what Coach always said. Show them your strength and power, even if it means hurting them. Sometimes you have to hurt them. That's what he taught me, Rose."

Suddenly, it hits Rose. "Coach Hutchinson taught you that. He taught you by showing you, didn't he?" Tyler is silent. "He dominated you, he controlled you. He didn't kill you, obviously, but he assaulted you?"

Tyler is silent.

"Was he … sexual with you?"

"Yes, to prove a point. To show his power. To show me that when you want something, you take it. What he did… what we did together… Coach was just doing what he had to, to make me into the man I am now. My training with him, my time with him, that has defined me, it has shaped the path my life has taken, everything I have, everything I've done."

"But it didn't have to be this way. This isn't you. You're a good person. You're better than this. You don't have to let what happened to you define you."

"You don't get it. I want to! If it weren't for Coach, I wouldn't have all the amazing things I have now. My career, Emily, Logan, Slone. He taught me to go after the things I want in life. If you want something, you just have to reach out and take it."

Rose sees that Tyler really believes this. He has lost his mind. "Tyler, that doesn't make any sense. That's not how life works."

He is getting frustrated. Angry. He starts screaming. "That's exactly how it works! You don't know what you're talking about,

Rose. I always protected you. You never had to worry about someone hurting you. You never had to learn to assert your dominance. It's hard work and it's not easy, but someone has to do it!"

"It's hard because it's unnatural. You can't just go around taking what you want."

"Yes, I can!" he shouts. He is red and panting, becoming aggressive and terrifying.

"Do Mom and Dad know?"

"Know what, that Coach was assaulting me? Turning me into a man, he said?"

"Yes," Rose whispers.

"Mom has no idea. She would freak out. I think Dad knows, but we never talked about it. Typical. Dad has no awareness of anything in his life. He thinks he was the perfect, loving father. He doesn't realize the shit he put on me," Tyler is shouting. "'Make sure you score today, Tyler!' 'You better play well today, Tyler!' 'Ninety-eight percent on a test? We're disappointed in you, son. You should have gotten a hundred.' And God forbid I wasn't MVP one year! You know my first year playing AAA hockey, he hit me when I didn't make captain? No one gets captain their first year playing. But he expected me to. He demanded it."

"Dad would never ..." Rose tries, but Tyler cuts her off. "Dad tried to make me the perfect son, and I was a fucking submissive, pathetic loser, until Coach took me under his wing. He taught me how to be strong, how to be powerful."

"Strong at what cost?"

"Who cares about the cost? It's not about that! You don't get it, Rose! Why can't you get it? Why can't you understand?" He is shouting and starts flying into an intense fit of rage. He is pacing around the room.

"Tyler, calm down," Rose starts, crying audibly now, but she can't calm him down. She doesn't recognize him anymore. He is a different person. She unconsciously has been backing up, and now sees that she is pinned against the wall. He is facing her from across the room.

"Rose, you need to understand."

"I can't."

"Please," he begs.

"I can't. I don't get it, Tyler. How could you?"

"Rose, you have to. You have to get it. You have to be okay with it." She is silent.

"What are you going to do?" he asks. She still can't speak. Tears are pouring down her cheeks. "You can't tell anyone, Rose. No one."

"I have to, Tyler. It's not right."

"You can't, Rose," he starts crying along with her. "You can't. You don't understand," he sobs.

"It's over."

"No, you can't do that to me."

Rose realizes he is holding a knife. She didn't even notice before that he had one. Did he take it from the kitchen drawer? Or was it in his pocket?

"You are a killer, Tyler." She doesn't recognize her own, shaky voice. "You are a murderer. You murdered eight people. You murdered Will! How could you?"

He is still crying as he approaches her. "How could YOU do this to me, Rose? Did your pathetic loser boyfriend Ben tell you to do this? Is he too much of a wimp to face me himself?"

Rose recoils at the sound of Ben's name. "No, he doesn't know anything about this. He doesn't even know I called you. Please, keep him out of this. He has nothing to do with this!"

"I can't. If you know, he knows. I need to take care of him once I'm done with you."

"Done ... done with me?" she stammers through her tears.

"I'm sorry. I don't want to hurt you. But you can't go telling people any of this. No one can know."

"Please," she sobs.

"I'm sorry, Rose," he sobs. "I'm so, so sorry." He is close to her. So close he can touch her, just by reaching out his hand.

"Please don't hurt me, Tyler. Please!" She pleads. He doesn't say anything, he just keeps inching closer to her, with a wild look in his eyes, a terrifying combination of sadness and anger and fear. "Normally I give my targets something to quiet them, calm them down. But my stash has run dry. And Emily's office has started to notice that vials of ketamine seem to be disappearing, so I can't go back there. I'm sorry. You'll just have to be awake for this."

"Tyler!" she is begging, hysterical now.

He is standing right in front of her. "Please," she whispers. They are staring at each other, both of them crying. Rose sees Tyler pull his arm back, the arm that is holding the knife. She closes her eyes tightly and braces herself for the sharp pain that she knows she will inevitably feel as he plunges the knife into her sternum. But before he can finish the movement and end her life, there is a loud noise and Tyler collapses to the floor. Rose looks up and sees Ben, standing in the doorway, gun outstretched in his hand, aimed directly at Tyler.

CHAPTER 41

Rose's screams had drowned out the sound of the front door opening and Ben rushing in, but nothing could muffle the sound of a gun going off in an enclosed space without a silencer. Her ears are ringing, as she stares at Ben and tries to force her brain to comprehend what is going on. Tyler is on the floor. She knows that he has been shot, but she can't see the wound or the source of where the blood is coming from.

Ben holsters his gun and rushes over to her, wrapping her up in his arms. He holds her and whispers, "It's okay. I'm here." She collapses into him, sobbing uncontrollably. But then she looks up and sees that Tyler has gotten up and is lunging forward toward them. "Tyler!" she screams.

Ben's reflexes are quick and he is able to push Rose away from him and take the brunt of Tyler's attack. The attack is low, as Tyler uses legs to propel his shoulder into Ben's gut, knocking him to the ground. But in doing so, Tyler loses is balance and falls down with Ben.

Rose can see that Tyler was shot in his right shoulder. Ben had shot to injure and disarm, not to kill.

Ben is able to quickly recover and jump up, but Tyler is only a second behind him. He lunges again toward Ben with a powerful right hook. Rose can hear the crack as Tyler's fist makes contact with Ben's face, clearly breaking his nose. Sheer adrenaline allows Ben to ignore the blood dripping down his nose into his mouth and he drives an uppercut into Tyler's stomach. Tyler is doubled over, and Ben uses this opportunity to grab Rose's arm and pull her out of the kitchen into the living room. "You have to leave. Go! Now!" But before he can even finish the words, Tyler is right there in the living room with them, charging at him. The two men fall over again, knocking the console table behind them. Ben uses the momentum and rolls, pulling Tyler along with him. The two men roll around a few times before Ben holds Tyler down, face-down, pulling one of his arms behind his back. The snap is audible as Tyler's shoulder is yanked out of its socket. Rose is screaming at both of them to stop. "Get out of here, Rose!" Ben shouts. But she can't. She is frozen. She thinks about some of the witnesses she has questioned when prosecuting assault cases, who describe a trauma-induced involuntary paralysis, preventing them from moving or running away when experiencing a trauma. This must be how they felt.

Ben lets go with his right hand, reaching for Tyler's other arm to bring it to the other to bind his hands together. Tyler senses the shift in weight and while Ben leans over to reach, Tyler throws his entire body to the right, throwing Ben off him. Ben is caught off guard and Tyler seizes the moment and jumps on top of Ben.

Tyler has Ben pinned down on his back. Tyler has a wild look in his brown eyes. His right shoulder is bleeding and the left shoulder is throbbing, but the adrenaline seems to numb the pain. He is strong. The years of playing sports competitively, working out, and continuing to train are clearly paying off. He is stronger than Ben. Tyler is throwing punches at Ben's face, which is spurting blood everywhere. His nose is definitely broken and blood pours out of it. His eyes are already swelling where they have been hit by Tyler's wicked right hook.

Rose jumps on Tyler, trying to pull him off. Tyler swings wildly and slaps her in the face, knocking her to the ground. Rose feels blood running down her chin and realizes that Tyler had slapped her so hard he split her lip. She touches the warm, sticky liquid, then looks at her hand. The blood is warm. She never realized how warm blood is.

Rose looks around her. There is blood everywhere. It's hard to tell whose blood it is, but it is everywhere. The two brawling men are both in terrible shape. All Rose sees is red. Red, warm, sticky blood.

Tyler is focused on Ben, still on top of him. At some point in their fight, he must have grabbed his knife that had fallen when he was shot and he now has the knife directly pointed at Ben's heart. Ben is using all his strength to block him, to push his hand with the knife away. But the knife inches closer and closer, Tyler's strength clearly overpowering him.

In a moment of sudden clarity, Rose realizes she is about to watch her brother kill the man she loves. For the second time. With a guttural throaty scream, Rose jumps up, grabs the ceramic gold-plated sculpture from the console, and, using all her strength, bashes Tyler on the head.

Tyler's grip falters and he collapses unconscious on top of Ben. Panting, Ben pushes Tyler off him and slowly grabs his zip ties. Ironically, hew ties his hands and feet behind his back, similar to how Tyler had tied up his victims before torturing, raping, and killing them.

As Rose hears the sirens of police cars and ambulances approaching, she collapses onto the floor, tucks her knees up into her and rocks in a ball, sobbing. Once Tyler is secured, Ben comes over to her and puts his arm around her. He sits there holding her, bloody and bruised, while she cries for a long time.

EPILOGUE

There is blood everywhere. Red, warm, sticky blood, oozing down Rose's finger. *Why is there so much blood? And why does it suddenly make me crave cherry pie?*

"Stupid paper cut," Rose mutters to herself as she instinctively sucks her bleeding finger. She was moving aside stacks of paper to make room for her laptop when she sliced her finger. While she waits for the computer to turn on, she glances out the window at the stately trees lining the street. It has been an unseasonably warm September. The leaves are starting to change colours to deep shades of red, orange and ochre, but the sun still shines brightly. Families take long strolls together, walking dogs, meeting up with friends on the street. Children flock to the parks after school, relishing the final few days of sun. Neighbours are outside in their backyards, grilling dinner on the barbecue, eating on their patios.

It has been about four months since Tyler's arrest. To Rose, it feels like it was just yesterday. She has remained in Toronto and is slowly settling into her new life here. She quit her job as Crown counsel (Charles is devastated but also extremely proud of her for embracing this new challenge) and took a job as a professor with the University of Toronto Faculty of Law. She teaches courses on criminal procedure, the laws of evidence, and trial advocacy. She loves her new job. She enjoys staying in her field of expertise but without not have the everyday stress and anxiety of running files herself. She also is removed from visiting horrific crime scenes, talking to traumatized victims, and examining dead bodies looking for evidence. She has a knack for teaching and is naturally charismatic. Her students already love her.

She sold her condo in Vancouver through a real estate agent. At the end of June, she and Ben fly out to Vancouver to pack up her belongings and bring them back. She introduced Ben to Paige, who insisted on taking them out for dinner that night. They laughed and cried, and Paige held Rose extra tight as they say goodnight. She whispered in her ear how happy she is for her. And how she better come visit regularly.

Rose moved her things into Ben's house and she stays there indefinitely. He insists. He has been incredibly supportive and loving to her, patiently helping her work through her emotions about everything that has happened. They go for walks every day, wandering different areas of the city, from the downtown beaches to Kensington Market to Unionville just north of Toronto, soaking up the final rays of the warm summer sun. They cope with their shared trauma the best way they know how: through laughter. They share silly jokes and sarcastic banter. They argue, like all couples do, and fight over who the better singer is. They have random dance parties after dinner in the middle of the kitchen, just like Rose did growing up. They discuss their work, art, and politics. No one has ever challenged Rose emotionally and intellectually this much. And physically. She still feels butterflies when he kisses her. Their sexual chemistry is off the charts. Months after meeting, Rose still cannot get enough of him, and he is more than happy to oblige her, to fulfill her every need and desire. When her friends probe for details on their teenage-like romance, she quips, "Let's just say we have gotten good use out of his spare set of handcuffs." Ben is waking up the desirous, sexual being inside her. She is thrilled to be exploring this side of herself, a side that she has not felt in a long time.

Her nightmares continue but they have taken on a new sickening twist. Almost nightly, she dreams of Tyler trying to kill either her or someone she loves. She wakes up screaming and crying, but Ben is always there beside her. He hugs her and she curls into him, panting and gasping for air. The heavy weight that she has felt for the past six years, that hand holding her down and telling her to give up, has lightened. It is still there, but it feels more manageable now somehow. Perhaps it is the finality of Will's murder being solved. Perhaps it is Ben, with his calming presence. He does not judge her during her anxiety attacks or depressive episodes. He shares the burden with her. He listens, sympathizes, and empathizes. He does not try to solve her sadness; he just lets her feel it. He does not pressure her to pretend everything is fine and to just move on. There is no need to put on lipstick and a smile and to get over it. With Ben, it's okay to not be okay.

Tyler has been in jail since that horrible night at their parents' house. He was denied bail. Her parents have gone out to the jail to see him a couple times, but Rose has not gone. She can't seem to bring herself to do it. There will be a trial, and she knows she will have to testify against her brother at some point. Right now, she tries not to think about that.

Rose brings her attention back to the computer and logs on to video chat. She has a virtual therapy appointment with Dr. Hill. She has been maintaining their regular weekly appointments, changing the time from 8:00 a.m. Vancouver time to 7:00 a.m., which is 10:00 a.m. in Toronto. Rose was surprised when Dr. Hill first agreed to this new time since it is quite early, but Dr. Hill explained that she is an early riser and was okay to start her day early once a week. Rose can see Dr. Hill sitting in her chair and she can picture herself sitting on the grey sofa across from her.

Dr. Hill starts their session the way she always does: "How was your week?"

"It was good, thanks! Ben and I enjoyed some quiet time together. We watched a bunch of movies and went for a run together. He and I are doing a baking class together, and we mastered tiramisu this week. And the craziest part of the whole week? I did not cry at all."

Dr. Hill smiles at Rose. "So, the usual?"

"Exactly," Rose says with a smile. Rose reflects on how much her "usual" has changed in the past six months.

"Has Ben asked your father about your dowry yet?"

"Not yet, I think he's waiting until I'm pregnant. Then I'll be good and worthless, he knows my dad appreciates a good deal."

"Seriously, how are you?"

Rose thinks about how to answer this. "I'm good. I still have moments that are really tough, but most days I'm good."

"How are your nightmares?"

"Horrible. As always. They're just so vivid. Last night, I dreamed that Tyler was strangling me, then Will came up behind and shot him. Tyler collapsed on me, bleeding, then Ben came running in and shot Will, who collapsed onto Tyler. We were like a totem pole of bodies. Just as Ben was putting a gun to his own head to kill himself, I woke myself with my own screams."

"That must have been very intense," says Dr. Hill.

"Yeah. It's usually some version of that. One of the three men I have loved killing someone else I love or killing me. I'm sure Freud would have a field day with these dreams."

"What do you think they mean?" Dr. Hill prompts.

"That I'm crazy?" Rose tries to laugh the question off, using her humour as usual to deflect. Dr. Hill gives a brief smile but does not say anything. She waits for Rose to answer.

"I think they mean that I'm afraid of losing people I love. I lost Will, and I lost Tyler. I'm worried I'm going to lose Ben."

"Are you actually worried about losing Ben?"

"Yes. No. I don't know. I feel like I don't know anything anymore. The only certain thing in my entire life was Tyler. And look how wrong I was about him."

"He went through a substantial trauma at a young age. That shapes a person, for better or worse."

"But how did I not know? Did I turn a blind eye? Did I miss the signs?"

"You couldn't have known. He hid it from you."

"But I wish I had known. I would have said something. I could have stopped him. Which would have saved him. And stopped him from becoming this ... this ... monster that he became. I could have stopped him from killing people. I could have stopped him from killing Will."

"Do you really think you have that much power? That you could have saved Will?"

"Maybe. I don't know."

"You are always trying to save people. But that's not your job, Rose. You can't put that pressure on yourself. You are trying to assume responsibility for everyone's wellbeing. You are not a superhero. You can only control your own actions and reactions."

Rose is silent. Then in typical Rose fashion, she quips, "Stop going all therapist on me, with rational, insightful guidance, calling me out on my craziness."

Dr. Hill smiles but pushes on. "You're not crazy. You want to do everything and be everything for everyone. Just like your mother. She always took on responsibility and never asked for help. And look how that worked for her."

"She has more anxiety than she knows what to do with. She's so busy doing everything for everyone and trying to make people happy, she forgets about her own happiness sometimes," Rose admits.

"Exactly. And it's natural for you to follow that path, after all it is what was modeled for you as a child. But I'm going to challenge you to fight that. Break the cycle. Be human. Acknowledge you have limits to your powers. Ask for help. Show yourself the same love and compassion that you show to others."

"It's hard. I have trouble asking for help. It's in my genes."

"But is it? Consider the interplay of nature versus nurture. You were raised the same as Tyler, right? But you turned into two very different people. You can have the same genetic makeup, the same upbringing, the same parents, the same education. But the experiences that you go through, and the relationships that you make, those are what allow you to become who you want to be. Those are the opportunities we have as individuals to define ourselves. And we get to choose the moments that define us. We choose who we want to be. Tyler chose to be defined by his abuse. It shaped the path he took, leading him down a dark path. If you think about it, you let Will's death define you for years. It dictated your career path, your relationships, even where you lived, moving across the country."

"Tyler didn't choose to be molested as a child. And I didn't choose to have my boyfriend murdered."

"You didn't choose for those events to happen to you. But they did. The point is you get to decide how these moments define you. You just discovered that your brother murdered your boyfriend. You can let that destroy you, haunt you for the rest of your life. Or you can use it to fuel you to be better, stronger. Or you can choose to not let this moment define you at all. You can be whomever you want to be. Ultimately, it is up to you: what are the moments that define you?"

Rose is silent while she contemplates what Dr. Hill is saying. "I don't know," she answers truthfully. "I hope I can be stronger from this. To create new meaning for my life. It's just so hard."

"It is very hard."

"I still can't believe that Tyler had this whole other side to him that I never knew. I never saw. I'm unraveling this twisted web of lies Tyler created that I had no idea existed. How is it possible to know someone your entire life, but not really know them?"

"He hid it from you," Dr. Hill reminds her. "You couldn't have known."

"How did my parents not know? Not do anything?"

"They're not perfect, Rose. Just like you are not perfect. You told me you think your mom had no idea and that your dad turned a blind eye, refusing to allow himself to think about it. No one wanted to confront the possible horrifying truth. Ultimately, it was up to Tyler reach out and ask for help. But he didn't. It was not up to your parents to save him, just like it is not up to you to save him. A parent's job is to love their children unconditionally and do their best to raise decent human beings who try to do the right thing.

"In fact, that's all anyone can do. Just try to love the people around you and love yourself. Try to do the right thing. And forgive yourself when you don't. All anyone can do is try."

"We're all a work in progress, right?" Rose says. "Except me, of course. I'm perfect." Dr. Hill laughs. She knows that, despite this humorous deflection, her words have resonated with Rose.

Rose heads back upstairs, hearing the familiar creak of the third step, and finds Ben waiting for her in bed. He motions for her to join him. He has taken the week off, using up years of accumulated vacation days, to spend time with her and she does not have a class until 1:00 p.m. that afternoon. She climbs into his arms, snuggling into the spot in the crook of his neck which feels like it was made especially for her.

"How was therapy?" Ben asks.

"It was good."

"Did you spend the whole time talking about me?" Ben asks, as he shifts his weight to look directly at Rose. He is leaning on his right elbow, while his left hand lightly traces her arm. She is temporarily lost in those teal eyes with the emerald green rings.

They were the first thing she saw when she first met him, and they continue to be one of the most mesmerizing things about him.

"Obviously," Rose quips.

"About how handsome I am?"

"Of course."

"And smart?" he asks, while he begins to kiss her neck.

"Mm-hmm,"

"And strong?" More kisses.

"Yes."

"And sexy?" he asks, nibbling on her ear.

"So very sexy."

"And good in bed?"

"Well, I have my doubts on that one."

"What!?" Ben pulls back, feigning insult. "I guess I'll just have to work on that." His kisses now travel to her lips and he kisses her deeply, passionately.

"We definitely need to practice. As much as possible, as often as possible," Rose says.

"I can handle that," Ben says earnestly. Then he lies back down and pulls her into him to snuggle. Rose puts on some music for them to listen to as they relax in bed, having a lazy morning. She closes her eyes as she listens to the beautiful melody and soothing voices of The Beatles singing "In My Life".

"I love you, Rose Davis."

"I love you too, Detective Cooper."

"I said it first."

"It's not a competition."

"Of course not. But if it were, I would win."

ACKNOWLEDGEMENTS

I feel so honoured and humbled to have an amazing support network of people who have encouraged me to fulfil my grandiose plan to write a book. I have always loved reading. I whip through books faster than my son whips through whiffle balls during his baseball practice. Occasionally, I would think to myself, I could totally do this. I could write a book. But I never had the time.

Until one day, in the middle of the COVID-19 pandemic, I decided to just do it. I'll never have time, I just have to do it. So I grabbed my laptop and started writing. And here is the result.

It was not a smooth road of writing. It was very hard to take an idea that had formed in my mind and turn it into something lucid and legible. There were bumps along the way, moments of fear and insecurity. Who am I to write a book? What experience do I have? But during these self-doubting moments, my family and friends urged me to carry on, and I'm glad I did. It was so much fun. I loved having a creative outlet to let my imagination run wild. To dive into a world with new characters and places that I got to explore. Through my literary world, I got to say things and do things that I've never dared to say or do. It was liberating.

Thank you to my family and friends for pushing me to tell this story. This may not be the perfect story, but it is my story. Thank you to my mother-in-law and father-in-law, for taking me in like I'm your own and for sharing my love of reading (and sharing your books!). Thank you to my besties, MARJ, for over thirty years of friendship, love and laughs. I can't wait until we're old widows in a nursing home getting kicked out of the lunchroom for being too loud. Thank you to Ilana for your sharp eye and editing skills, and for not being too mean after reading the first draft of this book.

I owe immense gratitude to my parents, who have provided endless love and support along this journey. You have taught me about hard work, perseverance, and resilience. More importantly, you have taught me about love and respect. I love you so much and appreciate everything you have done for us. Now please skip over all the sex scenes; let's not make things awkward. Also, Mom, I promise I put some lipstick on today.

To my sister, the Midnight of the Flash Club: like everything else in my life, I could not have done this without you. I'm sorry you didn't get a more prominent role in the book, but hey, at least you're not a murderer! And special shout out to my loving, intelligent, and responsible brother for not actually being a sociopathic serial killer. Much appreciated.

I have read other book acknowledgements where parents thank their children for allowing them the time and space to realize their creative process. Not my kids! Nope, they made sure I had as little free time as possible. If they saw me sitting alone, they made sure to hop on my lap so I wouldn't get too lonely. I adore them for their lovingness, their neediness, their silliness, and their contagious energy. Paige and Chase, you drive me crazy, and I could not love you any more than I do. My goal in life is to make sure you are happy and healthy and that you go to therapy for different reasons than those that led me to therapy.

Finally, I want to thank my husband Harris, who puts up with me on a daily basis. I'm a total pain in the butt, but for some reason you still like me. My life changed the day you sent me the grammatically incorrect message asking me out on a date. I was tempted to decline, but you were to cute to ignore. I'm grateful I didn't. You are smart, kind (most of the time), and funny (most of the time). You encourage me to go after my dreams and to stand up for myself. I hope one day I can see myself the way you see me. I love you so much and could not imagine navigating this crazy world without you. Also, I'll give you $10 if you can tell me the grammar mistake in this paragraph.

I identify with Rose in a lot of ways, but I want to be clear that I am not her and she is not me. Sure, I'm a competitive, overambitious, perfectionist lawyer with anxiety and depression. But I didn't move to Vancouver. That's something, right? I'm also way funnier than Rose. But like Rose, I am a work in progress. And I'm proud of who I am today. I hope this book inspires all of you reading it to be proud of who you are, to embrace your flaws, and to love yourself not just in spite of them, but because of them. May we all air out our dirty laundry together.

THE AUTHOR

Rachel Goldenberg is a lawyer with no impressive writing credentials or achievements. She is just an avid reader who loves the art of storytelling. At the start of a global pandemic, while balancing working from home, homeschooling her children, and battling the sheer terror of the unknown, Rachel decided it would be a perfect time to fulfill her lifelong dream of writing a novel. She lives in Toronto with her hilarious, loving husband and two impish yet adorable children.

www.ingramcontent.com/pod-product-compliance
Lightning Source LLC
LaVergne TN
LVHW091536060526
838200LV00036B/627